HIGH WATER CHANTS

TREVOR FERGUSON

HIGH WATER CHANTS

A NOVEL

HarperCollins*Publishers*Ltd

The Skincuttle Island in this novel is an imaginative creation and is not modelled on any other island of that name. The Cumshewa Nation is partly fanciful, and partly a mosaic of Northwest Coast and other North American Indian tribes.

The author is grateful to the Canada Council and the Ontario Arts Council for assistance during the writing of this book.

HIGH WATER CHANTS. Copyright © 1977 by Trevor Ferguson. All rights reserved. No part of this book may be used or reproduced in any manner whatsoever without prior written permission except in the case of brief quotations embodied in reviews. For information address HarperCollins Publishers Ltd, Suite 2900, Hazelton Lanes, 55 Avenue Road, Toronto, Canada M5R 3L2.

http://www.harpercollins.com/canada

First published in hardcover by The Macmillan Company of Canada: 1977
First HarperPerennial paperback edition published by HarperCollins Publishers Ltd: 1997

Canadian Cataloguing in Publication Data

Ferguson, Trevor, 1947-
High water chants

1st HarperPerennial ed.
ISBN 0-00-648079-9

I. Title.

PS8561.E759H55 1997   C813'.54   C96-931935-5
PR9199.3.F47H55 1997

97 98 99 ❖ HC 10 9 8 7 6 5 4 3 2 1

Printed and bound in the United States

For my mother and father

AUTHOR'S NOTE
This book owes much to Dennis Lee,
for his faithful encouragement
and critical eye. J. T. F.

And Reuben returned unto the pit; and, behold, Joseph was not in the pit; and he rent his clothes. And he returned unto his brethren, and said, The child is not; and I, whither shall I go? (Genesis 37: 29, 30)

1

DOC'S NEVER UNDERSTOOD IT HIMSELF *but he's right, I'm no ordinary historian.* Henry Scowcroft's breath came in hoarse gasps and his lungs were hurting. He ran along the road away from Lyell, past farms, knowing that this was not the shortest route, running with a leaping motion as he bounded high off his good leg then skipped quickly off the lame one, knowing that this was not the shortest route but he pretended it was, pretended too that he was not looking for a place to stop. *But this is no ordinary history and that's what he hasn't understood yet, that's what he's never dared to realize.* He ran down a low hill to the river with the forest on his right. The trees blocked the sunlight so that the woods were waiting for him in darkness and stillness, the air stagnant and close, the woods waiting quietly and issuing only sporadic signals. Henry Scowcroft stopped and breathed heavily. "I'm staying here a minute," he said aloud. His voice was stern and determined as if he were not speaking to himself. *Because what I'm talking about now is not the fire. What I'm talking about now is not the fire in my shack but the point of pain that became the fire, that could only become a fire given time and fuel. And not just time and fuel but the right circumstances to ignite it. I mean, maybe not even time and fuel and circumstances, but just somebody to recognize it or at least realize that it had been burning all along and holler it: Fire! Which I did.* Sitting on a boulder underneath a birch tree he caught his breath. Here the Oganjibra

River completed its descent from the mountains and escaped into Cumshewa Sound. Where the river slapped the rocks the spray glistened in the sunlight. The mouth spread wide and the shallow water bubbled over the smaller stones, then broke into whirlpools as it hit the sound. Fresh water into salt. Fast into slow, the whirlpools scurrying into the sound where finally, peacefully, they were absorbed. *That must be it then. This history is an ember, still hot, breathe on it and it flares up, becomes a circle of fire.* Henry addressed his thoughts to the river, but he had not stopped here to think or to catch his breath. He wanted to delay his entry into the forest, and so had run but had taken the longer route to the river, and so had stopped to think while his chest heaved. He could feel the forest waiting for him as a stern guardian, and his apprehension created a constriction in his chest and stomach, overriding once again his need and fascination for the woods.

Henry knew that if he turned he would still be able to see the smoke. It rose above the trees and cleared the top branches and the horizon too of the hill behind him, gathered in black, billowy balls that scurried quickly, like the water; and they were absorbed too, diffused into the skyway. But Henry refused to turn. The forest was waiting for him, and behind him four heads popped above the crest of the hill and watched him, but Henry stood and caressed the bark of the birch tree. *So, tree, what's your complaint? You think you've heard it all before?*

He was wearing a faded green jacket and a green cap that pushed his red curls down over his ears. In his left hand he gripped a cane which had a big black knob on the end. His baggy brown pants were too big at the waist and pulled in by his belt they accentuated his skinniness. The birch tree overhung the river slightly, and he could look up at the sun through the leaves.

You're wrong if you do. There's something different in it this time, and not just something different but something new. I don't know what it is. It's as new as that. Can history have something new if it's past? It does though.

A quick flash of colour attracted his eye. He knelt down. The glare off the water caused him to squint. Then he spotted the fish a few yards upstream; it darted quickly then stopped again, and a familiar pang touched him. Regrets mingled with memories and aspirations.

Maybe that's it! Maybe this is a past that has its future in it. Maybe that's the difference, what's new. And not only is its future in it but the future is motivating it now, too, actually pushing the past on, not then but now. Henry managed to smile. *Like this fish here.*

The fish shimmered in the water. Henry tried to sense the experience of the fish for himself. It vibrated in the water, seemed to detect and differentiate and read the currents, water currents and electrical currents too, seeking its spawning ground. He spied a second fish. Believed it to be female and he slipped off his boots, throwing them back behind the birch tree. But as he did so he saw the four men standing motionless on the crest of the rise.

Nope. You can't hold me back from this. If you've come out of the past or future or both, you can't hold me back from this. He took his socks off. *I mean I'm going because it's already beyond the point of no return—not that there ever was any point to return to except the point of pain, and look what that turned out to be, a circle of fire. I'm going to find Thomas, but you can't hold me back from this first.*

He stepped into the water. The cold sent shivers up his legs. He moved cautiously in his bare feet, seeking out the smooth stones. The female was sleeking in the shadows of a boulder. The cold water tickled Henry's feet and turned his toes white. He moved in a crouch, kept his weight on his good leg, stepped with his gimpy leg gingerly and quickly. "Come on, fish. Come along. Better me than the bears upstream." Henry Scowcroft plunged his hands into the water, missed, dived, and groped again. The salmon ducked to the shoreline then back around behind the boulder again. Henry waited for the fish around the corner of the rock. He squatted and the water splashed his seat and hips. He pulled the brim of his cap down to shield his eyes from the sun. He could see the fish when he peeked. Its gills and fins were working, the fish backing away it seemed, ever so slightly, as if anticipating the next thrust. Henry went around the rock and approached from behind. Saw the male coming back. Hopped, plunged, and frightened the fish so that it crossed over his hand. He grabbed it by the rear fin long enough to switch his grip to the belly and back. He touched the egg-full belly tenderly as the silver salmon squirmed in his hands and gleamed in the sunlight. When he turned, the four men seemed closer than the last time he looked, nearer the bottom of the hill, but they were still motionless. Turning his back to them, Henry did an awkward dance in the water with the fish raised high to the sun and to the sea and to the river, offering not only the life of the fish but its story too, its secret knowledge too. Returning the salmon to the water he delayed its release, squatting beside it with his hands encircling the body, squeezing firmly, gently, trying to read the tale, the history, to cull it from the water and the squirming of the fish as the fish culled the water for direction. *I might need you this time up. This time up we might have to learn everything. It's the Duffs again. That's right.* He released the fish. He squatted in the water and looked up the river into the forest. There was darkness, but there was light too, breaking through the tree-cover and summoning the vegetation. Birds anticipated him, they flew nervously among the higher branches. Flies and mosquitoes danced amid the stirring dust motes in the rays of light. The forest waited for him as a disciplinary parent. *I'm sorry, Doc. I got to leave you behind. You don't know what's up there or even why.*

When he stood, the four men were much closer to the river and he could see their faces, uneven and hazy in the bright light as in an overexposed photograph, motionless like a photograph too, not frozen exactly or mummified, but held still, captured by a single moment and bound to it forever, while the landscape behind them changed and evaporated. "All right!" Henry said aloud, calling to them, moving towards shore rapidly and laboriously, the water churning about his feet. "I'm going! Do I have to say it? I'm going, I'm going."

Slumping underneath the birch tree he pulled on his socks and boots. The four men stood above him, motionless as before, as if their descent from the hill had been accomplished by an erratic form of projection, like the interchange of photoslides, abducting them from one point to the next without movement in between. Henry Scowcroft twisted his torso, looked up. "I said I'm going. I already have one boot laced. Thirty seconds more, tops, then I'm not only going but gone. See?"

Henry worked to control his trembling. The sun blazed into the eyes of the four men but they did not squint. Their pupils remained wide open as if it were night. Only the mongoloid had his mouth shut; the jaws of the other three men were slack, and one had a twisted tongue that lolled from the side of his mouth. Each man's head tipped slightly forward, as if it overweighed the neck muscles. They waited. Their clothes brown and grey and baggy like Henry's and the creases of their shirts and the cuffs of their trousers lined with sawdust. Their clothes otherwise clean, but the lines of their necks and foreheads were caked with old dirt, and their boots were worn and broken. They did not seem to be breathing. They did not move. Henry Scowcroft jumped up and grabbed his cane and his canteen and his small backpack and stepped towards the forest. "See? I'm going. I'm on my way." He took several more steps without his eyes leaving them and he stumbled over a root. "There! You see! You see what this is! You see what it means? You're sending a cripple into the woods!" *To find a man, your brother, or half-brother anyway, though he might want to deny that, who's a hermit and a mountain man and more, a part of the mountain itself, an invisible strutting tree. And me, what can I say, except that I'm going and see no choice either? I say I'm a cripple and a fool and no match for that man, and between these three things I'm liable to break my neck. And you won't be there to catch me when I fall. That I know. I'd tumble from the tip of TaColl Mountain, break my back in a gorge before the fall would so much as register in your brain. That's right: brain. I've learned. It's one brain. You're a collective unit, right?* "All right, all right! I'm going! See? Another step. I'm a man of my word, unfortunate as that may be. Thank you for the send-off. Your good cheer is encouraging. Come on, fish. You swim, I'll climb. Tally-ho! Charge! Never say die! You see? I'm off."

Henry scampered along the riverbank, working his cane and gimpy leg strenuously. He felt the eyes of the four men impaled on the back of his neck. *Because you feel it too. You must. Not so much the pain and least of all the fire, but the empty space in the centre of both which must be sought out finally and at long last filled.* He looked sideways once. The black smoke had changed to grey and a sallow white. Behind him, the four men had disappeared. And entering the forest finally a tremor turned within his stomach and chest, and a sudden breeze sent a corresponding quiver through the woods.

2

INSULTS HAD BEEN HEAPED one upon the other, too many of them, too often, and now that the lights were out, Doctor Marifield felt lethargic and abused. Stripped to his shorts he moved listlessly through his house, his hair and back still wet from the shower, looking for his clothes to throw them out of the house. He had come home desperate to be free from the smell of smoke, but the odour lingered in his house and emanated from the hidden clothing. A shirt had fallen behind an armchair, his pants lay under the pine coffeetable, his boots and one sock had already been tossed out the bedroom window; locating the other sock by the shower-room door he carried them all to the front verandah and heaved the bundle onto the grass. The smell made him nauseous. He had inhaled too much smoke, and he coughed as if to prove it.

The sun gleamed brightly on the sound but Doc's house fell under the shade of cedar and pine and fir trees. Inside it was dark, a shadowy cavern he thought, and a glimpse of his face in the hall mirror startled him. Smoked eyes. Flared nostrils like a dying dragon's, with no fire left to breathe. Scorched cheekbones and singed hair. He did not study himself in the mirror for long, not wanting to define himself again, not wanting to be wrong all over again. Yet despite himself the mirror-image remained with him, provoking him, beckoning like some panhandler he wanted to avoid.

Doc slumped onto the couch and let the big sagging cushions absorb him, and when he spoke his voice was low and weak, and the words at first seemed to seek out a listener, but finding none they dissipated. "So. A fire. After all this it's come to that." Dismayed, he was thinking of Henry who had left without him, without saying where he was going or why. Unable to tolerate the darkness any longer, he wandered into the kitchen where a sunbeam illuminated the table, but the piece of mirror was there, the one he liked, the one with the rounded and smooth edge opposed to a jagged and flared side; it depicted a fireball or comet, and it caught his face and he glimpsed it, and this time he was immobilized, drawn closer as if hypnotized and floating with his feet off the ground.

He saw that he had exaggerated. His hair was not singed, it was wet. His cheekbones were not scorched, they caught the shadows of the room. And although his eyes were smoky and bloodshot and the scent in his nostrils was of ashes and his throat was parched, the face he saw was merely that of a tired man, a man lacking spark and spirit.

He drank and choked on the water. What bothered him most was not Henry's leaving or the fire or the sabotage of his powerplant, but the fact that he could wander about his house virtually naked and have no fear of anyone intruding. No longer was his house the centre of things. He felt ostracized, no longer a participant but merely an onlooker in the affairs of the island. It seemed a long time since he had been a leader and a catalyst. Now even Henry had not consulted him or informed him but had simply left. "We're supposed to be friends. At least. At least that!" Doc accepted that he was dying, not even dying but merely fading into a facsimile of death bereft of protocol and fanfare, a death without a funeral.

Returning to the main room, his log book nagged at his attention. And his great pulpit Bible lay unopened beside it. The room had not been tidied for weeks. The chairs were out of place, no longer facing one another. The area carpet had been kicked up at one corner exposing crumbs and marauding ants. Medical texts he had brought with him years earlier from Vancouver, reopened in a finalizing ritual of boredom, lay strewn about the room. Glasses and plates and cutlery occupied the nooks and crannies of the dark room, emitting stale odours which mingled with the scent of disinfectant from the examination room. Doc decided to gather all the dishes and return them to the kitchen. But the log book waited for him, looming in his mind as a last gasp of conscience. It lay on the far desk, unopened, black with brass hinges.

In the kitchen, the dishes were piled haphazardly in the sink. At the window where the sunlight entered he watched the movement of the wind through the trees, and he realized that he did not care if his spirit was restored or not. He had no interest in doing anything about it. And if there was no funeral, then so be it: there would be no trumpets on the other side now either. He fetched the log book, finally satisfied it would not change anything. He had fallen, and he clung now to his new station stubbornly. "Maybe when you come back, Henry, I'll be gone." The lights going out had proved it, proved something. "Now I'm a victim for sure, and that's what you thought when I came. So after all this you're right."

Flipping through the log, a trend was easily recognized. His collapse was clearly portrayed. The latter pages contained brief entries, spaced over weeks, that were morose and bitter. Sometimes the tone rose to an elegant solemnity, but he saw through his own lies. The language through the middle of the book had a strong philosophical quality to it, while the early stages, written during his first year on the island, bubbled with boyish enthusiasm, an energy that toppled over itself and was not so much concerned with direction as infatuated with the opportunity to be alive for the next breath. Feelings now remote to him sprang from the pages. Doc laughed out loud, mocking himself. He had aspired for this book to be a complement to the Bible beside it, a modern testament to righteousness and zealous exhortation, a thought he now found insane.

Standing, the silent echo of his laughter vanished into the timbers and dust, and Doctor Marifield suddenly felt hurt, a quick, emotional pain coursing upward through his stomach and heart. "Ezekiel!" he cried out. The name resonated among the beams, then drifted away. In the stillness, Doc heard a motorboat start up from Lyell. He walked to the landing at the front entrance and scanned the room. "Jeremiah!" he called. Again, there was no answer. He crossed to the hallway that led to his bedroom, turned, and studied the room again. Not so loudly this time, he asked, "Isaiah?" The room was still. There was no reply. Doc went into his bedroom and donned a clean pair of pants. When he came out he screamed—"Mal-a-chiiiii!"—and he gripped the doorframe like a man clutching the columns of a temple. His shout reverberated and died down, the emptiness and stillness remained. He felt like the room, vacant, a void. He detected the sound of a boat bumping his wharf and the engine being cut, and reluctantly he returned to his bedroom and put on a shirt. He thought he heard footsteps but when he listened only birds and tree-wind sounded. He plunked the log book down on its table, beside the huge Bible. The prophets had carried their visions through to completion and ultimately to their redemption, but he had succumbed, and the log was a witness to this surrender.

A board cracked on his verandah. "A less dramatic form of sabotage was conferred on me, Henry. I even pity myself for that. At least your rotting timbers were transfused into fire and smoke, but my fate is less heroic. Perhaps my gas was used to ignite your fire, while I'm left with a powerplant filled damn near to the brim with water."

He heard the screendoor creak and when he turned the door was already shut and the four men were standing motionless before him. They were staring at his log book. Doc moved in front of it. "Gentlemen," Doc said. "What can I—"

Only the mongoloid, Rupert Duff, was looking at him. The other three brothers stared at the log book even though they could not see it behind him.

"Some fire," Doc said. Then he saw that they had carried in his boots, had placed them neatly on the floor. "Oh. You must have seen them in the grass. Thanks." Doc tried to speak calmly but he was terrified. The boots were an obvious signal, but where did they want him to go and why? Doc was afraid he knew. "Excuse me a moment. I'll, I'll just be a moment."

He returned from the bedroom with a pair of socks. He sat on the couch and his hands were trembling as he put them on. He straightened the cover on the couch, which had come down at the back. "So. What can I do for you?" He wanted to intimidate them with politeness and manners. He was watching their profiles, except the mongoloid's, who was staring at the pack he always kept prepared for medical emergencies. Doc ignored this sign too. He turned his back to them and sat down at the piano. His fingers banged out a lively dance tune. When he stopped the men had not moved. They had not been listening. They did not seem to be breathing. Doc rubbed his palms on the thighs of his trousers. "I can't consider it," he said. "It's not possible. Look, it's out of the question." He left the room as if to end the discussion. He found his wrist-watch in the examination room and put it on. Returning, the men had not moved. Doc dropped himself onto the couch. "It's impossible," he said. "That's my final word. Thank you for coming, gentlemen."

In the stillness that followed Doc grew increasingly uncomfortable and nervous under the strain. He clamped a hand to his side to suppress a budding ache, his anxiety wrenching his back and tightening his leg muscles. The men were staring at him and he considered yielding, but he was afraid. He cursed Henry for not being here. He cursed Henry for abandoning him, leaving him to interpret on his own the signals of the brothers. To release some of his malevolent energy, he grabbed his boots and put them on, knowing it was a mistake, knowing that he was not appeasing them but strengthening their resolve. He hurried into the kitchen and glanced in the mirror. He was frightened by the terrified eyes he saw. He came out of the kitchen yelling, "I can't do it! I'm not Henry, you understand me? I'm not—Henry! Go find him if you can. Don't come to me. I'm through! Through! Take your troubles somewhere else. My days are finished here." They did not respond and Doc picked up a cushion and smacked it back down against the couch. "Damn," he said.

Three men were staring at his log book, as if eliciting its help and power. Doc ran over to it and waved the book in the air. "I don't care anymore, you understand me? Look!" He threw the book. It bounced off the large chair and tumbled on the floor. "You see? I don't give a damn anymore." The mongoloid had resumed staring at his pack. "Bloody hell!" Doc hollered, and he grabbed a jacket from the coat rack with one hand and the pack with the other and brushed past the Duff brothers and left his house.

He ran down to the wharf. He unmoored his boat and cranked the engine. A long look back at Lyell. No place to hide there, the brothers would only pursue him. He started off toward Cumshewa Town. When he looked back the Duff brothers were standing on his wharf. They looked as if they were studying the water. "Bloody hell," Doc said, but he spoke under his breath.

3

HERE THE OGANJIBRA RIVER QUIETED, its water diverting into a deep pool surrounded on three sides by a steep rise of scarred white rock. Beside the pool, smack dab in midstream, sat a large configuration of split and cracked rock, one encasement, but cut and divided and creviced so many ways that it looked like a huddle of smaller boulders banding together for warmth, anxious to keep their toes out of the water, fearful of a flood; and from the top of this outcropping grew a maverick jack pine, skinny and crooked, but determined to persevere and survive. *I can't stay here. No matter what it means. I've taken one reprieve already. But no matter what it means I can't miss it either. I got to stop and get going at the same time and that's the trouble.* Ahead of Henry Scowcroft, confronting him, the low-slung pine branches looked formidable and united in their solidarity, while below him the lucid and tranquil pool appealed to his senses. He dropped his cane and canteen and pack.

The spot was familiar to Henry and significant too. It affected him like the cemeteries at Lyell and Sockeye, mystified and intrigued him. At the cemeteries, a peculiar aspiration would creep over him, exhorting him to burrow into the graves and revel in the memories of the skeletons and bones; here, the spot marked the limits to the forest he had known as a child, and beyond, the forest loomed as impenetrable and awesome. *Lord knows I can't stay here. Even the forest knows I got to press on. If Doc was here he'd prod me. I'll say that much for him even now.* The origin of the two formations had always puzzled him. If the outcropping was turned upside down it would fit perfectly into the pool. As a child, Henry would dive to the depths of the pool, exploring, seeking a hole that would be a mate to the pine tree, so certain that the rock had come out of the pool, pine tree and all, that not finding the complementary hole had never discouraged him. The mystery tantalized his senses; it was more than the thrill of the unknown. It beguiled him into believing that the answer existed, thrived and flourished in some remote sanctuary, that someday and somehow the history, the story, might be visited upon him.

Henry stripped quickly and leaped. The cold water was a shock to his skin and heart and he gasped for breath when he surfaced. He lay on his back in the water and gazed at the sky. Annoyed crows and a frantic bevy of jays flew out from the forest and crossed above the river. *But Doc wouldn't know where he was going or need to know. For him it would be enough to barge in and arrive. Hang the consequences. I can't do that. I better not stay here long though.* He dipped the back of his head into the water and arched his spine and with a strong sweep of his arms he bore smoothly into the water, and with his eyes open he saw the sunlight penetrating the surface and dancing there, like the waving curtains of the northern lights, reminding him of the black nights in collusion with the woods ahead of him; and when he broke to the surface again his lungs gasped and he heaved for deep breaths. He swam to where the pool edged the stream and climbed the underwater bank and when he stood in the stream the water was only up to his shins. *But Lord knows I can't stay away from here either when we were bonded here, and the bond was sealed here too. Or maybe we were sealed in the bond. Either way. Either way I can never be free of it. It was your silly attempt at flight, your momentary ascent heavenward, that did it.*

Henry climbed the rock. He knew the way up by rote, knew which steps and twists to make, knew the footing well enough that at times he had been able to climb at night in heavy rain. He respected the rock as the grave and gravestone Gail Duff did not have. On top, he crawled to the far side of it, opposite the pool, and he lay on a bare expanse of stone and let the sun toast him. He lay on his stomach, his fists on top of one another propping his chin, and his view was of the pool and the steep walls of stone that surrounded it. His body was concealed from the pool and opposite cliff by the slope of the rock, by the trunk of the pine, and by the tall grass and wildflowers. Seventeen years earlier, he had spied on Gail Duff from this eyrie.

She had been naked above the pool and her eyes were slanted toward the sky. Slowly she tilted her head back as far as it would go, as if she were in a trance, her sandy-blonde hair falling back, closing her eyes then, then arching her back and standing like a ballerina on the balls of her feet, clearly wishing it was tip-toes, clearly wishing it was higher, above ground, stretching to the sky, then raising her hands slowly, exquisitely from her sides to above her head, and Henry's pulse beat rapidly, his body tensed, he was certain she would fly, rise up, suddenly burst with a splendid light that would radiate like the sun, the sun reflecting upon her upraised face and throat and her small, just-forming twelve-year-old's breasts and her thin chiselled torso as off a great and many-coloured jewel; just at that moment, at precisely the second of her flight, wings spread, she laughed and fell back on her heels, hand to her mouth giggling, and she jumped, a little girl again now, squealing, limbs scattering every which way, hitting the water hard on her shoulder and side, a lethal wave bounding up around her.

Henry had sprung quickly to his knees. Gail Duff had hurt herself in her half-jump, half-fall into the pool. But Henry was denied. He was bonded to her forever now but he was denied the rescue. He was denied the opportunity to climb down from his post like a wilderness apparition, a minor god from his lair, heroic and protective and male, each quality enriched and magnified by the forest and by the solitude of the pool, and his leap into the pool with his arms encircling, cradling that delicate and fragile wish, was denied too. Rupert appeared above the pool, Gail's brother, naked too, his deformed head like a foreign outgrowth of his body, thrown up by this body as rejected material, a vacant and purposeless bulge. Rupert jumped into the pool in desperation and he was fortunate that he did not land on his sister, missing her by inches, and the pool became a convulsion of thrashing limbs and churning water, and together they rescued one another, Gail calming her terrified brother, Rupert wrestling his stricken sister to the rockface. There was a crevice in the rock that was accessible for climbing. Gail Duff was laughing soon, one shoulder red and stinging, and she climbed carefully and slowly. The mongoloid ponderously made his way up the escarpment behind her. Henry Scowcroft lowered himself onto his rock and regretted his denial, but he was awakening too to a sensation which one day he would identify as a bondship. *Because in that one second before birdflight you were transfigured, transformed, not a girl and not a woman but a new kind of being altogether, not even an angel for you were more translucent than that—maybe it was your future I witnessed, that's it, your ascension.* Within two seconds, he had delved so deeply within her that he was bonded to her out of simple respect for so intimate a coupling. And the intimacy took on new significance that coming autumn with her disappearance and probable death, new meaning because now he held secrets of her being in himself alone, she was gone, and years after that probable death the bond had been sealed.

For once again he had lain concealed on the rock. Come to brood, come to ponder, to fret. Once again the sun had shone brilliantly although the horizon was black. Once again the girl who appeared was from Sockeye and not his native Lyell. She also exuded femininity, a quality rare in girls raised on the island; but both girls had been moulded in this tradition by their fathers. Once again the girl, no, woman this time, Evlin Oliver this time, stretched gracefully to dive, to fly, and this time she did lift from the earth, fly from the rock, curve and extend her body and limbs and enter the water with precision, a flying fish, the water scarcely disturbed around her. The similarity struck home and Henry's pulse mounted its erratic rhythm again. The sandy-blonde hair, the sculptured throat, the touch of innocence or grace that reflected the sun like a jewel—Henry's thoughts collided and jammed. Could he go down now, older now, climb out from behind the jack pine and approach laughing, a friend embarrassed but tickled by the unorthodox meeting, and would they play in the water, friends, trusting, and let the water and the sunlight and the approaching storm make lovers of them both?

Once again, he was denied. For appearing on the white rock, crouching, storm clouds rising behind him as if he himself had summoned them, was Billy Peel, chest bare, skin a deep brown, his muscles toned and smooth. They stared at one another for several minutes, as if hunting not only the temper in one another but in the meeting itself, with Billy looking down upon Evlin like a bird of prey, while Evlin swam. Until Billy stripped finally and leaped, and they circled one another, not speaking or wanting to, circled with short strokes, not taking their eyes from one another until Evlin swam to the crevice and climbed up. And Billy Peel followed. And Henry turned on his back and watched the sun disappear behind the storm cloud and the rain beat down on his chest, and when he looked once, quickly, they were coupled, and he knew then that it was sealed. *It was right too, the only way, for how could I love a sky-being, it took a complementary being, a bird of the forest like Billy Peel to do it for me and in the act our bond was sealed, Gail, I was sealed to you, because there on that rock Evlin was the sky-being, there on that rock she was taking the place of you, just as Billy was taking the place of me.*

Henry rose from the rock. He had stalled too long. Regrets, aspirations, old pains, contemporary fears—his usual companions—all stood up with him. He climbed down from the outcropping and stepped through the stream. He spied salmon slipping past him on their way upstream. He bellyflopped into the pool, swam across it, then scaled the white rockface. Alone and troubled, he dressed and adjusted his pack over his shoulders. The forest loomed as dark and severe, the air was heavy and dank; the woods awaited his return. Henry Scowcroft breathed deeply, nodded quickly at the pool and outcropping, then crouched low and ducked under the pine branches.

4

DOCTOR MARIFIELD TRIED ATTUNING himself to the cadence of the water. He had travelled ten miles, and his nervousness and impatience still gnawed on him like a tumour, eating him from the inside out, while the boat ascended and descended the full, tide-driven waves in an easy rhythm. The foam churned in the wake, swirling in circles that fought for traction. Waves slapped at the prow as the boat mounted them and shot out a fine spray coming down on their backs. Doc was approaching the sea and Cumshewa Channel was choppy, the wind picking up, whitecaps highlighting the horizon, and the cadence was a simple and reliable one, the slap of the waves on the boat, the clap of the boat on the water, and through it the percussive putt-putt of his inboard engine. Yet he failed to relax in it, failed to conform to a nuance he had discovered by chance, that the rhythm was like a heartbeat, and failing to calm himself furthered his exasperation.

The boat rolled, dipped, and rose again. The old timbers of the scow creaked and groaned. Doc had enjoyed this trip down the channel in the past despite his fear of water, he'd rub his hands along the polished, fish-stained ribs of the boat and listen to its story. So he blamed Henry for his present temperament, and felt abandoned. He figured that the Duff brothers had sought him out because Henry had already left. Surmised that Henry had abandoned the four idiot Duff brothers too, and his anger boiled. He fidgeted in the rear of his boat, sitting on an upturned crate now with his arm draped over the rudder. He rested his feet along the boat's rim, switched suddenly, and plopped his heels down in the water running to and fro in the basin of the hull. He banged the toes of his boots together. Time to bail out again and he took to the task rigorously, swinging his arm like a waterwheel until the bailing can could scarcely scratch a drop off the bottom. Doc locked the rudder and stood up, bending over for balance. He stepped over the engine compartment and sat near the bow. Standing a second time he crept right up to the prow. Watched the boat slice through the water, the splash of spray, the smaller waves rolling out from the point of impact. Then twisted himself around awkwardly and returned to the stern. He was pacing and the lack of room to manoeuvre annoyed him. The boat was his cage. Overhead the seagulls were screeching and when they flew close he got angry. They had trailed after him from Lyell, beaks open wide, terrorizing him with their shrill cries. They pestered him like distraught prison guards.

"Numbskulls! Idiots! You lunatics, you!" Doc shouted. "Who needs you?"

The boat was jarred by a crossing wave and Doc lurched forward, tumbling off his crate, and soaked by the spray he had to grab the rudder fast to steer back into the waves. Exposed to the waves he was rocked drastically before getting the awkward hulk turned about; the boat carried up only to be dropped flat, plunked down, and turning about he maintained a firm hold on the rudder. The gulls responded to his outburst with equal vehemence. Flying low to the water they dipped into the foam and cried out. He had never known gulls to attack but they seemed prepared to do so now. A one-legged sergeant had the audacity to mount the prow and screech at him from there. In its eyes was the look of the terrified witness, the being made vicious by what it had seen. "Shut your trap, why not?" Doc called. "I'm just as hungry as you are." He scared it off by rattling an oar.

Doctor Marifield hugged the shoreline, moving into the open water only where rocks forced him out, then quickly coming back.

Even in the channel he was afraid of the open water; whenever he was on the ocean he was terrified. "What do I have to do with you anyway?" he shouted, and he was thinking of the Duff brothers, but it was the gulls who screamed back. "With any of you?"

The image of the Duff brothers: like soldiers on guard knowing no reason or purpose to their duties, compelled by some inner command, its source long confused and lost, idiots on a rampage of silence. "They think they can push me around," he whispered, as if sharing a secret with the water and the boat. "Bloody hell." Doc resented his own passivity, discovered himself as if completely by accident allowing the rudder to slip slightly and slip again, so that he was cutting the waves at an angle, and as he let it slip further, the boat caromed off the tops of the waves, bucking hazardously, rising into vacant space, falling hard, smacking the water and jarring the old timbers. "Why should I heel to you too? I've had enough, you understand me? I'm finished! With you, with Henry, with the whole lot!" Caught sideways in the valley between crests, he was soaked again getting the hulk turned around, but he was pointed towards Lyell only briefly, the sun in his eyes now, the wind at his back only a few seconds before his anger emerged with still greater force, and he yanked the rudder hard, the boat spinning on the crest of a mounting wave and nearly capsizing as it slid into the depth of it then up again, Doc shouting at himself, "Damn it! Do it! Turn back why don't you!" and he knocked his fist along the top of the green rudder stem as if it was the boat he was fighting, and he was pointed away from Lyell once more.

Swearing at the Duff brothers then. Rupert. Whitney. Jackson Two. Jake. They had continually dogged his footsteps since he had arrived on Skincuttle Island. But he was confused, not knowing if he had become their nemesis or if the reverse was true, for he supposed that he did represent intelligence and learning to them, and they were the imbeciles. Moving on a course that would approach the shoreline gradually, he recalled his first meeting with the brothers. He had been taking a casual tour of Lyell and had ventured down to the sawmill. Wandering past the furnace, he looked in, fiery, he thought it worthy of a Nebuchadnezzar crematorium. He passed the sloping tiers of lumber, planks, and two-by-fours and two-by-threes to where the chain saws screamed and planks shot out, jostled into position on a pile by two men. One scarcely moved, the head and neck and torso stationary, but the arms worked, the hands nimble and so quick they were like extensions of the machinery and not of the man. Wandering farther he came around in front of the man with the large head, noticed the eyes, the sadly fat and puffed face, mongoloid, and he observed the smaller man from the side and saw that his feet were moving too, out and in, out and in, keeping time with the planks as they rocketed from the slice of the saw, yet the body even more still than he had perceived at first, without breath or sweat or notice. Down at the other saw the two-by-fours were spewed out like atomic lances, the saw an apocalyptic horseman, a charging black mechanical knight, and two more brothers combined incredible quickness to duck and corral the spears with a minimal degree of movement, not moving one muscle extraneous to their work, not appearing human but resembling prototype robots that were still in the planning and developing stage. Doc stared, he studied them, they did not respond and finally he had to check himself, realizing that he had been examining them as if they were specimens grafted with an occult mind or skin disease and he awaited the outbreak. So he turned and walked away, but the one big saw sent out such an incredibly piercing scream that he spun quickly, and they were staring at him, motionless, breathless, without a twitch or a falter in their eyes, the saws whirring down now, switched off. Fear gripped the new doctor and not knowing which way to turn he said, "Gentlemen," and turning quickly he hurried away, averting his face from the wafting heat waves of the furnace.

Avoiding a boulder, Doc eased the boat very close to the shoreline. Gazed into the water and saw the rock bottom. The water was clear and bright and reflected the clouds. Bluebirds in the trees and squirrels too were observing him. A passing crow cawed to affirm its presence. "I'm going back," Doc said aloud. "To hell with this. Yep. I'm going back and to hell with the Duff brothers too. They can solve their own problems. They can solve them better than I can. I don't even know what their problems are. What do they want from me? I'm not Henry."

But he did not turn suddenly as he knew now that he could. He intended to take the entire width of the channel to execute his turn. And doing so, he was thinking of his second encounter with the four Duffs, his mind drifting, as if concentrated thought would somehow miss them, as if even within another man's mind they eluded contact, and only by permitting the mind to drift, absently, could it sort out and surround and fuse with their absence, which was their being. Approaching Rogg House, lost in thought then too, staring at the ground, he had walked right through them. He entered Rogg House and cried out a greeting to Henry sitting across the beer parlour, and then it struck him. He felt uneasy. He went back through his mind and sensed a presence, like a man stepping through a hidden mist on a road then turning, wondering what it was. He sat at Henry's table but he could not stay seated long. He went outside. He reentered Rogg House. He repeated this performance twice more and was left with the tingling sensation that entering the first time there had been two men standing on his right and one on his left, and the inexplicable feeling that he had passed neither between them nor among them, but through them, or at least through something. Like a membrane. To Henry's query, Doc said he did not know what was wrong. The next day he saw them for certain. Three Duff brothers, squatting on Lyell's green eating sandwiches. Two sat together and there was a gap between them and the third. They stopped eating when he passed. They held their sandwiches in midair. At night on his way through the wooded area to Henry's cabin an eerie, night-forest feeling befell him, of moonlit, elongated shadows moving in conspiracy; he looked sharply to his right once, then ran. Puffing, laughing nervously, he told Henry, "They're crazy! I think they're following me around!" Henry looked up at him. "Who?" Doc slammed his hat down on the table. "The Duff brothers! I keep coming across them. They're always staring at me. They're out in the woods right now!" Henry stood up, concern mirrored on his face, the shadows on his face dancing in the dim yellow light from the lantern. "Why? What's up?" Wood crackled sharply in the stove. "Who knows? They stare. They don't move. It's the damndest thing." Henry gripped Doc's shoulder hard. His voice was low and urgent. "Fast, what details?" Doc shirked under his friend's rising fear. "No details—there were three of them—" Henry's body jerked in a spasm. "What! What do you mean three of them? What's the matter with you?" Henry was already moving towards the door. Doc shrugged. "Nothing. There were three of them—what else can I say? Every time I've seen them lately there's been three. A couple of them were standing on one side of a tree, one on the other." Coming back, Henry pulled Doc out of his chair. "Run get your bag. No. I'll get it. You run like hell to their house. Now! Fast! Now! Hurry!" And he did, frantic, his pulse wild and erratic, feeling the fear now too, swearing to himself for taking so long, for not catching it in the first place, or at least not consulting Henry, who would have caught it immediately. It was Jackson Two who was injured, motionless on the cot, pain and fear keeping him prone, the little finger of his right hand missing. They had kept it in a can. When Henry arrived with his medicine bag Doc sewed the finger back on, his eyes straining under the sallow yellow lantern light, tying the tendons together, incredible work, wrapping the bandage, the best work of his life. Finished, Doc was exultant. "There! How about that!" But Henry was already tugging on his sleeve. The Duff brothers were sitting at the pine table and staring at a central point between them. Henry gave his arm a quick yank.

Coming out of his reverie, Doc was coming out of his circle, and he realized suddenly that it was a full circle, that in a moment he would once again be heading away from Lyell and not returning, and he hesitated before pulling the rudder in, hesitated and the circle was completed. He eased the rudder to his side and bore a course for the mouth of the channel, for Cumshewa Town again, staring ahead of himself dully, admitting now that he did not have the heart or courage or cunning to face the four idiot Duff brothers. Somehow they had the ability by their combined silence and stoicism and something else that he had refused to apply to them before, their vision and determination—which Henry had insisted might be connected to their culpability, their mutual sin, which Doc had not understood—somehow they were able to turn him back in upon himself, and he had no place to go. But he felt he was following a course already charted for him.

Doc was not certain if he intended to fulfil what he had begun, first he would seek help—Henry was gone, he would talk to Evlin at Cumshewa Town—he would not entertain a confrontation with the Duffs again without her advice and support, painfully accepting that the dissipation of his enthusiasm for life on Skincuttle Island had dulled his spirits and his mind, his prayers too. And when he approached Cumshewa Town, ten minutes ahead of a squall that was pressing in from the west, he spied Evlin on the pier, hands in her pockets, the wind at her hair, and he waved, relief finally cracking through the static of his nerves and releasing his muscles, and he approached and docked and accepted her hand up and hugged her with a swift enthusiasm that surprised them both.

"Evlin! It's good to see you!"

"Hi, David. How're you doing?"

"Great! Just great!"

Evlin looked at him closely. "Well, come on up to the house then," she said. "I've been expecting you."

5

THE FOOTING ON THE ROCKS BY THE RIVER was slippery, sluggish on the forest floor. Henry pushed himself forward by choosing a landmark ahead of him, a boulder, a prominent tree, a bend in the river, then concentrated all his efforts on achieving it, a mental technique that kept him moving, kept him from sagging under the prospect of the entire journey and climb, kept him from resting needlessly and dwelling on other things. But when he looked back after each success it seemed to him that he had spent too much time and too much energy to garner only forty, fifty feet, a suspicion that agitated and exhausted him all the more.

He was approaching the chute—he could hear the blast of water. Around a bend, the Oganjibra River narrowed and the water churned in white rapids. The land rose sharply here, the first serious thrust of the mountains, and Henry's pace slowed in proportion to the incline. His crippled leg hurt him when he stretched to climb, the strain on the knee shot currents of pain into his feet and through his hip. The next bend revealed the chute, sighted through the monotonous grey sheets of rain, a waterfall that adjusted the Oganjibra from the foothills to the plateau. But a fault down the centre of the riverbed had caused a V-shaped gap to appear, cut through and chiselled by the water, so that only thin streams came over the falls; the bulk of water plunged into the narrow gap and roared through the chute as a powerful white fury.

From a distance, Henry spied the silver bodies flapping gamely in the air, the great blast of foam and mineral and sand and water tossing the fish back with little grace, the fish no sooner airborne than they were whipped downstream, spun, twisted, and dropped.

Henry squatted near the base of the chute and watched the struggle. Spray that was colder and sharper than the rain stung his face, and sometimes a small stone or a speck of sand ricocheted and bit his cheek. He was enthralled by the rush of water, excited both by its power and by its precision. The salmon were impotent against the turbulence, but he was captivated by their effort too, the curl of their bodies, the contraction and frantic flap and extension to propel them in flight, only to be tumbled topsy-turvy and thrown back, to return time after time, equally resolute, not pausing at all except to regain their forward momentum. *I see them like this, Gail, with you, riding the currents, more curious than afraid, twitching near your drowned body as it somersaulted, then unwound itself, going down. Another human lost at sea, but this one so young! so frail!* Eventually many fish learned, rushing headlong to the base of the falls and along the edge of the river to avoid the chute, then leaping straight up the rockface. The strong ones made it quickly, leaping the twelve feet on their first try and landing on the top rock and desperately flapping there, wrestling for the deeper water. Smaller fish and heavy fish required practice to find the range and flew gallantly in the air, only to fall short, and slamming against the rockface they were jettisoned into the rocks below.

Once up, the fish were sometimes sucked into the chute again, Henry seeing them rocket out, curled up, like balls whacked by a batter, and he laughed at their sudden surprise.

I never told you my secret wish. I was waiting until we were both old enough, I'd tell myself. So much would have changed—everything, different. When I used to watch you from close up or even from far away, it was always from an angle, askance, secretly. When you died, I didn't believe I couldn't follow you anymore, and what stays with me most is visions of your death and hardly your life at all. When we were kids I planned to marry you someday. A delicious, fantastic secret. Now it's like you never existed, as flesh, only as some nagging compulsion or amputated part of me I feel I haven't really lost yet, but have. Damn. Damn! This hunt means I resurrect you again!

Henry commenced climbing the cliff alongside the waterfall. The rockface was slick and cold. It felt like the scaly backside of a fish. He stumbled once and fell back. Trying again, he made it half-way, with the top of his head flush with the plateau of the cliff, and he was looking into the wet snout of a large and curious black bear. The animal was blocking his access and staring down at him. They were nose to nose, inches apart, the bear examining him vacantly, and Henry squeezed the rock with the tips of his fingers and held on, not moving. The bear swung its head from side to side and shifted its weight from one front paw to the other.

"Easy, mister. Easy now. Or is it missus? Look, I'm on my way. I'm going. I'm backing down this rock here, see. See?"

The bear's eyes were small in proportion to the massive head, black like the head too and immersed in the body, as if they looked inward and not outward or perhaps nowhere at all, the gaze steady and detached and indicating nothing. The fur was sticky and matted, soaked by the rain, and a line of sharp points through the fur, between the ears and around the neck like a collar, resembled a porcupine's quills.

Henry managed one step lower but as he did so a cub ran up, spotted him and panicked, fled, then turned and charged. Henry fell. The cub leaned over the cliff and Henry picked himself up and backed away. He moved away slowly, discreetly, trying to disguise the movement, his body overtly still while he judged each step carefully. The mother loomed behind her cub, formidable in the rain, and Henry was scared. The cub was attempting to negotiate the climb down the escarpment. Henry fell over backwards, his crippled leg collapsing, and before he could break his fall he had smacked his chin on a rock. He had to untwist himself and now the cub was coming down the bank and the mother was right behind. He scrambled to his feet and ran, set his sights on a cedar grove fifteen yards away. And running he felt ignited, afraid but wild too, and he galloped with abandon. Looking back once, he was suddenly stunned and he landed on the seat of his pants. Picking himself up off the forest floor, one eye closed from the blow, he ran again, sloughing off his backpack, then diving for the cedar grove; the long branches brushed the floor and Henry slid under them, slithered along the floor, pulling himself along by gripping the lowest branches, his face and back scratched frequently, and he sought what might be the deepest tree in the grove and wound himself about its trunk like a snake and waited there.

The cub came close, bounding into his vicinity and thrashing upon the branches that covered him, but the mother bear never entered the grove, and Henry heard her snorting and mauling his pack. The cub became interested in this diversion too and left him alone. Soon he could hear them moving away.

He picked out the pine needles from around his eye. Sometimes everything was just too much, Henry thought. Somewhere he had lost his cane, and the moment he realized it his leg rebelled, pain shot up from his calf through his thigh and he cried out. He clamped a hand over his mouth as the pain mounted and reached an intense and critical peak before subsiding. Sap from the tree was sticky on his face. Henry felt as though the entire forest was converging upon him, pressing him to the floor, the mountains, the rocks, the vegetation, all contracting, folding in upon itself and upon him, and he wondered how long he would be able to bear it.

He left his hiding place, sliding over the wet earth on his belly. His swollen eye was tender to touch. And napping in a cramped position had created minor aches and sorenesses that were expressed when he stood up. Henry flexed his bad leg, working out the stiffness.

Back-tracking the route of his flight, he found pieces of clothing first. Then a shirt, a favourite that had been torn previously but it was shredded now; a jacket with one sleeve neatly torn off at the seam; his cap; he found his pack next and tins of food surrounding it, but the bacon slab was gone and the faint white trail ahead would be the flour. Slowly he was able to gather most of his belongings. He mended the rip in his backpack by wrapping a cord around it. Where he had smacked into the tree limb he located his walking cane. It waited for him propped against the trunk.

Henry did not venture back to the river but climbed under cover of the forest. The land was level briefly, then it dipped low, and it was a different forest he entered now, an older forest, a forest he cherished, steeped in the myths and history of Skincuttle Island. He could sense the passing of the great warrior tribes and the beating of the drums, feel the stirring of vision and prophecy. Underfoot, the duff was spongy, yielding to his steps like soft carpet, and he pressed ahead against time.

When he finally did stop, he was out of breath. He knelt down and leaned against a fallen fir tree. The enormous root system lay exposed on its side, ten feet in diameter, a neat circle surrounded by an array of points, its upturned face directed toward the setting sun like a forest mandala. He sat in a puddle but he was too tired to move and too wet to care. He looked up through the towering trees that teetered against the sky and in the narrow space of sky visible to him a raven passed. The forest quieted considerably in the few minutes that he rested, here and there the crackle of branches adjusting themselves for the night. He concentrated on a woodpecker's drill for a minute.

Henry found it difficult to get moving again. He hoisted his pack over his shoulders but he was conscious of each movement. The trees stared down upon him. Elders of the woods, disciples of the ages, guardians of a higher discipline. He walked slowly, his shadow weaving and bobbing alongside him like an erstwhile prophet who had not been heard for centuries, frantic by comparison to the staunch and dignified colleagues surrounding it.

Hearing the river. The force would be stronger now. When he reached the Oganjibra again, it had taken on the tones of dusk. He could see the tips of the TaColl Mountains emblazoned by the red beams of sunset, and the lower reaches of forest were dark, relinquishing the spectre of day and dusk, becoming indistinct and massive: a dense conglomerate of shadow and bulge and gloom. And the water reflected the red rays and shadows too, hinting at depths more secret than those traversed by daylight, the white foam on the rocks acting as centres of conversion, the currents bubbling over and turning themselves inside out, light into shadow, day into night.

Before long he came out on an open stretch, the river bending deep to the east to expose a wide swath of sand and rock. Further ahead of him was canyon.

Soon the dusk lingered in its final moments, the darkness growing in overhead waves, the mountains diminished from view, the forest a resilient curtain on either side of him that seemed to waver and contract on the periphery of his vision, spring back when he glanced at it directly. The darkness hovered, as if pondering its final descent, and the illumination of trees and rocks and water and sky appeared to be an afterglow, without a source of light. An eagle soared overhead and disappeared into night. Henry walked to the sound of the water now, seeing nothing, finding his way by his feet, seeking out the smooth and stable stones.

The light through the trees would be the rising moon and Henry stopped and squatted on the rocks. He breathed heavily. Breathed the currents and undulations of the night. The night and the forest together had always been a source of mystery and inspiration to him: he felt the rolling back of time, the breakdown of traditional barriers to sight and sound, and he sensed a stirring, a rise of the spirits that haunted his thought and the ghosts that plagued his memory. He believed he could communicate best here, in the depths of the forest at night, not only with the forest and the river and the night, but with himself too, as if entering here he was stumbling upon a hidden chamber where secrets were kept to be revealed only to a surviving intruder. But he feared this depth at the same time, recognizing it as treacherous territory.

Walking on.

Sometimes he suffered from sensations that were too multiple and subtle to decipher. Sometimes it seemed that someone was marking his steps and stopping whenever he stopped short to listen. Usually he experienced the opposite, a striking sensation of walking in the footsteps of all those who had gone before him, the Indians, the great visionary chiefs like Connehawah and Leegay, and the great hunter and warrior Klakow, and before them, before the whiteman came, the mythical Yestiglee, and more recently the white trappers and prospectors, the gold-seekers, and also the centuries of animal life, the bears and the deer and the wolves, a continual criss-cross in the lives and deaths of nations and brothers and enemies and friends. Yet now he felt someone dogging his steps and he felt afraid, and scolded his imagination for seducing his mind and upsetting his perceptions.

It took nearly an hour to reach the canyon, the white water bubbling through it, and he could go no farther in the night. The forest was dark, the thick, black evergreens shielded the land from the moonlight, and he found a spot under a cedar tree to make camp, to stretch out, pulling down a few sweeping boughs to lie upon. Resting, he opened a can of beans and ate them cold. And the night took him over, drifting around and through him, a kind of hypnosis that left him weak and light-headed, returned him to the state he had experienced during the rain: a numbing, a fusion with the landscape, a loss of body.

He listened to the forest breathe, conjured images of animated trees and humanized animals, and drifting into sleep he thought he heard the shuffle of feet, steps over the rocks and sand, the approach of a man, but sleep conquered the realization before it had a chance to take hold.

6

SOMETHING HAD CHANGED. Doc saw it in the way she moved about the room, as if drained or exhausted, recrossing the kitchen floor to the sink and returning with the lantern, her serious expression regressing into a frown whenever the light and shadows caught her face at certain angles, and her movements created a crossing pattern in his own mind. He wavered back and forth between wanting to blurt out his feelings and wanting to sit quietly and contentedly, as if everything was under control, himself included. And he did not know what exactly was different, changed, knew that he had changed and was duller, dispirited, but did not know if this accounted for what he saw in her or not. Perhaps it was his perception that had been altered. Doc said nothing and listened.

"The fishing has been good. It's a good season. But—the same old problems, David. Some men have already demanded money from the cannery—even though we arranged that nobody gets paid until the season's over. I guess things are working out right now. But when payday comes—"

What bothered Doc was that she had not questioned him. He was relieved but at the same time suspicious. Were the spaces in her stories intended as opportunities for him to speak up? to confess?

The stink of fish pervaded the room, as it did all of Cumshewa

Town and now the night air. "There's only so much I can do. I may be the wife of the chief, but I'm still white." Evlin laughed lightly for the first time. "I know what you're thinking. That that bothers me more than anybody else. But it's still true that we're oceans apart sometimes. It's too bad because then so much of the burden falls on my husband, and Gerald already carries enough."

Doctor Marifield nodded sympathetically but he was suddenly scared, vulnerable, because he believed he had no help to offer, the reverse of his usual role here. And now Evlin's gaze was steady on him, like an exploring hand.

"Tell me more about Morgan Duff," she said. She folded her hands together on the table.

Doc smiled. "There's not much to tell. His scar is frightening. Mostly he's minding his own business."

"Really?"

"Sure, sure. He drinks a lot. Yells. Takes target practice from his hotel window—but that's all."

"I don't know, David. I don't know."

"What's on your mind?"

Sighing, Evlin massaged her forehead with her palms. Telltale lines marked the corners of her eyes and lips. She pushed herself up from the table. Moving through the room again, something tired and defeated in the slow motion of her body, as if her limbs had lost their sensory capacities and worked lifelessly, but not like the dead or the aged, like the weary, the body relinquished to fatigue but trudging on anyway, spirited by an effort that was no longer physical, fuelled by determination and need, speaking, "How have you been feeling, David?"

And with the question upon him now, like a net he thought, hindering all attempts at freedom, Doctor Marifield knew that he was trapped. A lot became clear to him as he squirmed in his seat. He had come here to escape, to nestle perhaps in some old affection they shared together, to escape not only the agonized glare of the Duff brothers, but Lyell itself and the summer itself, Morgan Duff and the townspeople and the spectre of the sabotage. Things had been bad enough, and with Henry gone he did not want to be there alone. But he had found Evlin not as he had expected, found her alone too and labouring, not laughing and talking a blue streak about plans and hopes and dreams, but doing the very work that he had skirted and avoided in Lyell. He wanted to escape again, flee into the abyss of night and darkness, where his terror would break out finally, ride like a manic black spirit upon his spine. He had come to lie, and Evlin had caught him at it, and straining against her net only entangled him further.

"Well?" she said.

Doc shrugged, said, "All right, I guess."

Evlin smiled, shook her head. "David, David. All I've heard all summer long is that you've been lagging. People who don't know you think you're sick, and those who do say you're depressed."

"Look—"

"How come you have nothing to say to me? What's happening with the mine? Morgan Duff? The sabotage? With you? So much is going on and you have nothing to say."

"It's not a simple thing."

"I didn't say it was."

He hated being in this position, looking down at his hands now and at a loss for words, knowing that his lies only compounded his difficulty, that to Evlin he was transparent and exposed. "Henry's gone. He left today. Don't ask me where—he just left."

"How come?"

Doc shrugged, said, "Somebody burned his shack down."

Evlin surprised him by laughing. "Well it's about time! That old thing. You sure he didn't burn it himself?"

Shrugging again; reduced to it he thought, his usual light speech thwarted by his fears and anxiousness to defend himself. He said, "My powerplant was sabotaged. Somebody filled the tank with water."

"Maybe you deserved it—from what I've heard."

"What do you mean by that? What the bloody hell—"

"Somebody's concerned about the mine! You, you haven't done a damn thing all summer! I don't blame whoever it is for being fed up with you. I know I'm fed up with all the stories I have to listen to."

"What stories? What—"

"That you're sitting on your rear end growing splinters! The same as the rest of them in that town."

Doc jumped to his feet and his chair fell over backwards. He picked it up roughly, slammed it back into position. Waving his hand in the air to punctuate his words, he said, "All right. You want to hear it? Okay—I'm finished. I'm through. I've had it up to here with this island! I, I damn well have it in mind to leave altogether."

"You—you—" Evlin shook her head as she spoke, jutting out her chin, struggling to find the right word. When it eluded her she hurled the word first in mind, like a handy weapon. "—quitter!"

Brushing past Doc she crossed to the far side of the room. She rested her head in one hand while keeping her back to him. Her back was shaking: tears that Doc did not see, but he felt them as his own, wanted them to be his own. But there was nothing he could say.

Gathering herself together again, as if collecting disassembled pieces fraught with fatigue and strain, Evlin wiped her eyes and rubbed the back of her neck. When she spoke she turned, although she still did not face Doctor Marifield. "Listen. I'm sorry for yelling and being frantic. But we still have children here sleeping in their parents' vomit, and . . . women beaten by their husbands . . . men still get drunk with money their children need for food. So I don't have time to keep track of what goes on at Lyell. Now that Gerald and Walter are out at sea constantly—no time at all. But it scares me, David, it really frightens me, you know! I thought we shared—Well, I thought we could trust each other. But you come here and try to weave a happy tale—the carefree and brilliant Doctor David Marifield, without a worry in the world! David, what's wrong? Don't you—don't you care any more?"

Pulling the chair out, Doc sat down. He squirmed in his seat as if unable to find a comfortable spot on it. "What do you mean?"

"I made myself clear, David."

Doc glanced furtively about the room. Evlin's words made him hot and uncomfortable. Heat smouldered along his spine. He scouted the room and searched down the corridor, learning why he had felt uneasy here, for the room and house had adopted the attitude of a battle station, people laboured and warred here against encroaching defeat and misery. Doc realized how much his own condition must have stood out to Evlin, juxtaposed against the contrary state of mind, the man in retreat visiting the camp of those who fought on, pretending to be a warrior himself. He felt like a fool. "Sure I care," he said.

Evlin only looked at him steadily, and Doc turned away. And he tried to refrain but his tension forced him to swallow, a lump in his throat feeling like some huge obstacle or beast that had wedged itself and gripped tightly. "All right, so I've been down a little lately. I admit that."

"You admit nothing," Evlin said flatly, and she took three quick, long strides and sat on the stool by the sink. Watching her, Doc noticed how the light glowed on certain strands of her blonde hair, cast shadows under her eyes and over her throat. And he was touched unexpectedly by memories, recalling suddenly and with renewed vividness the first weeks and months after they had met, after he had arrived on Skincuttle Island and they had become close friends, he helping her to keep up her spirits while she battled against her father's will and hold on her, and this rush of sentiment caught Doc by surprise, he longed for that time again. "You admit nothing," Evlin repeated. Their roles had been reversed then. Evlin's words returned him to a vacant and nullifying sensation. Once he had encouraged her and reprimanded her when she faltered; now, he was the one to sit and witness the strength of her emotions.

"So Henry and I needed your help and you gave it and we received it," she said, as if she had known his thoughts. But it was more than that. Knew *him*, he realized. "That doesn't make us your children. That doesn't mean you can't receive our help when you need it. Does it, David? Does it?"

Doc looked down at the floor. The ties were splitting and losing their corners. He would not allow himself to speak, suppressing conflicting and confusing emotions, anger mingling with self-reproach, bitterness with shame.

"Think of it, David. You tell me Henry's shack burned down, your powerplant was sabotaged, all this is happening and you haven't a clue who's responsible or why."

"Look—it's not easy! Even Henry doesn't know!"

"But you don't even care. You don't care that you don't know."

"That's not true. It bothers me, sure. And anyway, we do have a clue."

"Thomas Duff?"

"That's right."

"So why don't you go find him? Two years ago you wouldn't have hesitated. It's because it doesn't really bother you. Does Morgan Duff bother you? Does the mine . . . *bother* you? Tell me what does bother you, David?"

Light from the lanterns reflected on the window panes behind Evlin's head, reflected in the glass and they were like the eyes of the darkness looking in; wind whipped the door and shutters and even in the room they could feel the presence of the approaching storm, perhaps a quick squall with its controlled fury and swiftly spent rage. Doc stared out into the blackness, into the night, already knowing that he was going there, already knowing that he was trapped again, and not by the house or by Evlin or even by his own fears and weaknesses, but by that familiar rising spirit, rising now within him, impetuous and frantic, spoiling for activity, even bedlam, no matter how mindless or ill-conceived.

"David."

And looking at her she seemed far away, remote, like the lights in the glass, somehow intangible and inaccessible, and it was not her but everything, everything he had ever known or shared, that began to fade, disappear as he floated past.

"David?"

Even his name hung in the air, failed to reach him, failed to strike some note of recognition or accord, and Doc already sensed the mounting sea, the massive waves, already experienced his fear of the water churning within him and trying to dissuade his nature, to keep him here, keep him in this house with this friend where he belonged.

But he already knew that he was going, soon, that the next stop would be Kloo where he still had prestige. Billy Peel might question him but not assault him like this.

Evlin was standing. Doc looked into her face. It frightened him that he could not see her eyes, that they were concealed and protected by the tricks of lantern light. It frightened him, and his defence of himself welled within his chest and he eagerly awaited its outbreak, anxious for a final explosion of force and violence to propel him into the night and upon the havoc of the sea. He would carry this quarrel to its furthest limits, until there was no other solution but flight.

"David!" Evlin called, and Doc looked up at her, and he relished the fright apparent in her voice.

7

RAINDROPS TAPPED ON THE BRANCHES, quick, spirited messengers rapping on his windows and doors. And hesitant streams poked their way over the earth, nudged the twigs and fallen pine needles, swooped into miniature valleys and mounted tiny hills. Henry awoke in the middle of the night and immediately began to burrow, frenzied, desperately building a dyke around himself, plowing the earth and twigs into parallel barricades the length of his body, two inches high, joined at his head to the tree trunk and protected at his feet by the downward slope of the land. Finished, he sipped raspberry juice from his canteen nervously, gasping from his sudden exertion, then located his flask and drank brandy. The brandy burned his throat and stomach and sent a warm glow through to his fingertips and toes, and lying back he tucked an arm under his head and listened to the rain on the leaves.

The moon did not penetrate the cloudcover at all. The rain reminded him of childhood nights—left bedridden by his crippled leg he would lie awake listening to the constant patter on the roof. But here the darkness was total and Henry was forced to battle fears, of the forest, of the blackness, of the impending storm. He listened to the sounds behind the rain, hoping to cull some favour from the forest, some reprieve from the oppression of the night. The forest seemed awake too, and active. Easily he imagined the forest alive and the trees uprooting themselves and cavorting around his bed. The animals too, the bears and the deer and the beavers and many racoons, abandoning their common habit and strutting on two legs and communing in an elaborate, mystical language. The images became so intense and distracting to him that Henry was tempted to run out into the rain to reassure himself. Instead he allowed the images to develop, preferring their birth and dance to the alternative of blackness and incessant rain. And he viewed a council of the forest where the trees gathered to compute mathematical equations concerning the solar system and the galaxy, and the deer arrived with advance reports on the regeneration of mankind, and the bears, in conference, proposed that mankind should not be permitted more than a decade to continue believing that they were the sole custodians of the universe. The animal kingdom and the plant kingdom would have to reveal themselves to the human mind. And the eagles and the ravens were granted the responsibility of plotting the course of action, the means to accomplish this transition.

A fallen branch cracked sharply, and Henry, almost asleep again, jerked to an upright position, banged his head on a limb. He thought he detected a disturbance in the undergrowth, but he was not certain, and save for the steady rain it was followed by stillness and silence. But his heart beat frantically, and he was conscious of his heavy breathing, as if his heart and lungs and nerves knew what he did not. Henry lay back and pulled the blanket around himself tightly, reasoned that whether the intruder was imaginary or real he was at his mercy, nothing could be done. He drank again from his flask, the brandy soothing his frayed nerves.

Rain worked its way through the trees. Whichever way he turned, drops of water found him, smacking an eye, exploding off the tip of his nose, running down his cheeks. This was the aspect of wilderness he feared the most. Not the physical challenge, because it was quickly neutralized by the exhilaration and joy felt, but the challenge to his psyche, the bombardment of the forces and manifestations of life in their fullest intensity upon his mind. His shack had been a protection against this, old and familiar and decrepit, reeking with memories and past dreams, concerns of a childhood that had bloomed once but swiftly faltered the day he lay pinned under a rockslide. When he had sniffed the smoke, startled from his dream, and discovered the thin, red flames encircling him, not sure yet if this was still dream or physical, it had been the demise of this security that had scorched him, and he hollered, "Fire! Fire!" while he grabbed his pack and stuffed it with food and clothing, running then, only to stop and go back and find first his canteen, which he filled with raspberry juice, then his brandy flask, fleeing again, still shouting, "Fire! Fire!" but stopping again and going back, coughing now and choking on the smoke, throwing his books out the window, then running for dear life and the woods, while others hurried to extinguish the flames. A maudlin spirit circled, entered him. Thinking of the shack, seeing it burn now for the first time in his mind's eye, realizing that he could no longer return to it, that it had been reduced to ash and charred timber, Henry drank again.

He was unable to sleep. Insistent thoughts, the presence of the forest, kept him awake. Henry repeated a prayer taught to him by his missionary father. But the words only raised feelings of loneliness and despair. And he could not submerge himself in these feelings when he tried, he could not drown in his sadness, he kept bobbing to the surface again, a branch pulled down by the currents but springing up again. It seemed to him that the wilderness would not permit him to sink, to indulge in despair. Such a thing would be a sacrilege, and the forest was the church, and Henry felt compelled to shift his thinking. He wondered if these woods were not more distinctive than he had allowed, perhaps their history and memory made their expression unique, so that it was not the wilderness with which he had to deal, but specifically the Skincuttle Island forest. This intrigued him, it returned him to his personal territory of history and mystery. Perhaps there existed a special connection between him, the historian, and the forest, the holder of the secrets. For the forest had witnessed all that he had recorded and much more. Maybe he was not an intruder here, a mere stumbler into the deepest chamber of this inner sanctum, maybe he was a trusted friend, and perhaps all the movements and undulating currents he felt around him now were actually the expressions of a desire to communicate and not to frighten. Long ago he had sensed the mind of the forest, a practice into which his father had guided him, and he had credited sudden flashes of inspiration and insight to his attempts to commune with that mind. Usually he had undertaken these attempts from the safety of his shack, on the mere edge of the forest, and always he had felt fear afterwards despite the warm glow of the initial meditation. Now he was right in it, immersed in the depths of the rain forest, there was no escape, and slowly, bit by bit, he eased his tensions, allowed them to fall off like dead leaves, and he reached a point of quiet, progressing to stillness, and he felt his body drifting. When he woke the rain was fierce and the water had soaked through his blanket and clothing. He moved against the tree trunk, curling himself into a tight and shivering ball.

Henry's leg reacted to the rain, his knee serving as a kind of signal centre that shot sharp pains either up or down in sequences that followed no pattern. Individual currents were so intense that sometimes he saw flashes of tiny white lights before his eyes. He touched his damaged eye and the swelling had increased during his sleep, moving up through his eyebrow and placing a neat, round bulge on one side of his forehead. Over the jacket he wore, he pulled on the jacket that had only one sleeve. Again he thought he detected movement in the undergrowth, but when he concentrated he heard only the drone of the constant rain. He hugged the tree as if trying to nourish warmth from the contact and to reassure himself of his own presence and being. Water was collecting in pools and rivers and, reaching out, his hand landed in a stream already two inches deep. His dyke was being inundated.

A game. Conjuring the images of other people. Doing it at first for companionship, holding two-way conversations in his mind, but soon he was portraying them and putting other people in his situation. Doc thought this was a grand adventure and told himself stories of his own frolics as a city-slicker. Jonas Gatenby, a cantankerous Skincuttle seadog Henry had known all his life, bellowed and swore and cursed not only the rain but the trees and the island and the planet too. Henry took a swig of brandy to fulfil the role and broke off laughing. He considered being Thomas Duff, the hermit, and mussed his hair and closed an eye, the swollen one, but to accurately portray Thomas he would have to get out from under the tree and walk through the forest as if it was the sunniest day of the year, allowing some inner radar to direct him. Then Henry imitated Billy Peel, folding his legs under himself, straightening his back, sitting stoically and staring into the rain and darkness. He refused to yield an ounce of dignity to the onslaught of the elements. And imitating Billy gave him strength. He realized he was better off than huddling and shivering and allowing the storm to terrorize him. So he sat and waited for the dawn, mindless of the time.

A disturbance close to him again—this time Henry responded. He rolled his blanket quietly, cautiously, and returned it to the backpack. Located his flask and canteen and did the same. He fastened the pack, positioned it over his shoulders, and tightened the straps to a snug fit. Sitting cross-legged he laid his cane on his lap. Clutching his cane like a club. He removed his small hunting knife from its sheath and stabbed it into the earth in front of him. Henry waited. Hearing the movement again, the sound of bushes being trampled. He did not expect an animal. Henry changed to a crouch position and gripped his knife, balanced on the balls of his feet.

There was no light. He could see no farther than the edges of the branches that concealed him. And failing to distinguish details, his eyes resorted to elaborating the inner and interwoven currents of darkness, giving credence to black forms protruding from the greater darkness. He closed his eyes, concentrated all his senses on listening. A branch cracked. On his left and ahead a bit. A step splashed in water. On his left. He knew the intruder must be very near to be heard through the rain. Henry concentrated so hard he could hear the blood in his ears, the beat of his pulse in his throat and temples. He discovered himself hoping that a trespasser lurked, that this was not a trick of his mind which would be more difficult to tolerate.

A sound—a voice?—like a muffled shout through the rain. Cautiously, moving with the slow deliberation of a slug, he crept forward.

Toward the—it spoke again, closer this time so that he knew the voice was real. The voice ceased but Henry detected movement, steps: the man was approaching him. Crouching on his knees, Henry kept his cane and knife ready. The voice again, and Henry was shocked that it was so near, the man could be no more than two or three feet from him, yet he could not see a thing but heard only his name, summoned and repeated, "Scowcroft! Scowcroft!" And for a moment he thought he could make out the man's form but he was not sure, he clenched and unclenched his grip on the knife, considered striking, the swift bite of a snake. "Scow-croft! I'm waiting for you, ya!"

The man moved a few steps farther. Like a town crier moving from house to house—from tree to tree—to make his message known. Suddenly an upper layer of cloud was blown away, the moon did not appear but a faint aura of light was evident, made bright by the hyperexpansion of his pupils in the pitch blackness, and Henry saw the man's silhouette. The man raised a bottle to his mouth. Henry thought for a second that his predator had a cane also, but he quickly corrected himself and concentrated on the rifle. *The gun!* It was not too late to spring. He could wait until the darkness was total again. Jump him, grab the gun. *The gun! The gun!* Without his rifle, Morgan Duff could be pacified, perhaps, perhaps—beaten.

Henry memorized the terrain, the trees, the branches, the slope. When the moonlight was obliterated he shouted with the fullest velocity he could muster, "Mor-GAAAN!" then he scurried back behind his tree, cut across to the next tree, finding his way by locating the branches first then pulling himself underneath.

"Scowcroft! That's you?"

Henry expected the man to remain still, to turn and try to locate his voice. "Morgan!" he cried, a quick staccato shout, loud enough to be heard. Immediately he moved again, crawling on his hands and knees, knife and cane held in front of him. He travelled fifteen feet and called again. "Mor-GAAAANN!" And he dove behind a line of ferns, landing in a deep puddle.

The blast of the rifle rocked his senses, he was up and running in an instant, but his panic buckled his knees and he fell, colliding with something, for one horrible instant he thought it was an animal but it turned out to be a loose root, and he saw the second blast of the rifle, fire from the muzzle shouting out, the sound of it cutting through the rain and forest and his own mind like a heraldic blast, a proclamation, a salute to the bullet that now tore through the night seeking to burrow in warm flesh and bones. *Right, right, right! I already heard it! I should have known it and never been surprised at all because I heard it before you ever fired, heard it not as a gunshot or even a blast but as a bump, a gentle nudge of the boat on the wharf and the groan of the timbers and the pinched squeal of the rubber tires, you back on Skincuttle Island, returned, so this isn't even it but only the continued reverberation of it, I should have expected nothing less!* Morgan was only five yards away and Henry continued to circle, until he crouched only three or four feet from him, he could hear him laughing, and Morgan wheeled and fired in the opposite direction, a response perhaps to a sudden fear or a ghost.

Henry coiled himself. Returned his knife to its sheath, gripped his club. He wanted the rifle. He was burning with his desire to possess it. Understood that the man had followed him out, kept track of him enough to know that he had not gone beyond the canyon by nightfall, and so had camped in the same vicinity. Drunk now and angered by the rain he had revealed his presence, Henry aware that it was not a mistake, they were both captive here, nowhere to go, aware too that it was Morgan's privilege to taunt him, that if he and Morgan set out at the first light of dawn, he would be no match for this man and soon would be left behind. His only chance was to get the gun. The night and rain and forest worked on his side to neutralize Morgan's superior strength and power, and the sheer chance of this opportunity thrilled him.

Suddenly, Morgan spun in a short circle and fired a volley of shots into the air, the fire from the hammer lighting his face, creating eerie shadows and skeleton patterns, his scar looking like an open wound, a great gap in his face, his eyes like flickering candle flames.

The gun! The gun!

Henry hesitated. He knew his move. The element of surprise, the thick knob of his cane swinging fiercely into the other man's face, breaking his nose or knocking out teeth, and in the same motion he'd yank the rifle loose. His flight into the woods would be a simple one, the darkness converging behind him. But Henry hesitated. And when Morgan laughed it seemed directed at him. And as Morgan moved away Henry did not chase him down, leap upon his back, and drag him to the earth as he knew he could, but he waited until he was gone then slammed his fist into the mud.

Fool! You fool!

He lay on the ground in the water and panted.

I could have had the gun! I could!

But he soon stopped chastising and berating himself, for he knew if given a second or third chance he would fail again. It was Morgan. The scar. The man's intense, manic laughter. He was afraid of him, terrified, in awe of him, his presence numbing his reflexes and stopping-up his heart. *So really, what's the shame? I mean that man's fought a Bengal tiger and has the marks to prove it, so what match would I be against a man like that? Yeh. Well. I had him. I had him! I could have the gun now!*

An idea stirred, beckoned to him as if from a corner of his mind. He resisted it at first, but thought it through after a while. A way to travel at night. A chance he had to take. *Thomas. I'm coming after you. I hope you're worth it. I hope there's enough left of you that's worth anything at all. Glimmers of memory and hope at least. And I hope Gail's dead seaplundered body is worth it too, and not her body but her memory, and not even her memory but her presence, and not just worth it to me, but worth it to you too.*

Henry walked with caution, using his cane like a blind man's, working his way among the trees and rocks and limbs, following the sound of the river. He was able to trace the rise of the canyon wall with his cane when he reached the shore. He dipped his hand into the water. Cold. He checked the laces of his boots and the stays of his backpack. The rain had tightened the knots securely. He stepped into the water. In the darkness it felt like entering the chilling swirl of a black nightmare.

He moved out until the water was above his knees. He was praying to God and entreating the water too to be kind. Lowered himself into the cold currents, the force of water striking him now, stinging his face, the cold sending a sudden alarm through his body and he had to gasp for breath. With his hands and feet on the bottom of the river he pushed himself forward. Reaching deeper water he still used his feet for traction, using also his cane like a paddle but digging it into the riverbed to push himself forward. Water splashed into his mouth and nostrils and the cold continued to constrict his chest, and reaching an obtruding boulder he pulled himself up and caught deep breaths, the rain on his back feeling warm now and he laughed, and laughing he swam into the water again and battled the rapids, keeping to the shallow water, and slowly, tenaciously, he worked his way up the gorge in the dead of night.

8

SPREAD OUT IN THE BOTTOM OF HIS BOAT and lashed to it, with his shoulders propped against the stern, his neck and head bent back over the side, Doctor Marifield managed to open one eye. A wave rolled the boat upward and he saw light, the early glow of the false dawn, and for the first time in many hours he felt that he would live. But looking west he could not see land, panicking then, perhaps he had gone right past the southern tip of Skincuttle Island, Kloo, or had drifted far out from shore and was lost. But he was saved by another wave that lifted him high enough to sight land only a hundred yards away, concealed by the darkness and by the rising, falling sea.

 Doc looked long and hard to make sure that the shoreline was real. Throughout the night it had become difficult for him to distinguish between what was hallucinatory and what was real. A one-armed pirate had risen from the ocean with a screaming mermaid tucked under the stub of his arm, and had approached waving a sabre. Doc had closed his eyes to the attack only to view a sea-monster loom on the horizon of his mind. Doctor Marifield had expected to hallucinate, he was prone to doing so, as in earlier days on long drives through the countryside, winding mountain roads and evening, suddenly set upon by riderless horses sporting brilliant gold and silver saddles; or at a party where he had been drinking too much, balancing his plate and glass as he sat down, glancing up in the nick of time, the moment a mountain lion leaped from the chandelier. He had expected to hallucinate but he had not expected to lose his ability to know what was actual and what was not, and he blamed the rain, blamed the eternal roll of the sea, blamed his boat, the boat and the rain and the sea becoming a single, coherent entity, made so by a lavish intercourse in which he was merely a timid and confused spectator. Waves rolled out from his boat to collide with the sea-waves, foam sprawled into the air, a celebration, the splash of spray like gaseous fires on the sun, and the continuous rain became the curtain between the illusory and the tangible. Through the night his searchlight had followed the shoreline until he lost connection between the beam of light and what was his own vision, one became so deeply fused into the other, he lost understanding of what was shoreline and land and what was shoreline and sea, and his own position along that frontier.

Nine hours on the sea from Cumshewa Town, his watch still ticked but Doc imagined such movements were foreign to him now: heartbeat and pulse, blood pressure counts, functioning rhythms spewed out along with his vomit and guts and swallowed by the scavenger waves. His body felt limp, numb, soggy. In a lucid moment he had lashed himself to the boat, and so had relinquished control of his life to the boat, presumed it to be in control anyway, hobnobbing with the waves, prancing through the rain like an old man on a picnic with his grandchildren, a kid again, the arthritis forgotten for a day. The boat was familiar with the ocean and with ocean storms, it was clumsy and awkward and too fat for the inland waterways, but on the sea it was spry and congenial and puttered through the water with a confidence garnered from long experience. Doc simply kept a light hand on the rudder, bailed-out every few minutes, refueled every few hours, and let the boat do the rest.

At dawn, the true dawn, just as the red sun's brilliance broke over the horizon and shone through a sliver of open sky, Doc sighted Kloo. Below the cloudcover and amid the red-tinged rain, mists rose and fell along the mountainous shoreline, and at Kloo smoke from many fires mingled with the wafting layers of mist. The village emitted an aura of peacefulness that hung about it like the mist and smoke, an aura which was more than just the promise of shelter. The village had the appearance of being rooted, as if the poles supporting the teepees had sprouted from the earth and possessed intricate and penetrating root systems, as if the shacks enjoyed a special awareness in knowing that they had been hewn from trees grown here over centuries, knowing too that this, the newest of Skincuttle villages, was actually the perpetuation of a village that had thrived throughout those centuries.

Doc rammed his boat onto the shore. His legs wobbled when he stood up and he had to clutch the boat quickly to steady the dizziness in his head. He stepped into the water to drag the bow further onto the rocks. He lashed the bowline to a tree, wobbling still, feeling as if his body had been emptied of all its organs and entrails. Among the trees were the hollowed-out cedar canoes of the tribe at Kloo.

You never had the courage to finally take something of what you learned and apply it. I mean to yourself.

Look. Evlin.

What? Well. What?

Doc stepped back into the water to collect his gear from the stern. He pitched forward trying to pull it out and had to crawl from the boat on his hands and knees. Down on all fours on the shore, he breathed deeply and tried to summon strength. He pushed himself to his feet and walked through the trees that lined the shore, past two ancient and moss-covered totems that leaned to one side, supported now by ropes, and onto the clearing at the base of the Kloo hill.

Kloo rested on the slope of the hill, a winding path threading its way among the teepees and shacks and the two large longhouses. A pack of barking dogs ran towards him, and Doc walked only a few yards further when he stumbled. He thought he could right himself with a little skip but he tripped again, and as he put out his hands to break his fall, a blankness, a grey veil crossed his eyes and he hit the ground hard, unconscious.

9

OPENING HIS EYES, he saw rocks, a piece of driftwood, the rain splashing in a sheltered pool of water; and Henry breathed deeply, cautiously, felt the air enter his windpipe and expand his lungs; his exhalation was a sigh of relief too, for everything seemed to be working, there were no broken ribs or punctured lungs and he was still alive.

The rain was warm on his face, gentle. Lifting his head, he saw mist, he saw the canyon, he saw the sheet of rain. A grey landscape, everything dominated by the sky now, by the layers upon layers of cloudcover, grey mingling with black, mists rising and descending, flirting with the clouds, the forest and the river and the rocks reflecting this uniform and dismal greyness. Henry wondered how long he had lain here.

He looked up, twisting his neck to do so but remaining prone on the ground, lying on his stomach. He recognized his location. Years earlier the side of the canyon wall had collapsed, dumping itself into the gorge, forming a beachhead but convulsing the flow of water around it. Henry had been swept into these convulsions, his feet suddenly lifted by an undertow, and he was carried into the rapids, pulled downward, deep underwater, and finally spirited up again. And scratching, clawing, he was washed onto this promontory. He had almost drowned; he had swallowed a lot of water so had pushed himself up from the ground repeatedly, fighting off delirium and unconsciousness, panic and fear, dropping his chest onto the hard surface to slam the water out of himself, until finally the hacking and gagging and coughing subsided.

Henry made no motion to get up, and he did not bother to check himself over, knowing that he was in bad shape, the details would only be superfluous now. He was content to lie still and close his eyes. But something tugged at his mind, appealing to his attention, a nagging thought amid his many aches and sorenesses, a circular kind of thought that wheeled around him. Trying to identify it, his mind suddenly slipped into a sickening swirl and he remembered again and again the sensation of being pulled downward by the water, as if the thought was a moving thing inside of him, waiting for him to be drawn into its domain.

Opening his eyes again—the piece of driftwood, and that triggered something too. Closing his eyes he saw Gail. Her image popped into his mind with astonishing clarity, and taken by surprise he sprang to his knees. His body was wracked by pain. Pain centres in his crippled leg administered it all, sending messages in sharp, caustic commands that were quickly received by other areas and a response given. But he knew when he had entered the water that this would be the price. Gail. He remembered now, her boat broken and scattered on the rocks like driftwood, her body sucked into a void of gushing water—exactly what had happened to him.

The landslide had created a slope from the riverbed to the top of the canyon, and looking up, Henry saw his escape route. Daybreak meant a return to the forest, he chided himself for resting. Looking down the gorge the way he had come, he was struck by his accomplishment, overwhelmed suddenly by his success. Laughing, he shouted, "Ya-hoo! I made it! Morgan! I'm over here! Hey! I made it!"

Standing, he cheerfully removed his sopping-wet jackets, his shirt and undershirt. Because the rain felt so pleasant he removed his boots and pants as well, bathed in the falling water. His backpack now weighed a ton. The blanket alone had absorbed gallons of water. He would have to leave almost everything behind.

He drank a can of soup, then sorted out what he needed and what he could afford to leave behind, settling on one jacket and a shirt—he wrung them out in the pouring rain, twisting them into tight little balls which he stuffed into the corners of his pack—no socks, his pants and his boots which he put on again, the canned food and his cane. Both his flask and his canteen were gone, and he had to rearrange the straps on his pack to cover a tear.

Henry looked around but it was no use, his cap was missing too, and he felt disappointed; for a moment he weakened, growing sad and angry at the same time as a wave of self-pity coursed upward through him. He had considered his green cap pushed down over his curls as a kind of personal signature. Felt the loss not of identity but of security.

"Come on!" he yelled, slapping his thighs hard, once on each side. "Let's get moving! Let's go!"

And Henry Scowcroft climbed the slope of fallen rock on his hands and knees, and when he reached the top he did not look back but entered the forest quickly in his pursuit of Thomas Duff, and miles downstream, Morgan Duff plucked a green cap from the Oganjibra River and turned it over in his hands.

10

I ALREADY TOLD YOU that I'm not your child and neither is Henry. You should see that.

How far do you think you can carry this, Evlin?

David, for heaven's sake, you're falling apart at the seams.

Smoke in his nostrils. And he admitted with some reluctance that he found the scent enticing and invigorating, his body was quickening and strengthening too.

Doc opened one eye only at first, saw the young girl stirring food over the open fire. She was staring into the black pot and stirring absently. Doc opened his other eye and he was not surprised to be here, he expected to be here, for this teepee had become his personal guest room whenever he visited Kloo. And the same girl was looking after him. Doc raised his head and looked down over his body, over the familiar multicoloured blanket covered by a bearskin this time. Someone must have thought he was sick. Propping himself up on his elbows he was overcome by a coughing fit and the girl came around from behind the fire and slapped his back. He had to spit out phlegm before the fit subsided.

"Hi, Carol. How's the patient?"

The girl giggled, smiling so that her whole face lit up. "I'm not the patient! You're the patient!"

"That's what I mean. Tell me, nurse, do I live or die?"
Shyly, the girl said, "People call me Wogeena now, not Carol anymore."
"Who?"
"Wogeena. Do you like it?"
"An Indian name. Sure I like it. It's different. How'd I get up here?"
"You were sleeping in a puddle. The dogs find you or maybe you drown. Billy carried you up here." The girl giggled again and attended to the fire, poking it here and there with a stick. "You want some soup? It's all ready now. It's fish."

The girl passed him a wooden bowl filled with the steaming soup. Cupping the bowl with both hands, he sipped, and his body responded to the warmth in a split-second of ecstasy. But he began to cough it up and Wogeena whacked his back again. She sat beside him. "We think you will live. You are a good patient."

Doc smiled and gave her a quick hug. "Nothing can kill me now, Car—whoops! Wo-gee-na. Wogeena. I like it!"

"Why did you come at night?"

A charge, a shock, opening a space through his body. He looked at her sharply for an instant, but he wanted the question to slip off him and he shrugged, smiled. "I got lost for a while. The rain—it took me a long time."

Wogeena traced patterns in a patch of bare earth exposed between the bearskins and blankets that covered the floor. The easy motion intimidated Doctor Marifield, he felt uneasy about his lie, as if the girl was scrawling the truth on the ground, or summoning it. "I better tell Billy you're awake now," she said.

Wogeena moved across the teepee and pulled a wolfskin over her back, the head of the wolf with its eyes and teeth exposed resting on the top of her head, a startling apparition. She pushed back the flap of the teepee and the rain danced in a big puddle right where she stepped. She was quick to close the flap behind her and Doc finished his soup.

I don't believe this!
You! You don't believe it!

Once, you know, your perceptions were sharp. You could cut right through to the depths of any false movement. Now your senses are dull, David, dull. You speak without an iota of sense. I mean, I haven't heard such a ridiculous tirade in all my life.

Doc crawled out from his pallet and ran his hands along his clothes; everything was still damp so he pulled the bearskin around him and sat by the fire. He had always enjoyed coming to Kloo but he was not sure why. He found the teepees cozy and the old men and children pleasant and the food satisfying, delighted in the beauty of the setting, the simple and primitive village juxtaposed against the mountains; yet he experienced a zestful spirit that went beyond all this, for he walked with long, energetic strides and often felt tall and proud when he climbed the peak of Kloo hill and looked down. Looked down over the smoking teepees and cabins, the barking dogs and playful children, the women arriving from the forest with kindling and the men coming in from the sea with their catch, looked down and felt elated and proud. Thinking about it now he arrived at a point of satisfaction, of comfort, felt independent here, autonomous in a sense, as if being from another civilization granted him a peculiar distinction, not of superiority exactly, but of separation and regard. Separated, he was still acknowledged, and he liked that. As a doctor he was the only whiteman permitted in Kloo, and it was not the esteem he enjoyed but the security, here he had his own gait and speech and duties and there was little, few opportunities or openings, into which he might be drawn or with which he might be fused.

Sometimes he feared the chanting. He had been swept into it in the past. Sometimes it rolled over him, wave upon wave, hollowing a path through him so that he felt overcome, experienced his heart quicken with the drums and his mind reel under the onslaught of the voices, but he had learned to tolerate the chanting too and benefit from it, because he had learned that always it ended and he was released back to himself again. The chanting was something he could follow and lose himself in but ultimately survive, ultimately be squeezed out the opposite end of the ritual like a triumphant dancer at the end of his movement, and ultimately the theatre would be emptied and barren and he could be alone again, expelled with his own thoughts and disturbances.

Moving to the entrance, Doc kneeled and opened the flap slightly. The rain. The bent grasses were slick with running water, dancing pools and puddles everywhere; the pathway up the hill was a thin meandering river and he looked up into the rain, saw it falling not as a steady downpour but as the spray of finely timed waves, precise and intricate workings. He viewed the edge of the forest, the first line of trees like brooding confederates guarding all that lay behind. He tried peering around the flap to see if he could see the mountains, but the rain beat on his face and all he ever sighted was the mist and smoke. The forest. The mountains. He wondered if they were not already alert to his arrival, if they did not lie in wait for him, prepare to close behind him after his entry, sealing escape routes, converging behind him like time passing, the very processes of dying, and he wondered too what loomed ahead, a skirmish? a battle? a truce? a handshake from the forest or a nod from the mountains? or would the mountains avert their faces once again and refuse to recognize his presence? That's what bothered him about Henry, he thought, his reverence for the wilderness, which was something quite different from a tacit respect, or even love. He had always respected and loved nature himself, or so he believed, but Henry feared it too, as if it were an abiding and discerning presence, as if it held him accountable. The closest Doc had come to this intimate kind of relationship was to sense the forest and the mountains ignoring him, simply refusing to participate with him in anything at all, turning their backs to heartlessly echo and thereby ridicule pleas for recognition.

And Billy was no better. But different though. Doc had not determined the essence of Billy's relationship to the forest. Billy did not fear it, and reverence, respect, and love were not appropriate words, they did not fit; with Billy it was something that was more concealed, and Doc had never been able to uproot it and expose it to the light of day. But then he had never been able to uproot Billy Peel either, their friendship based on respect rather than understanding.

Billy. Coming soon. Doc anticipated his approach nervously, a new and unsettling experience. Billy disturbed many people, but Doc had accepted the contact between them as something vital and nourishing. He had never feared Billy as he had the Duff brothers, at times, or even Henry; questioning himself, he understood that it was facing Billy that scared him now, fearful of his questions, fearful of admitting that the Duff brothers had intimidated him, and Henry had abandoned him, and Evlin had upbraided him—knew that Billy would not laugh but would find it deeply ironical that he had had to come to him, adversary and opponent, to get help for this mission into the mountains, would perceive it all as an immense comedy. He would hate admitting to Billy that he had faltered, even failed.

Doc let the flap fall and sat near the fire again, shivering. He would have to give up something to ask Billy's help, and Billy would see it but not acknowledge it. Anticipating Billy Peel's arrival, Doc felt the bewilderment that islanders, like Henry, like Evlin, had been feeling for many years, and it annoyed him. He added kindling to the fire, watched it blacken and burn, felt his nerves vibrate again, tensing, felt the tumour again, and hearing the footsteps he pulled the bearskin more tightly over his own skin, and with his thumb he pressed and rubbed the bear's paw.

Remember. For a moment. Please. When you first came here I was the one on the limp. It was me, David, who needed the help. You gave it. Remember? And I thank you for it. But now the tables are turned. So what? Is that so hard to accept? Look at it this way and remember. You never would have come to Skincuttle Island if it wasn't for your troubles. Your coming here was an escape, you shouldn't forget that.

Billy Peel stepped into the teepee, bending low then straightening up, flapping the front of his jacket as he did so to shake off the water, a bird rising into flight, a raven, Doc thought. Doc noted that Billy's coarse and jet black hair was much longer than he had seen it before, and his black eyes smouldered like coals in the light from the fire. Following him in, Wogeena tossed the wolfskin off her back and sat away from the fire. Billy sat across from Doc with the fire between them; the flames shimmered on his brown face and gave it darker tones, offsetting the smoothness and roundness of his features that usually made him appear child-like, even babyish. They exchanged nods across the fire and Billy put more wood on the flames. Doc found himself flustered, already scurrying within himself for explanations, an accounting.

"You hungry, Doc?" Billy asked.

"I could use some solid food. I'm a little woozy."

Billy nodded, said, "Wogeena." The girl adjusted the wolfskin over herself again and left the teepee. He smiled and rubbed the back of his neck, said, "When we found you this morning we thought you were dead."

"Thanks for dragging me up here, Billy."

Laughing, Billy looked up, his eyes following a burning ash as it floated up through the smoke and out the centre of the teepee. "We didn't drag you, Doc. We carried you."

Doc returned the smile. The wind shifted momentarily and rain fizzled in the fire, creating smoke. Doc coughed. "I was just wondering how I was received."

"You were lucky the dogs saw you. Maybe you still be down there now." Billy waited before speaking again. Doc scratched his whiskers and thought he saw a shape moving beside him: shadows from the fire. He wondered how it would come, the probing, the questioning, had Wogeena already told him of his lie? Probably. When he looked up Billy was watching him. "We would understand you coming at night if somebody was sick, but you're the one who's sick, so nobody understands."

Billy's speech was flat and stilted, and as usual Doc did not know if he had raised a question or issued a command. Doc rubbed his hands together and looked alternately into the fire and around the teepee. "Different things have been going on lately. I don't know how much you know of it." He delayed a moment to see if Billy would answer, but the young chief remained quiet, staring at him. "For one thing, Morgan Duff's back on Skincuttle Island."

Nodding, Billy leaned forward so that his chin was directly above the rim of the fire. The shadows changed his eyes into deep black caverns and Doc was startled by the effect. "We heard he come back. He's gone a long time."

"Hmmm. Henry said seventeen years."

"Yes. Henry keeps count. Morgan works for the mine company, we heard that."

"Not exactly. He and two of his brothers, who didn't come, they have their own business. The mining company hired them to build whatever transportation facilities they require—roads, railways, maybe a port. So. That's one thing that's been happening, but there's something else too."

"The sabotage," Billy said. Outside there was movement and chatter, people passing along the footpath.

"So you know about that."

"About the fires we know and the mischief. What we heard was people suspected us. Then we heard they were suspecting Thomas." Billy shrugged. "It makes sense. The mine will be in our territory and Thomas's territory too."

"There were notes. Thomas left notes saying it was him. Well. Pieces of paper with his name scrawled on them."

Poking at the fire, Billy looked at Doc sharply, about to deliver a strong statement, but he checked himself and continued poking at the fire.

"Did you hear? Thomas burned down Henry Scowcroft's shack."

Again Billy looked at Doc sharply without speaking, returning to his interest in the smoke and flames.

"That's what it seems like anyway."

"Where's Henry?"

Doc still rubbed his hands nervously, rearranged the bear hide over his back. "I don't know. That's another thing. He disappeared."

Billy was quiet for several minutes. He picked fistfuls of earth off the floor and let it slip evenly through his fingers to form an inverted cone on the floor, let it slip through his fingers like sand in an ancient timer, only to be picked up again, as if turned upside down to continue its measure of the minutes and hours. Doc considered Billy, the chief of the Raven clan, as a raven himself who flew over this island and its mountains and forest and lakes and hamlets, flew over and oversaw it from an altered and distinctive point of view, from an alien view of life and time, and he wondered if Billy did not have a hold on time. Perhaps this was his weapon and his strength, as if somehow the time allowances existing in the space between planets and galaxies, between birds and land-creatures too, had been acquired by him, which is how he had managed to return his clan to patterns of life that long ago had been obliterated and virtually effaced from memory, which is how he was able to wait upon a time that even he did not consider to be at hand. "Why have you come here, Doc?"

"Well—I thought I could help Thomas and—"

Doc stopped abruptly; Billy was shaking his head. "The sand. You see it falls a certain way." A quiet and restrained voice. He had been through this many times before. He knew that patience was required to deal with Doctor Marifield.

Suddenly, Doc got mad and he slammed a piece of kindling against the ground. The bear hide fell away from him and exposed half his chest, dividing his chest down the middle of his body. "Look, Billy, what difference does it make? I need your help to find Thomas. I want to get him and I figure I won't find out why until I get there. I don't even know the reasons yet. The idiot Duff brothers in Lyell pressed me into this, and Henry and Evlin haven't helped, I mean, Henry's gone and Evlin's on some kind of crusade and I have to play this by ear. If I spent half my life in the forest I'd never find Thomas. So I'm asking for your help. You're the only person left I can approach. Walter, Gerald, the others, they're gone with the fishing fleet. I mean, if anybody knows where to find Thomas it's you. I mean, you share the same territory, you said so yourself. Ah, hell—I don't know. I don't know any more."

Billy nodded and gazed into the fire. After a while he looked up, said, "If Henry says seventeen years, that's right. A long time since Thomas Duff became a hermit. A long time since Morgan Duff left Skincuttle." He looked up and followed the smoke through the smokehole. "That's a long time, seventeen years. A long time between—Do you know what this is all about?"

Just then, Wogeena entered, with a large bowl of hot stew, venison mixed with potatoes and carrots. But Doc only sipped the juices on the spoon and attended the food with little interest. "It's about opening the mine, I guess."

"No. That's partly right but that's not it, Doc."

"I heard about the young sister probably drowning. And some of the family disappeared in the search for her. And about the rest of the family disintegrating after that. Is that what you mean?"

Staring at Doc for a moment, Billy seemed to fade away, seemed to merge with the shadows and the dancing forms. Whenever Doc looked away from him, down at the food, it triggered the impression that Billy was absent, suddenly gone. Then Billy got to his feet. "Eat your food. When you finish, we'll go." Billy moved to go outside.

"Billy!" Doc called, speaking for the first time with strength. "Why?"

Billy Peel stopped, turned, looked at him. Then he looked at the smoke again, into it this time and through it. "No. Our reason won't work for you. You still have your own reason to find." He ducked and in one movement the flap opened and closed behind him. Doc smiled at Wogeena. He was annoyed when she did not smile back.

11

WHAT IS IT?

"You were never here before."

The skeletons were covered by a dark green moss, and the mortuary poles were mostly rotten and crumbling and covered by a brighter moss, and some bones dangled from their ledges and others lay on the ground. The grass was waist-high but criss-crossed by beaten paths.

"An old graveyard."

"Not only old." At the extreme end of the open space were new poles, supporting new coffins. Three little coffins.

"You didn't bury the children! Why not? I thought—I presumed you would bury them."

"They have the right to lie here."

"What if their disease was contagious?"

Billy shrugged, said, "It's gone now."

The two men walked on, skirting the rim of the mortuary ground. The old and faceless and colourless totems were content in their death watch, secure in the rain, contemplating the rain and the deaths and protected by the rain, warmed by the deaths. Doc felt strange here, the bones of so many men and women and children ejaculating testimonials that were beyond him; he did not wish to cope with them, preferring gravestones with their mysterious names and discreet reckoning of dates. These bones, skulls, and rib cages — and the exposed coffins of the dead children that in time would rot away and present their skin-stripped bodies too—created a rebound in his mind so that he found himself sensing his own bones, felt the warm rain washing his tissue away to reveal his skeleton and space. But Billy, Billy walking ahead of him with sure strides, diverting his course now to pass between sets of mortuary poles, Billy striding among the bones, plump and short with the rounded flesh and the deep black eyes, he would not become a skeleton, recline and peacefully grin in the rain, no, Billy Peel would stiffen and petrify and change into one of the breathless, eternal totems, their mystery and knowledge fading into the deeper recesses of time.

The path sloped downward. Because it was well-trodden the two men were able to move quickly, jogging down the incline then taking strong strides where the land levelled. The vegetation was thick and luxuriant here, the earth soft and pliable underfoot. The sound of their steps was muted and rhythmic. They splashed through the many small streams rushing to the sea and maintained a brisk pace. The land rolled up and down, an imitation of the sea. After a couple of hours the pace began to tell on Doc. Although he enjoyed the exertion and found the rainfall pleasant, he finally had to plead for a rest and Billy relented.

"How many miles is it, Billy?"

Billy shrugged, said, "This rain will stay."

"Do you know where Thomas Duff is?"

"We have a hard place up ahead."

"What about my question?"

"Sometimes a long rain washes the trail away. It's along a cliff."

"I asked you a question."

"But when we get to the river it will be easy to climb."

"Does that answer my question?"

"When we get to the river it will be nearly night. You tell me how many miles that is."

"What?"

"Never mind."

Doc thought that Billy did not understand, could not understand, could not comprehend the effect of this forest on a stranger. He needed to talk, fearing silence might give credence and power to forces he did not understand or even know about. Doc lay back and rested his head against a bulging root, moping, and closed his eyes. He saw dancing girls frolicking on clouds, but even above the clouds and under the sunlight it was raining. Billy kicked the sole of his boot, said, "Let's go, Doc."

Reaching a cliff-face, they were forced to climb along a narrow ledge. Billy went first. Doc glanced timidly into the gorge, the wash from the mountains churning through it. He could not see around the bend in the cliff, but he presumed the path would soon jut sharply downward. He followed Billy's example and walked sideways, a step at a time, his face and stomach pressed to the wall of the cliff. Rounding the bend, he said, "Bloody hell."

"The footing is good," Billy said. "We're lucky."

"Bloody hell."

"What?"

"I said no. I'm not going over that."

The fallen fir tree spanned the gorge. It sloped downward about fifteen degrees and rested comfortably on the side of the hill opposite the cliff. "Sure you are," Billy said. "Don't walk across, Doc. Just sit on it and pull yourself along."

"Walk across," Doc muttered to himself. "I was thinking of walking across. Bloody hell!"

The end of the tree at the cliff seemed secure on closer inspection, the tree wedged between boulders so that it would not roll, and the first five feet were firmly imbedded in soil. A hundred feet long, the tree was suspended at least seventy-five feet above the gorge. Jumping on it, Billy calmly walked across, his arms outstretched for balance, his feet quick and sure, each step placed directly in front of the other down the centre of the log. And watching him, Doc observed his lithe step and was captivated by his movement through the rain, the great trees on the opposite bank the overseers of this initiation, a vista not only from another time but from another world. Doc dared not mount or touch the log himself, afraid of disturbing it and of interfering with the moment too, but Billy was across in less then a minute, hollering, "Come on! Let's go!"

And looking down the length of it the distance increased, the tree stretching and being made more narrow at the same time, and touching it Doc was startled by the crust of the bark, it seemed alive, like skin. "Well, why don't we rest awhile?" he called. But Billy said no. It was striking Doc now that he was in this for good, no matter what, that he had not expected a pleasant excursion but he had not really considered the prospects either, all that he might have to face and endure. Suddenly his imagination was rampant. He climbed onto the tree thinking of it as a horse, mounted it tentatively, as if the first impulse of the timber would be to buck him off. He glanced down into the gorge once, then shook his head and looked up into the rain. A desire to be away from here, to be free not only of this situation but of time already spent on Skincuttle Island, surprised him violently, and staring at Billy, hatred flared for a moment. He straddled the tree trunk. Pulled himself along by his hands. Billy was sitting with his back to him at the opposite end of the tree, and even half-way across Doc wanted to somehow turn himself around, abort this mission and vanish, miraculously accomplish the manoeuvre. But the forceful countenance of Billy's back drew him forward. He felt he was being called in, as if riding a dutiful horse heading for its barn. And near the end of his ordeal he felt exhilarated, still plodding along, timid and slow, but tremendously impressed with the view and the height and the drone of the wash below him and with his own victory, so that when Billy finally turned to face him, his expression stony, something altered in his face and his attitude too, as if now they were beginning, leaving behind once and for all their comforts and warmer, cozier thoughts. Doc was overcome again by the need to talk and battle this seriousness. "Carol!" he shouted. "I mean Wogeena—that's her new name, right? She's grown! But she still has that damn crush on me. You ought to find her a nice Indian boy, Billy. Tell her to stop fooling with old whitemen like me. We don't want to interfere with the purity of the clan now, do we?" Doc jumped off the end of the trunk. "Do we, Billy?"

Billy looked directly at Doc for a moment, said, "You made it."
"Do we?"
"Let's go, Doc."
"I'm right behind you, Billy-boy, Billy-boy."
On the side of a mountain they could look out over the forest and see the fog-covered ocean in the distance. Roaming mists played about the woods and hills, lifting suddenly or scattering in a flurry, and Doc stopped once to watch them and he fell behind. When he looked up again, Billy had disappeared. He hurried quickly, broke into a run, arrived at a fork in the pathway. One trail headed down toward the sea, the other veered higher along the hillside. He could not spot Billy anywhere.

"This way," Billy said, coming from behind Doc and brushing past him, taking the higher trail, and this time Doc thought he had detected the trace of a smile on the younger man's face.

Doc continually wiped water from his eyes. Both he and Billy were hatless, but Billy's thick and matted black hair offered more protection against the rain. The trail narrowed and dropped steeply and twice Doc stumbled, sending a cascade of stones and pebbles rolling that Billy had to dodge. After the second time they changed positions with Doc in the lead. They reached another stream where the tree crossing it was twenty-five feet long, but at its highest point the drop was only six feet. Feeling brave and ambitious. Doc stood up on it. He took a moment to find his balance, wavering from side to side, finally straightening his body and spreading his arms wide to clutch at the air. Moving one foot in front of the other carefully, he glued his eyes on his destination. He moved cautiously, laughing a little at one point, unable to sustain concentration for so long, but when he reached the middle of the crossing he froze. Hands spread out, feet rigid but in the pose of a runner at the wire: the stance of a statue.

"I can't move," Doc said.

Billy was several feet behind him. "What's wrong?"

"I'm stuck!"

"Just keep going, Doc."

"No. I'm stuck. I can't move."

Billy waited silently a few moments. "Lower yourself down slowly, Doc. Crawl like you did before."

Doc tried but his knees shook as they bent. "Damn it, Billy, I'm stuck!" Doc still had his eyes front, staring at his destination, trying to wrench it out of the ground and bring it closer. Behind him, Billy backed off the log. "What are you doing, what?" Doc heard him jumping down the bank by the stream. "Where're you going? Billy!" Glancing down, the turbulence of the water made his head spin and his entire body tremble. He could not hear Billy anymore and he caught his breath in frightened gasps as his knees quaked. Then his Indian companion appeared at the end of the log, right in the line of his stare.

"Come on, Doc," Billy said. "Let's go." And Billy left, tramping through the woods and disappearing among the trees.

Doc shivered. Slowly he began to lower himself. His foot slipped and his knee cracked against the bark; falling, he was able to react quickly and grip the log. His body hung partially over the side, one leg dangling and kicking the air, his hips sliding off the tree. Breathing heavily, he righted himself and while his heart pounded he crawled across, hands first then body, hands first then pulling the body up. This time he did not run after Billy but walked at a steady pace and checked behind the trees and dense vegetation along the way. But after a half-hour he was worried that he was lost. He resisted the temptation to holler Billy's name, but he moved more quickly, hurrying along the path and glancing sideways only sporadically.

"Doc," Billy said, and he was sitting slightly off the path on a large boulder that had a flat tabletop, looking like a bird guarding its nest. "You want some food or not?"

Doctor Marifield laughed out loud, relief coursing through him so that he thought he would shriek, uncontrollably let his energies loose in a rampage of noise and bedlam. He could not remember the last time he had felt so buoyant and happy. The food came from a cache the Kloo Ravens maintained—heavily salted venison and seaweed. Sitting down, Doc bit into the meat with a vengeance. "So," he said. "You're not going to wait for me."

"Thomas lives near Lake TaColl."

"What? Oh . . . from what I understand, nobody's seen him in years."

"This trail goes to the Nistee River and we go up there."

"How far is it?"

"We go straight."

Walking again, Doc matched Billy stride for stride and chewed on a clump of dried seaweed, feeling stronger now that he had eaten again. Where the trail widened they walked side by side. Doc shot furtive glances at Billy periodically, noticing his skin and eyes and the way his hair stuck together in the rain, wondering if the other man was thinking or dreaming or involved in something that was not either and was foreign to him, wondering if he dwelled in another land while he walked in this one. The top of Billy's head came only to Doc's shoulders.

"Don't worry about the purity of the clan, Doc."

"What?"

"You should have a wife. There's lots more girls than Wogeena."

Doc was so startled he gave Billy a light shove. "What are you talking about?"

"Every Skincuttle doctor before you took a squaw. You should too."

"I'm still married, you know that. Technically."

Billy grinned, said, "We're a long way from Vancouver, Doc."

Doc was flabbergasted. "I don't believe it! I'm surprised at you! Foisting young girls on marauding whitemen. You're joking. You're joking, Peel."

"Who says? It's no joke." Billy grabbed his arm. "Look there!" A doe through the forest. Ears perked. In an instant it leaped and slipped deeper into the woods. "Many deer are coming to this end of the island. We don't know why yet."

Darkness deepened, established itself, but it was only a premonition of nightfall. Although the clouds darkened the rain became less heavy. The wind picked up through the trees and gusts blew in their faces. Another hour and Doc grabbed Billy's arm. "You were joking, right?"

Brushing off Doc's hand, Billy Peel continued walking. Later, climbing a short escarpment, he said, "Maybe they already sense the mine and flee now. Maybe they've learned how to do that."

"The girls?"

"The deer."

"What about the girls? What—"

"No. They haven't learned to flee yet."

"But you're teaching them, I bet."

Billy grinned. "An Indian girl would have a better life with you, Doc, better than with some miner who's only passing through, who wants her drunk and crazy."

Doc shook his head, said, "You surprise me sometimes."

Billy tapped him on the shoulder. "That shrub won't hold you. Come around this way." Going ahead of him, securing his feet and hands in the steps of the rocks, Billy said, "We wonder why you never took an Indian girl."

"Come on, Billy!"

"Why not? This is not Vancouver. We think it's because you are going back someday. Someday you go back to Vancouver, so you still live like you're there."

"Henry has a theory on that subject. He says I chose Skincuttle Island in the first place because I'm so scared of the water I'd never have the guts to get in a boat a second time and leave. He says I wanted some place where I'd be trapped, where I couldn't get home."

Billy offered his hand to Doc and pulled him up a high step. "You could take a plane. I see you leaving Skincuttle in a seaplane."

"That's why I brought my piano, Henry says. Because I'd never leave without it."

They reached the top of the rise and Billy sat with his feet hanging over the edge. He said flatly, "You'd ship it."

"That's what I told him! But he said I'd only leave on an impulse and I'd never manage to arrange all that."

Billy struck off into the forest again and Doc had to hurry after him. They came to the ridge of a hill that overlapped a broad valley. Sweeping trees as far as they could see. Billy indicated with his hand that they were going down, then up again. The vegetation was less dense, the fir trees taller, and their branches formed a cohesive ceiling over the forest floor.

"Is it much farther to the river, Billy?"

Billy studied the cover of branches and limbs, reading a map there. "People have seen him."

"Who?"

"Henry's smart," Billy said. He leaped and Doc flew after him, and they ran down the hill into the swoop of the valley, dodging trees, hopping fallen logs, jumping streams. Stopping, panting, Doc resting his head against the fungus on a fir bark, Billy laughed, said, "You're right, Doc. We're not going to wait for you this time."

Doc laughed with him. "Okay, okay. But how much farther to the river?"

Billy pointed with his thumb, said, "It's that way."

"Okay, but how far? How far!"

"Yes, we still think you live like you're in Vancouver."

12

THE GUNSHOT EXPLODED in the forest and reverberated wave on wave. The doe died in midflight, crashed into a birch tree. Anticipating a second volley, Henry dove for the cover of the grass, and he expected his head to shatter, the pieces to float downward gently like leaves while the sound echoed through the woods. But the forest was suddenly still, huddling now, the quick, panicked flight replaced by the hush of trepidation, the fury of the violence transplanted by the meditation on the death, and the waiting.

Henry listened to his own breathing and the patter of the light rain in the trees. Even the rain was hushed and quietly anxious. He slid, seeking adequate cover. His crippled leg had locked at the knee an hour earlier, it lay exposed along the bank of the mountain stream, and he dragged it behind him, a dead weight, a sleeping python, sliding it into the deep wet grass and he panted there.

The quiet continued, the hush, the sound waves rebounding now as silent shocks, stiffening the trees and his body, the forest and his mind becoming a vacant chamber in which the waves brutally advanced. Opening his eyes, Henry watched a pair of slugs creep slowly towards him, yellowy backs moving like marauding tanks over foothills and plains. Big drops of water that formed in the branches above bombed his face, with uncanny accuracy they sighted and smacked his eye. A shout. Then a piercing cry, so chilling and demented that involuntarily he rolled, through the grass and water and into the forest. Then hoots, derisive cries, shouts, and from behind a tree trunk Henry saw Morgan Duff appear on the other side of the stream, twenty-five feet away, at the ridge where the mountain stream disappeared, knife drawn, splashing through the water like a runaway locomotive, his rifle tossed on the bank, crying out shrilly— and Henry flinched as the upraised knife was plunged into the warm body of the doe.

Morgan laughed loudly, his voice riding up and down in a frenzy. Henry flattened himself on the forest floor again, needles and leaves sticking to his bare chest. He gripped the tree with both hands and squeezed, the bark coarse and brittle in his hands, squeezed so that the pain shooting from his knee darted into the tree like an electric charge, squeezed so that not only his pain entered the tree but his hope, his memory too, signals reacting back and forth between mind and tree, vibrating down the network of skull and neck and shoulders and arms and fingers, squeezed and felt the tree receiving his panic and fear and hopes and memory and accepting it whole. Henry followed all of it through the maze of roots and tendrils, through the bloodstream of the tree, down, into Skincuttle earth, into Skincuttle past, through underground waterways where bones sailed like upturned canoes on the rapids, down, among the fossils still waiting for a quick movement of liberation, down, gold and copper and soft black earth; he squeezed and felt his life slip through his fingers and into the tree, rise up, journey through the maze of branches and leaves, return, succumb, go back into the belly of the soil and mud and memory and rock; he could feel the tree return the grip, welcome him like a friend, and the moment passed. When he stood he saw Morgan lying beside the butchered carcass of the deer, surfeit in his laughter and passion.

Henry's fingers and palms pulsated. Sitting, he cuddled next to the tree like a child to a parent, nestled his back against the trunk and drew one knee close against his chest. The other leg lay immobile in front of him. He peered around the tree. His view of Morgan was obstructed but he could distinguish him on the opposite bank of the narrow stream, resting next to the deer and using the flank of the deer as a pillow. The tug of fear still persisted in Henry's stomach, but he was thrilled too by his moment of rapport with the tree and kept it alive.

Henry had not looked up through the branches of the tree and he did not do so now. He preferred to remain within the lingering sensation of their intercourse. *We could march it right back, Morgan, this tree and I, this forest and I. We could march it right back and what would you do then? What could you do then? Would you be confronted by a ghost you created yourself? We could march it back just as far as it's necessary. You know it too. That's why you're here. To stop the backwards march into time, into history. Hey, Morgan! It burns! A tiny ember, an ash, it's warm and in the pitch black it still burns. Breathe on it and watch it glow. The point of pain, a glowing light, a red dot in time, get close to it Morgan, closer still, and it's a circle of fire. Feel it around you. Feel the heat. Feel the flames scorching your throat. There are more witnesses than you can name. More witnesses than you could ever identify. The fish, the ocean, the forest, the sky, the birds, the bears, and even killing one more deer won't help. They all know, Morgan, and I will learn it too. I must. Feel it scorch your throat. Your temples are on fire. Your tongue burns. Your back crumbles in the heat. Feel the fire and know one thing: what I'm talking about now is not the fire but the point of pain that became the fire, and we're going to know it. I'm approaching it because my shack burned, my pathetic shelter, my compromise between past and present; but you, you're coming to it because your body burns. Thomas knows it and that's why you're here, because he knows, but there are more witnesses than Thomas, more witnesses than me or this tree watching you now. What I'm talking about now is the blood on the sea coagulating into one tight ball, a point of pain, Morgan, a fiery point of pain, and your seventeen years of flight, of absence, has not dissolved it, has not hidden it either, no more than Thomas's seventeen years of reclusion or Rupert's and Jake's and Whitney's and Jackson Two's seventeen years of practically total silence.*

Behind the tree, Henry rested but he did not sleep. He kept a vigilant watch on Morgan. Morgan's proximity across the stream alarmed him, proved that his fast pace throughout the day had not been adequate. Checking his station and circumstances, Henry decided to wait. To ponder. Cutting straight back into the woods would bring him downhill, eventually he would lose time and energy climbing again. Following the stream up would lead him into the kind of mountain country—sheer cliffs; splendid, smooth, and enormous escarpments—in which he could not travel. He had to cross the stream, which would expose him to Morgan's line of vision and therefore fire. Morgan was unaware of it but the deer had saved Henry's life; Henry was aware of it and he still felt the pulse of his life acclaiming itself, juxtaposed now against the moment of its death. He waited, not crossing the line of fire, calculating that Morgan would still follow the Oganjibra River, fifty feet below this ridge from where he had looked up and seen the doe framed against the clouds. Henry, having seen it too, and by avoiding it so as not to disturb its feeding, had avoided the sights of Morgan's rifle.

Morgan slept for an hour, a contented and spent man curled beside his lover. Slowly he pushed himself up, laboriously, and he wrapped the meat he had cut from the deer and stuffed it in his pack. With his bad leg working like a crutch out to the side of him, Henry moved through the forest, bending as much as he could, bobbing up and down. Circling, he came out by the stream again, closer to Morgan and the deer. The water was clear and cold and it mirrored the windswept clouds and his face, he could see his puffed eye and the bruise on his chin, and when he peered over the ridge he spied Morgan sauntering back the way he had come.

Henry splashed through the stream, his eyes on Morgan's back, came beside the deer and he was stricken. The deer had been decapitated and the face smeared in its own blood. Henry averted his glance from the deer's head. A wind gust chilled his bare skin and he wiped rain from his face. He withdrew his knife to salvage meat for himself, but just as he raised his knife and saw the water skimming on the steel blade and his fingers tightening on the white bone handle, just as he reached down into his coil for the velocity to strike, he stopped. It was Gail again. Her face again. Popping into his mind again with startling clarity, and when he turned it was Gail's body awaiting the thrust of the knife, and Henry did not hesitate, he scampered into the woods, head low to duck the swinging branches, legs and cane pumping, squirming through small spaces like a darting snake. He heard his own breathing, heard audible grunts and low cries utter from his mouth, rise up from his diaphragm and escape against his will, and he felt the pain of it welling upward in him like the night welling within the day, and it was not enough to run, not enough to cry, not enough to mingle his own tears with the rain, and he crashed into a thin tree and hugged it tightly as he fell. *All right! All right!* The tears came then, his body shaking, his chest heaving as he cried, the tears came and he had no strength remaining to fight them; pains from his leg and eye and rain-saturated body expressed in the crying too; and he knew it was his fate, his nemesis, to live with one foot still dragging in the past; the past moved inside him, the pain of it heaving in his stomach and breaking his body down to tears, whimpers, and minute cries. His throat and chest ached from the crying, Gail's visage still floated in his mind's eye, a look of astonishment behind the eyes, the curiosity yielding quickly to a rising horror, the throat and mouth attempting to shriek but there was no voice, no sound, the silence echoing through the vacant space of the years, past now and future then, and Henry's nerves and senses collapsed his body in upon itself. *All right! All right! Enough for now. Please! Forest! It's too much at one time. God, it's going to be night soon too.*

Pushing himself up, he dug his cane into the soft earth, strode forward, weaving from side to side, clutching branches and pushing off on trees to keep his balance, moving too quickly for his legs to support him properly, his stiff leg sliding out from under him and he fell often, slamming the forest floor hard, pulling himself up again and continuing. He knew where he was headed. Knew the spot exactly. Knew that this shortcut might return his advantage over Morgan but that was not it, not why he had returned here. He could not fool even himself, drawn back to the spectre of his own turmoil. The forest grew thinner and bare rock showed through underfoot. *Rocks. Trees. Roots. Earth. Blood.* The terrain steepened, mountain country now, sometimes through the trees he could see the TaColl Mountains disappearing under the cloudcover. One low crow passed overhead and cawed in the rain, the plaintive cry carrying through the woods and sky as a signal that all was well, the intruder toting the gun was replete and satisfied. But Henry knew better, knew that the sky and clouds and rain might occupy themselves with routine but the woods let nothing pass, knew that the forest stored its experience in a great expanse against the advent of another day. The forest knew Morgan, as a child once and now as a man, knew his breath and scent and the weight of his steps and Henry could feel the information and knowledge being transmitted to all groves and mountains and plains and valleys, to all trees and shrubs and grasses and roots, and he felt protected and alert, believed that if he remained sharp he could detect the forest's own inner communication as it followed Morgan, and thereby be safe from him.

Thinking it out further he wondered if the doe might not have been sacrificed to save him. He shook his head, told himself to be reasonable, but he could not shake the thought free, it continually flew back and stuck to him. Climbing around the perimeter of a boulder his fingernails scratching for a hold, the thought advanced and he perceived a movement over his head, like a passing breeze, the subtle lifting of a veil, gossamer on the wind, he looked and it was gone, but he sensed Gail's presence, wondered if she had been here. The thought became insistent: that it was not the deer who had been sacrificed, but Gail herself, again.

If that's what you are. Maybe not your self at all or spirit, but some redeeming part of me I sense—knifed, extracted from his carcass. I want to make you real again! real again! The memories are not enough. Remember, remember the time your father rousted me out of bed to put you in it? I couldn't walk so he threw me over his shoulder, marched me right down to his boat in the pouring rain and slapped me into his cot. That boat stank of fish. I stank of fish. I stank of fish for a week! He wasn't about to let you sleep there. What I remember though is the look on your face, you were sorry I had to be bothered.

Stories from that night had been embellished over the years. Jim Duff had come to town to release the hand of doom upon his sons. He rampaged through the beer parlour, clearing them out, including Morgan and Thomas. He intended to keep his sons in line, no matter what. No more drinking, no more swearing, no more carousing with women. Henry had heard Jim Duff's story from his father. He had been raised in a Newfoundland convent. As he grew older, he began noticing the ankles of the novices. Men he was fishing with put ideas into his head too. One thing led to another, and he was banished, and the pain of it hurt him so badly that he could do nothing less than place an entire continent between himself and his shame, the humiliation was so great that he foresook one ocean for another, and he came to Skincuttle Island when he was nineteen. He did not repent, however, not immediately, living wildly for nearly forty years, and siring twenty-one sons with four wives before Gail was born. His life abruptly changed when his daughter was born. His youth, his lost home, haunted his older years. He could not raise a daughter as he had his sons. He knew only one way to raise a girl, so he tried turning his house into a convent, raising Gail in rigid piety, attacking his sons' bad habits with a vengeance, deriding them for his own mistake, ruthlessly demanding that they change, while Gail grew up amid their hatred. She was the focus of all their bitterness and anger and confusion too. *It was not you, Gail. Not your fault. It was your father relentlessly correcting his mistake and not seeing the larger one created in the process. It was your father broken down—I saw it myself—sorrowful for abusing the home he had loved, ashamed and feeling damned. Maybe that's why there was always that look of bewilderment or astonishment in your eyes, you never really knew what was going on from the moment of your birth. You never had a chance. You never knew that your father hinged his redemption on your piety, your femininity, and your sainthood. I believe, I have a hunch—visions of your death again—that maybe he got wind of his error with you; out there, on the sea, tearless but mournful, scouting back and forth, back and forth, searching for some sign of your missing boat or body, back and forth, but one time not returning, one time continuing straight out to sea, never to be seen or heard from again, taking his wife and youngest sons with him.*

There were no shadows. Darkness had a way of taking the daylight by surprise, the day dark and gloomy already under the layers of cloudcover. The sunlight penetrated it less and less, steadily and without drama, so that the nightfall was very close before Henry realized it. Climbing was precarious. Sometimes the clouds blew about in several directions at once and he put on a shirt and jacket for warmth. At the edge of the forest he looked up, his eyes scanning the great boulders and smaller rocks that spread across the surface of the incline. Once it had been a mountain. Erosion had created a cavity and the mountain collapsed during an earth tremour, disintegrated into a massive pile of broken and crushed rock, and Henry had been submerged under it. He had come with his parents and many others from town on a holiday, an annual outing to Lake TaColl, and he had run ahead with his mother close behind.

There were trees then, a fire years earlier had made this area of forest sparse but there were trees on the slope, and he saw one rock that was no more than a yard in diameter topple from near the peak. It seemed to hang for a moment in mid-air, not defying gravity exactly but stalled by its great surprise, then it fell in an endless, perfect arc to suddenly splinter where it caromed off the side of the mountain. He hollered back to his mother and she approved of his route; she would follow him up. The others would take the gradual path that circled the mountain.

Now, climbing, the rain on his back, he had to reach back often to grab and pull up his gimpy leg, had to rely mainly on his hands and arms as he crawled over the boulders and squeezed between narrow crevices in the rock. He had not travelled this route since the landslide. The apprehension worked on his nerves and bones—when he accidentally kicked a group of small stones his heart leaped. He watched as they tumbled out of view. Reaching up and pulling, the jut of rock gave way and he slid back. Rolling to escape the rock he bruised his shoulder.

The sun had been in his eyes then: first had come a trembling that he felt through his feet.

Henry stopped. He threw his pack over a rock then crawled through a gap under it, and under it he paused, remembering. *It's because the forest held me, buried me and held me in its womb that we are learning of one another now. That was the day, the hour the forest gave birth to me, deformed, one leg forever in the past, that was the day the forest became my adopted mother. My father, my new father of this marriage, was the Indian.*

His mother had cried up to him, pleaded with him to return. But he felt hypnotized. The earth moved again, and again the mountain rumbled like approaching thunder and far in the woods there were voices, and one of them would be his father's frantic cries. But Henry had walked forward. Fear made his knees weak, but the sun was so bright and the movement of the earth so fascinating that he could not stop: the rumble was like a calling and he could not refuse it. The precise second he looked up the mountain teetered, teetered against the azure sky, and Henry had thought it was his own dizziness; then an overpowering roar, the great tear and agonizing rip of rock, and the mountain loomed large against the sky, but it collapsed, falling forward. Henry flattened himself upon the earth, clutched the ground for help, tore tufts of grass out of the earth as he sought to hide in it, his eyes screaming terror, his mouth open and emitting sounds but nothing could be heard now, only the horde of rocks as they pounded and smashed and obliterated the woods, trees breaking like splinters. Looking up he saw a huge boulder, a mountain in itself, roll through the spindly forest and approach him, but a small stone hit him first and he was knocked unconscious.

Henry crawled over the rocks. He felt enlightened and renewed. *I didn't get it before, it escaped me, the understanding of it. That's why I've been so afraid of the deep woods, so hesitant to give myself up and yet so drawn, because I mistook my birth for my death.*

When he woke up there were voices and he was in a dark cavern. He did not discern where he was or what had happened, presumed he was at home and nothing had happened, and there was a hole to one side of him where a light shone through. Looking through it he saw a beautiful Indian chieftain on a stunning black horse. Henry thought he was looking through a crack in his house and he wondered who the Indian could be, why he was looking back through the crack at him. He would not be able to see into this darkness. Suddenly the realization struck home. He tried to cry out but he was petrified and lost his voice. He stared through the hole at the Indian and the horse lowered and raised its head several times. The Indian wore a magnificent coloured deerskin suit and the horse had a golden harness and a brilliant green jewel between its ears. The jewel glittered in the sunlight. Henry heard voices. He uttered a sound and it surprised him, the cry that he had attempted earlier but had not managed, suddenly springing from him as if it were not his voice at all.

His father and other men dug him out, pulling him out eventually through a narrow gap in the rocks, headfirst. He cried out in agony as he was born into the sunlight again, the light blinding him. He had never known such pain, and his leg was shaped in an odd way with his knee bent backwards. Henry noticed the huge ball of rock farther down the hill; it had passed right over him. The search continued through the days and the coming weeks, but his mother was never found.

Attaining the height of the land, looking down over the destruction lying inert now in the wake of the landslide, Henry was pensive. His new understanding enchanted him, he was at once mystified and concerned by it. *You, forest, became my adopted mother, you gave birth to me, a second birth, and now I'm here.* Somewhere under the mass of broken rock was his mother's grave, and he could visualize her now: he remembered her calling to him, imagined her running after him and being caught in the crush of the landslide. He thought about the Indian, believed he had been real, somehow and in some way real, stationed there to watch over him. But he could not comprehend it further.

Still faint light. The deep woods were darker. He was close now to Lake TaColl, and close to Thomas Duff, for this was the hermit's ground. Morgan coming up the long way by the Oganjibra River would be trapped by the night, trapped probably by his own drinking and delirium and by his craving to cook and eat the venison he carried. Henry stopped a moment. Listened. Checked his thoughts. He headed into the forest, compelled suddenly by a recurring sense of urgency and by more than that, by a returning vision of Morgan, realizing with a shock that it was a mistake to be underestimating him again.

13

THE BRANCH SLIPPED. Losing his grip Doc fell on his face. The water was cold, icy cold, and it scared him. Billy's hands under his armpits, pulling him back up, but Doc fought him off, feeling something that was not anger and not desperation but between the two, which was his distress gnawing on him from the inside. But it was not that either, it was his own rebellion and refusal and he knew it now too; fought Billy off and he cried out, "Leave me alone!"

"You hurt, Doc?"

"Leave me alone, Peel!"

Billy swung the branch and it smacked Doctor Marifield in the chest, swung and Doc saw it coming like a black spirit in the moonlight, but he could not move to stop it. "Grab it!" Billy commanded.

Doc hesitated. Billy Peel coaxed him by hitting him with the branch again, it thumped against his coat and his thick shirt. This time Doc clutched it tightly and Billy jerked it hard, pulling him forward.

They walked on through the night. The moon through the roving clouds offered them enough light to see a few feet ahead and distinguish the outlines of the treetops as they followed the Nistee River into the mountains. A shallow river, only occasionally did it become as deep as three or four feet. Along the shore the water was only up to their ankles and freezing. Billy established a pace and he would not slacken. They had joined themselves by clutching a six-foot branch. Billy in the lead and pulling Doc along, Doc resisting and mainly trying to keep his balance. The wind was brisk and sudden gusts blew the rain in their faces. Overhead the clouds were moving quickly, the storm not abating but rearranging itself, as if concerned about weaknesses and strengths. The darkness and the darker forest intimidated Doctor Marifield. The forest loomed like a recurring and lifelong menace. He could only think of quitting this journey and finding a dry and tranquil place to sleep, but he doubted that the forest or the night would permit him a rest, he would be afraid to try now, afraid the night and the woods would absorb him while he slept, diffuse his body and mind, float him away. The forest was no sanctuary: his legs and neck continued to ache and his feet were numb splashing through the cold river. He tried concentrating on Billy, tried keeping the black silhouette of Billy Peel's back within his vision, hallucinations again disturbing him, first a timid dragon appeared and shuffled past into the forest, then a princess in a black gown who had lightbulbs for eyes, but he battled the illusions hard, desperately worked them to one side and struggled back to the image of Billy's outline.

The branch was cold and sharp. Whenever Billy pulled quickly and Doc lunged ahead, the branch cut into his palms and fingers. He started pulling back on it, thinking he could surprise it out of Billy's grip, thinking the stick represented a kind of bondage that had to be fought. But he paid the price for his idea, Billy responding with quick jerks that nearly knocked him off his feet, knocking him awake at the same time, which made him think he was being punished for his dreams. He wished he could sleep. He could not comprehend Billy's zeal and did not share it. Then he spied out of the black outline of Billy's form Billy himself raising a lance to stab him through the heart. Doc dropped the pole and ran and leaped onto Billy's back, and they both tumbled into the water. The cold water on his face startled Doc awake again and he yelled as Billy grabbed him and banged the top of his head using the base of his fist like a hammer. "Billy! Billy! Stop! I didn't mean it! Stop!" And Billy unclenched his fist and pulled Doc to his feet. They yelled at each other and their faces were only inches apart. They strained in the light to reach each other's expressions and eyes. "I'm all right!" Doc said.

"Stand straight then."

"I am!"

"No you're not, Doc. You wobble like a piece of rubber."

"What do you expect? You've been banging me on the head." Doc draped his taller body on Billy and let his weight sag against him. "I can't. I'm going to stay here."

Billy wrestled with him to keep him on his feet. "Stay then. I go alone."

"No! I'm coming with you."

This time they walked side by side, Doc with an arm wrapped around Billy's shoulders, Billy helping to hold him up at the waist. Their branch had floated away downriver. Their progress was difficult. They stumbled finding their footing, and frequently their bodies tilted and reeled, usually in opposite directions.

The foam bubbled in the moonlight. There were several bends in the river and once Billy ducked into the forest to cut across one. Doc felt strange in the woods, it was very dark and alien, to be suddenly released from the river made him alert and edgy. A branch brushed his forehead and he panicked. He tried to run but Billy hurled himself into Doc's legs and dragged him to the ground. Doc tried to beat him off but Billy overpowered him. Billy kept slapping his face. When Doc came to his senses, he hollered, "Let's get out of here! Let's get the bloody hell out of here fast. Billy!" Billy pulled him up and they fought their way out of the woods, but Doc was disappointed to be marching up the Nistee River again. "Let's stop. Let's rest."

"We cannot. You'll fall asleep."

"No I won't. Let's stop and eat, I'll eat."

"Those rocks there."

"No no. Can't make it that far. Let's stop . . . right . . . here!" Doc broke from Billy's hold and collapsed against the riverbank. He crawled up. "Right here. Here's fine."

Sitting beside him, Billy Peel passed him a piece of dried venison. In the darkness Doc could not see where Billy got it, it seemed to appear out of the air, the darkness, a stroke of magic. It worried him.

While he chewed on the strip of meat he wondered about Billy, felt afraid of him again, for here he was definitely in his element and had power over him. Doc looked around. Considered letting Billy leave him behind and somehow he would catch-up in the daytime, but he didn't think he could tolerate being alone for too long. In the woods and darkness. The darkness and the woods might overwhelm him and he would wake up in the morning with his sanity washed away like the branch. He perceived his sanity being washed out of him, drowning in the water, carried all the way down to the ocean. "I don't get it," he said. "What's all the fuss? What's the big hurry?"

"Let's go, Doc."

Doctor Marifield followed Billy lamely. Stumbling and tripping forward. Once he spotted a salmon in the stream beside him. He splashed his face with cold water to keep himself awake. After awhile the ache in his legs spread through his hips and chest and when he stopped to cough, he felt he could not lift his foot one more time. Billy pulled him by the arm and Doc angrily shoved him away. "Why, Billy? Tell me that at least! I can't go on, you understand! I cannot—physically—go on. That's it."

Billy spun quickly and slapped Doc's cheeks simultaneously with both hands. Doc lunged for him but Billy laughed and slipped away. He ran after him, ran right into him and Billy was laughing. So he was tricked again, and Doc wondered how many ruses Billy could present to keep him going, aware that even with the branch gone and floated away Billy had ways of tugging him along. Doc wondered if he reached a point of absolute and final exhaustion—death, say—if Billy would have a method of blowing life into him again and quickening his muscles. Doc tried to wrestle him into the water but Billy squirmed free, and Doc, mad and frustrated and angry, followed after him.

They walked on.

After another half-hour Doc saw a mountain peak twirl upside down and he fell into the river. Billy rescued him but he could not lift him up. He slapped him but it did no good anymore. Doc slumped in the water and endured a coughing fit. His stomach heaved and he vomited again, and when the retching was over he remained in the water, down on all fours and looking into the water. Billy gripped him under the arms and pulled, but Doc was dead weight. Billy knelt in the water beside him. He held Doc's chin between his hands and rocked his head from side to side, said, "Doc! Doc! Listen to me! Doc!" He pinched his cheeks hard and splashed water in his face. Just as Doc began to fight back, Billy grabbed him by the hair and stood over him and forced his head back. He hurt him and Doc cried out. Billy yelled, "Doc! Doc! Listen!"

Doc struggled against Billy's hold to no avail, eventually calling out, "All right! I'm listening! I'm listening!"

Billy put his face right up to Doc's so their noses touched. "Thomas! It's Thomas!"

"What? Billy, what?"

"He can't write, Doc. He used to sign his name with an 'X'. Thomas—can't—write!"

Doc stared blankly into Billy's face. The words slowly entered through his delirium and pain. With Billy's help he managed to stand up again. He breathed deeply several times. His back was hurting him and sapping his strength. He wiggled his shoulders trying to ease the tension up and down his spine. "I thought I'd—I thought I'd go talk to him." Doc reached out and rubbed his hand on the back of Billy's neck. He laughed, but the laughter had a tone of disappointment and meanness to it. "Some joke, eh? I had the idea I'd straighten him out." He shook his head and rubbed the back of his own neck. "I thought that would show Evlin. And Henry too. And the idiot Duff brothers too. But I'm the dope, right? Because if Thomas didn't write those sabotage notes, then who did?"

Doc was on the verge of babbling; Billy said, "Come on."

"No. Wait. Let me figure this out. Billy? If it wasn't Thomas. . . . Well then somebody. . . . So that Thomas is maybe in some trouble that maybe he doesn't even know about yet."

Billy squeezed Doc's elbow to get his attention. "Doc. Let's go."

"Yeh. Okay. We better get going."

They walked beside each other, each one quick to support the other when he stumbled, and they moved slowly but they did not stop again until they reached Lake TaColl.

14

He set about building a fire.

The dawn had come quickly and passively, the silhouettes of the mountains visible first, then the lake, the mist on the water. Slowly the forest formed again, began to individualize and colour, and the small waves on the lake broke on the shore and washed among the rocks. Bird calls. Birds crossed and recrossed Lake TaColl: eagles, hunting here for feeding lake trout before their downriver search for salmon; ravens, exchanging positions and shaking water from their wings. Across the lake from the mouth of the Oganjibra River a moose waded into the water and swam out from shore, turned, and swam back at a right-angle to his original line of entry, head and antlers disturbing the mists. The animal lumbered onto the bank and disappeared again into the forest and rain.

He did not have much luck beside the river, beside the mouth of the river where it flowed from the lake, but he worked his way deeper into the woods where he found dry twigs and branches under the cedar trees. He came out of the forest in the pouring rain with an armful of wood and the larger branches were damp but not soaked through. Bunching the small twigs together, he leaned over to protect them from the rain.

Taking a match from a tube. The match was coated in wax to keep it waterproof and he scratched the wax off the head with his fingernail. He retrieved a can of lighter fluid from his coat pocket and sprayed the twigs, and it took him three matches but he got his fire going, and he put on the larger branches and they caught fire too. Sticking a chunk of venison on the end of a stick he cooked it over the flames, browning the meat although the centre of it stayed raw. He ate one piece while he cooked another, and he just got started on a third when the rain extinguished the fire. After that he ate several pieces raw.

Morgan Duff removed his coat and shirt. Looked down at the suppurating boils on his chest. He had six in all, four on his chest and two more on his back. Hard crusts, miniature volcanoes that inflamed his chest and tore into his flesh like knives, like knives being twisted. He had done that once so he knew. He could see the knife twisting, twisting. It had happened along the Skeena River, east of Prince Rupert, not long after he had left Skincuttle Island years ago. He was hiding out in the woods, on the run from the police, having looked for and found trouble in Prince Rupert, when two Indians investigated, an old man and a girl; after he had strangled the grandfather, the girl had taken the old man's knife and stuck it upright in the ground and thrown herself upon the blade. Morgan had kicked her in the face while she was still alive, and he twisted the knife while she writhed and died. Indians. Indians, he thought. He carried medication, a cream a doctor had given him for the boils, and applied it carefully. The sores stung as he did so; the ointment never did much good but he used it anyway, garnered relief from the activity itself. Dressed again, he picked up his rifle, ran his hands along the stock and barrel. He cherished this gun; it had a carrying-case, but he had left it behind in Lyell and he worried that the constant rain would damage the steel. The gun was a thirty-ought-six and he had chosen it for its versatility. Never knowing where he'd be from one year to the next—North America, South America, Africa, Asia—he had wanted a rifle good for any situation. And he felt like shooting now. Enjoyed the sounds of the gunfire, especially the way mountains and woods vibrated from the blasts. He slapped his rifle and his pack over his shoulder and walked down to the shore. Removed the cap from his canteen and drank the whiskey straight; and he looked out over Lake TaColl.

The paddle dipped smoothly into the water and the cedar canoe skimmed over the water in a precise and even movement. Billy Peel watched the water running off the blade. Leaned over and studied the floor of the lake. Rocks and long weeds here. Dipped the paddle into the water again and pulled. They had crossed the lake under the protection of night, Doc paddling too, and Billy held tight to the shoreline now, hoping to conceal his presence by ducking behind the bends and curls of the lake and forest. The doctor slept in the nose of the canoe. A sleep of exhaustion, undisturbed by the rain or by their movement.

Billy did not work strenuously or hurry, preferring to meditate on the symmetry between himself, the canoe gliding over the water, and the dawn surfacing over the forest and mountains. The fresh morning air was not so dense on the lake as in the depths of the forest, and breathing deeply had the effect of clearing out his head, like the darkness dissipating around him. He envied the canoe its movement through the water, its sleek lines, and he admired the lapping of the waves on the rocks and exposed tree roots along the shore, felt soothed by the motion: morning was the best time of the day for Billy. He stripped quickly and rolled off the side of the canoe into the lake.

The water was freezing, but he swam to where it was deeper and dove to the bottom repeatedly. Each time he broke to the surface he shook his head like a bird, like a duck or a gander, shaking off the water and the weeds too. He swam back to the canoe before it washed on the shore and pulled it out to the open water again and hoisted himself up. Dressed, he paddled on through the rain.

The day became brighter, the cloudcover not as thick as yesterday, and occasionally the clouds blew off the mountains and left the peaks exposed. Erect and solitary, the peaks were like the castles of great and remote kingdoms. Doc finally stirred and Billy watched him struggle out of sleep, murmuring and groaning, wiping away water and grit and stretching, yawning, taking in the morning slowly, bit by bit, a small sample at a time. He sat up and rubbed his whiskers and face.

"I got it figured out," Doc said and Billy laughed. "No. Really I do. There's only two possibilities." Smoothly, casually, Billy paddled, resting a moment after each stroke. "It's like this. Either somebody's been framing Thomas to get Morgan to come in here after Thomas and threaten him or maybe kill him—I mean if this business with the young sister and the mine too is as drastic as all that, a man like Morgan might be prompted to kill, don't you think?—or maybe Morgan himself framed Thomas to give him an excuse to come in here after him and bring him out, take him away from the mining territory. Or maybe even kill him and call it self-defence and on the evidence nobody could dispute that claim, right? But he wouldn't even have to call it self-defence, would he? He'd only have to dig his grave and say that was the least he could do for a dead brother. That's why we're here, right? To act as witnesses, so he can't do anything foolish. Right?"

Billy Peel looked across the lake and up the slope of a prominent mountain. He could not tell Doc that there were more than two possibilities. At least of the kind he was talking about. He could not tell him because it was something he felt in his marrow and had not thought out, did not have to think out because it was something true and just and alive in his bones and he had always known it, grown up knowing it, faced each day knowing it and was thankful that it was still true. There were two possibilities, but within them possibility itself was infinite. Billy could not tell him because it involved more than the affairs of the whitemen, of the Duff family, of the mine, more than the affairs of Doctor Marifield or even Henry Scowcroft who must have been called to this business too, his people were involved, and the forest, and they were both one and the same thing. He could not tell him that if there were two possibilities then one was life and rebirth and the other extinction, because the life of his people existed in such delicate balance, and that the movement of things, of his people and of the forest, already leaned towards the death and the final and ultimate capitulation. His people needed more than two choices. He could not tell him that more forces and possibilities had to come into being because his survival depended on it, the forest's survival depended on it, he and the forest one couple, mated, as one went so would the other. He could not tell him because he had not thought it through himself and did not need to. The truth of it existed, in his bones and in his blood. It was a way of life. White people could think of two choices, because they never considered extinction as one of them. His people had to keep open a multitude of possibilities to keep their hopes alive, and it had become a part of their state of mind and intuitive sense. He could not tell him, but often Billy desired to reach this man, felt his spirit as bottled and distorted but nevertheless perceived a kinship, for his own spirit had been tormented and tested to a greater extreme; said, "There's a lot of people in it, Doc."

Doctor Marifield was scratching tobacco from a corner of his pouch, trying to get enough together to fill his pipe. He matted the tobacco down and flicked his lighter about ten times before the wick caught and the pipe smoke was immediately picked up by the breeze. Billy enjoyed the aroma. "That's it. There are two options and for my money I bet on the latter. I bet Morgan Duff, in league with his surveyors, set up the sabotage to discredit the hermit, to make everybody think he was a dangerous and delirious lunatic. What do you think?"

Billy paddled. He had told Doc what he thought he needed to know and Doc had ignored him like he always did, assumed he was talking about something else simply because he had spoken of something else. They shared the same canoe, but Billy believed he moved ahead of Doc, felt that Doc didn't know what was front or back, what was up or down. Doc never caught up with him because he thought that he, Billy Peel, was behind him, slow and evasive, and consequently was always trying to pull him down, thinking it was up. Sometimes Billy felt like a bird, circling in the sky, reciting the glory of distant green pastures while Doc was an agitated and grumpy bear, repudiating his wisdom, deriding him for not being able to see the mountain range that was so evident straight ahead.

"Look!" Billy cried. "Look there!"

Doc turned quickly in the canoe. Low to the water and rising, three beautiful and immaculate snow-white whooping cranes, gathering speed and height, great birds with twelve-foot wing spans, low to the water and rising, elegant, exquisite necks, the drift and flap of the wings a motion of beauty and precision. Billy felt a joy stinging him and he raised his paddle high above his head. A salute. Doc Marifield was captivated and he felt he had to pay a tribute too. The beauty of the sight was a shock; he was already afraid of losing the moment, of surrendering the emotion to a duller condition.

Henry Scowcroft saw the cranes. Watched them stepping in the marsh, feeding on the wild rice. They cleaned their wings and breasts, then struggled to be airborne. In flight, it was as though the forest and the mountains and the lake and the sky all paused in their one coordinated and concentrated movement, all stopped to admire the beauty ascending. Henry was dazzled. He had not seen the birds in twenty years and he felt honoured, the birds moving as through a corridor of honour guards, as through a respectful and joyful silence, and Henry watched and could hardly believe the radiance and something else, the glory of their flight. The shock waves of the rifle blast hit him and he jumped in a panic and cried out, "No! No!" and the three birds worked hard for higher altitude and the second volley resounded.

Billy flung his paddle at Doc and retrieved the other one for himself, and they bore hard for the shore, eyes peeled on the fate of the birds. They hit the shore when the third shot was fired. One bird dipped in flight but it rose again, falling behind slightly as they battled for the clouds. "Canoe up!" Billy called.

Henry ran through the woods in the direction of the gunfire. A pain pierced his hip and he fell, slumped into the branches of a cedar tree.

"Who?" Doc yelled. "Who is it?"
Billy did not respond. There was no need to respond. He stretched and hoisted the canoe onto the bank, shoved it into the bushes. "Push, Doc!"
Doctor Marifield put his back into it and the canoe was quickly submerged by the foliage. "Billy?" he said.
"What?"

When he got up the pain was still there, only shooting back and forth between kneecap and hip now, a new pain, one he had not experienced before and he wondered what the outcome would be, the knee had never been locked for so long. He stumbled ahead.

The birds flew high; the fourth shot rang out, a deep, earth-shaking blast that echoed off the mountains. Billy and Doc jerked their heads up. They followed the flight of the whooping cranes and none of the birds had faltered. "They're safe now," Doc said.

Flat on his stomach, Henry pulled himself along to the water. Poked his head out over the water and searched the sky for the birds. The last shot had been fired nearby. At first he saw only two birds and he was scared. But the third appeared out in front of the others and he felt happier then. He lowered himself further and sipped from the lake. He gripped the branch above his head to pull himself back up. He figured that Morgan was very close.

"Well at least now we know one thing," Doc said. Billy turned his back to him and cut down a cedar bough. He covered the canoe's nose protruding from the underbrush. One end of the branch he ran back into the tree so nothing seemed out of place. "Whoever it is can't shoot straight. How can you miss birds that big? I don't care if they were in flight, they were big birds. Big!"

Billy Peel turned slowly and faced Doctor Marifield. "Maybe he didn't aim at their bodies. Maybe he aimed at their heads."

Doc laughed. "Sure, sure. Stick up for him, why not? The fact is . . . What do you mean, their heads?"

Billy tossed Doc his pack. It contained food now. "Maybe it was too easy to hit the bodies. Maybe he aimed for the eyes, Doc."

"Sure. Now you're telling me he's a sportsman. Bloody hell. If it's Morgan, if he's up here at all, he shot to kill. Eyes, guts, wings, he wouldn't care." Billy started walking and Doc caught up to him. "Do you think it was Thomas?"

"No. It was Morgan. If he wanted the birds dead, I think they would be dead now. So he aimed for the eyes. If he didn't aim for the eyes he tried to tell us something. I think he tried to tell us something or he aimed for the eyes."

"Tell us something! He doesn't even know we're here! We don't even know he's here. That was just my theory."

"So," Billy said.

"So," Doc said.

Billy said, "So."

Henry crawled up a tree trunk to make himself upright. He forced himself to stand on two feet. No support. He keeled over and he couldn't employ his cane quickly enough to break his fall. The pain in his hip was much sharper, somehow more precise and refined than his usual aches and sorenesses. Because it was new and so intense he was concerned. He tried again. This time he managed to stand straight and after a moment he walked, hobbling, working his cane to support the bad leg. The new pain disappeared as quickly and as unexpectedly as it had come, but Henry feared it still, feared its return at any moment. He decided to head towards the caves where he could find shelter for a few hours and rest properly.

"Where are we going now? Do we find Thomas now?"

"How do we find one tree in a forest? We go to the caves."

"What for?"

Billy did not answer. They walked on. The slope was steep through the dark-green forest, but before long they encountered broad patches of bare rock. Billy stopped to listen and Doc caught his breath. "Billy. Why don't you tell me where we're going?"

"I told you, Doc."

"Yes, but not why. Why the caves? Do we find Thomas there?"

Billy listened. Then he looked at Doc. "Maybe we find nobody. But somebody might find us."

"Thomas?" Billy stood and commenced the trek higher into the mountains. Doc, his pack slapping on his shoulders, bounded after him. "Or Morgan?"

"Maybe," Billy said, "but I want to find Henry." Suddenly Billy clamped his hand over Doc's mouth. "No," he whispered. "Don't yell back at me. Morgan's close."

15

HE WAS WALKING AMONG THE BIG TREES and his heart was flapping. Coming down from the rocks where he had been listening and looking too, his heart flapping, but there was nothing to see, no one on the lake and no more shooting either. He tucked a hand between the buttons on his red shirt and pressed it against his skin, felt the beat of his heart. It was flapping like a wounded bird.

Tobacco juice dribbled onto his wild grey beard. He walked among the big trees and listened to the woods, and the woods were not settled yet. The little birds were still flapping because the forest had strangers in it. He knew the forest had more than one stranger because the birds told him so. Over a big section of woods the birds had not settled yet and that told him there was more than one stranger and they were spread out. Breathing in, breathing out heavily, his heart was flapping. Ever since the shooting his heart had been flapping.

The man walked up the slope to his cave and went inside, and the mouth of the cave was concealed by the big woods and by the contour of the rock. Looking at it directly nothing was revealed. The entrance was hidden behind a corner and fold in the rock and from any other angle by the trees. The cave was large and shaped like an egg, and the ceiling was from fifteen to thirty feet high. On the side of the mountain there was another opening which looked up into the sky like a window. The man lay down but he could feel his heart still flapping, and inside the quiet of the cave he thought he could hear it too. A scratching sound across the floor: the squirrel jumped on his cot and ran up his body. The squirrel sat in his beard. Sat up on its hind legs and chittered at him. He picked up the squirrel and pressed it down on his chest so the squirrel could feel his heart flapping too. The animal nipped his hand and he released it and listened to it scurry across the floor to the food table.

He had constructed all the furniture himself. Two tables and the cot like a box and four chairs and a meat rack and a long counter. Dark and shadowy now but there were many unlit lanterns about the cave. "Hunters," the man said aloud. "Must a ben hunters." Which was unusual, because no hunter had to come up this far from wherever he was coming to shoot, because whatever he wanted he'd most likely come across it before he got here. But it could be the other men. The man got up and his heart was still flapping, but slower and more quietly now, and he stood in the mouth of the cave. It could be the other men. The ones who carried the big spy glass on three legs and waved little red flags and one said, "Higher!" and then he hollered, "Lower!" and then, "Got it!" and scratched in his book. They banged stakes with red ribbons in the woods and some stakes had green ribbons. Whatever they were he always took them out, and days later they were putting them back in again. Whatever they were doing he didn't like it. And he didn't like the airplanes every now and again flying overhead, and he didn't like the plane that landed right on the lake once. His heart started flapping then too. He spat tobacco juice and ran his fingers through his beard. He didn't like any of it, he decided, and mostly he didn't like the shooting. The rain beat down on his face. He was just like any other tree in the forest now, and he didn't like the intrusions.

The man walked down the slope of the hill among the big trees, and he was a tall man and his hair was long and wild. He planned to go down and take a look for himself because it was the only way to discover who had come. If it was those men again he would take their stakes out again. While he was walking his heart stopped flapping. The waiting always disturbed him the most. He walked with soft steps. Once he had traded with an Indian for the moccasins he wore. He had counted his birthdays; he was sixty-five years old, but he walked through the forest in his moccasins like a young man. His legs were very thin. His chest was broad and heavy but his legs were like a young boy's, and the deerskin pants he wore fitted him tightly. His head was big also and one eyelid drooped over the eye, and whenever he wanted to look out for something he had to use a finger to prop the eyelid open. Kneeling behind a large cedar tree he listened to the birds. The big birds, the crows and the ravens, were undisturbed now. A long way off he heard a crow cawing. But the little birds, and especially the bluebirds, were still very nervous and didn't fly at all but chattered in the trees. Waiting behind the tree his heart started flapping again so he walked on. He walked very slowly now, listening with each step. Listening, walking slowly, he placed his hand between the buttons of his shirt to feel his heart flapping.

16

Thaat! Thoo! Rack!

Passing time, guessing the sound his steps would make on the forest floor; the *tramp-tramp* of his steps and the regular *ha-shooo* of his breathing helped Doc establish a tempo within himself that he found comfortable. Rescued now by the daylight, he was able to ignore Billy and be undisturbed by him or by his silence; followed and remained equally as quiet as his guide.

Their route climbed onto several rocky plateaus, and it occurred to him that the terrain resembled a staircase for a giant, one of such immense proportions that his kneecaps would touch the clouds. This was a giant's country too, the mammoth trees and high mountain peaks, the skies patrolled by the enormous ravens and by eagles too. They cut sideways across a slope, and it was difficult to find traction in the soft earth, it gave way so easily, and when they reached the crest their boots and pants were coated in mud.

"Now. This way," Billy said.

"Of course!" Doc said, and Billy glanced back at him.

"The caves begin near here."

"Certainly!" Doc said, and he smiled. And he did not feel that he was here at all. He felt more like a child exploring the remote boundaries of his neighbourhood on the first day of a summer vacation. Billy looked at him quizzically from time to time, measuring him, Doc delighting in playing the buffoon, his concerns evaporating in a delicate euphoria that had overcome him. Content to day-dream.

Catching him by the sleeve, Billy said, "Please, Doc. We got to be quiet here."

"What do you mean, 'we'?" Doc retorted, but Billy's sober tone put him on the alert again, and alert he became tense and frustrated, and he resented his companion for it. "You're already quiet."

They circled around a rock face, then mounted a ledge that carried them up gradually. Suddenly Billy ducked and disappeared, and Doc followed him into the cave. The mouth was about four feet high and five feet wide at the base, and as soon as he turned Doc saw the intelligence of Billy's strategy. Their vantage point was a good one. Wedged between two of the giant's stairs, the mountain was cut in such a way that they could see a fair distance to both sides, a relatively unobstructed view, and they held a strong position over the terrain below them as well. Here the weave of the land seemed straight up and down, but around them the land subtly sloped inward and towards them, so that any man seeking the most convenient access would be channelled through here, perhaps without ever being aware of the mountain's influence.

"Let me in on it," Doc said. "Why the hell Henry? Why are we waiting for him?"

"In the back, you find a box. There's food in it."

Caught between his question and the temptation, Doc shook his head and crawled into the darkness of the cave. The coarse floor was wet and cold on his hands. Twenty feet into the rock, Doc found the box and pulled a sack out of it. And looking back and squinting in the darkness, he was struck by the same sensation he had experienced looking down the length of the fir tree that spanned the gorge: the cave seemed to elongate and become an extraordinary tunnel, and Billy at the head of it was the guard. Time again, reaching back again and returned suddenly to another age, to a quiet and prolonged movement in time. Billy the magician, Doc thought, fabricating and distorting illusions of time, the high-flying raven disguised as a man. He hurried back and they ate the raw potatoes and kelp, and Billy opened his fist to reveal blackberries secretly and mysteriously picked along the way. Doc held the berries in his fingertips, studied them, expected them to vanish before his sight.

"You think Henry's up here," Doc said.

"I think so," Billy said.

"Why?"

Billy brushed his hands on his pants, flipped his head to throw hair off his eyes. "Where else would he be? Anyway, I can see him."

Doc's head jerked sharply up. He hesitated, required some further confirmation or explanation from Billy, so that when Billy grinned he jumped up and scraped his head and hair along the ceiling of the cave, then flattened himself on his stomach and peered over the ledge.

"Don't shout," Billy warned.

And a flurry of emotions passed through him in such quick succession that he was not able to identify them immediately, feeling something of it fire out of him like a shot, an accusation, so that he was at the point of screaming his friend's name, "Scow-croft!" and plummeting down from his perch and confronting him with treason. But it turned inside him, his bitterness, his pain, his shame and guilt too, twisting before he knew it or could grapple with it, the thrust of it cutting inward and forged against himself again, and toward Henry he could only direct his unhappiness and his need, identifying it finally, already secretly citing Henry as his protector here and not his prey at all. And wafting in the midst of this disturbance, he examined the form trudging like some broken, prehistoric figure through the depths of the forest, the red head bobbing but not smoothly or with rhythm, and there was something about his friend that seemed odd, his appearance—no—his walk; and he realized too, suddenly, something unusual not in Henry but in himself, unusual but familiar too, he was watching him clinically, as if studying a slide through a microscope. Doc shook himself from his spell and saw it—the bad leg, the limp much more exaggerated than normal. Once, twice, he glimpsed Henry's face. It bore marks.

"Wait," Billy said.

Henry passed below them. Choosing a round red pebble, Billy tossed it down. It skipped over the rocks and buried itself in the lush green foliage. Henry stopped. He looked behind him before looking up. Leaning over the rock, Billy gave directions with his hand and a slow sweep of his arm. Henry cautiously retreated the way he had come, followed Billy's route. Doc watched Henry working with his cane and free hand and bad leg, and the sight hurt him, his anger burning against Henry again not only for not taking him with him but for daring this venture without taking anybody. Because in Henry's state he saw a tribute to his own defeat.

Like looking up and seeing a great black bird about to swoop and anticipating the talons: Henry climbed carefully and he felt a giddiness and relief at finding Billy Peel, climbed over the slick rock and felt a trepidation too, an uneasiness accompanying the relief. For he did not know what to expect. Billy was a mild enemy, a lifelong adversary, boyhood disputes extending into their adult lives, but under these conditions he perceived him as a friend, figured that Billy had heard the shooting, and for once they were on the same side, brought together by a greater and mutual foe.

The fear of Morgan prodded him on. His heavy breathing was a curse to him, preventing him from listening to whatever lay behind or might lay behind, but he managed the hill and crouched and worked his way behind boulders and discovered the ledge. Billy leaned out from the cave and beckoned, said, "It's clear."

Fearing the height he crept close to the rockface, then ducked low into the cave, pulled in his bad leg behind him, and tripped over Doctor Marifield. "What the—Doc!"

Doc was startled too, Henry's face looking like it had been lacerated and pummelled—one eye nearly closed, an ugly bruise on his chin. "Bloody hell!"

Henry continued in his own dismay. "It's you! What are—"

"Your face!"

"How'd you get up here?"

"What happened to your face?"

Henry laughed out loud, joy buckling his tension, and he was greatly relieved and happy to see these faces again. "I don't believe it! I don't believe it!" he said.

Billy touched the side of Henry's face to look closely at the eye.

"See, this tree was in league with this bear, they planned to kidnap me but I escaped. That's the eye. The chin? Well, a rock jumped off the earth and smacked me. But you don't look so hot yourself, Doc."

"Why'd you leave without me, Henry?" Sharp, caustic, the repressed anger sprung from Doc with such velocity that even he was surprised. But Henry ignored it, winced.

"It's my leg, Doc. I need your help. The knee's locked."

Billy smiled; while Henry stripped and Doctor Marifield examined the knee, he scanned the forest, smiled because Henry had the same trouble as he did with Doc, steering him away from what was trivial and worthless into the immediate and real. The forest was too quiet. Maybe Morgan had followed another route. Maybe he was very close. Henry cried out and when Billy turned he was flexing the lame knee.

"How's that?" Doc asked. His tone was professional, neutral.

"It works. *Ouch!* Hurts like hell though. Sorry for the holler, Billy."

Billy Peel turned so that his back rested against one wall while he searched the forest, said, "I don't think he's near."

And Henry asked, "Who?"

Doc said, "Morgan. Didn't you hear the shots?"

"Sure. And I've seen Morgan for myself. But how did you know it was him?"

"Who else?" Doc said. He still worked on Henry's knee. He felt he was immersed in the centre of activity again. "Who else would shoot at those birds? God, they were beautiful."

But Henry was looking at Billy and Billy stared back, said, "I think he was shooting for their heads." A chance. The cave was still and the forest was too quiet and he put his words out to see what would be returned. He needed to take the chance. "He was shooting at the heads for a challenge, or for a warning."

Henry nodded, followed the line of Billy's thinking, imagined him reading the shockwaves of the gunfire and discovering meaning in the misses.

He said, "I thought he was shooting behind them. Just behind their tail feathers. But not for a challenge and not for a warning." Henry listened to the light echo of his words in the cave. Doc was working on his knee and looking at him with a question, but Henry looked back at Billy.

Billy thought. Saw the man aiming his gun near the tail feathers. He said, "To scare them. He was shooting behind to scare them."

"Yeh. It had nothing to do with us but with him."

And Doc stopped; he looked at Henry and Billy and the two men were looking away from one another, Billy over the forest and Henry into the wall of the cave, and it seemed to him that the two men had reached an agreement, but he did not know how or what it was about. Henry pulled his pants back up. He crawled to the front of the cave beside Billy. Billy pointed out the food sack and Henry munched eagerly on the potatoes. Doc moved next to them.

"The rain will keep the smoke down," Billy said. "We can make a small fire." He gathered twigs and small branches that had blown into the cave and he used Doc's lighter. They built the fire in the entrance, and Billy and Henry sat across from one another, their backs against the walls of the cave, and Doc sat behind the fire and faced out. They warmed their hands over the flames. Henry removed his boots to warm his feet and he turned back the ankles to expose the insides to the heat. Doc noticed that Henry wore no socks, which amazed him. When Billy spoke again his tone was formal and he paused between each word as if following each word along its wavelength and behind its journey, as if he planted the words carefully and firmly. "We heard about the sabotage. We heard people suspect Thomas Duff."

"Yeh," Henry said. He waited, studied Billy, the movement of his head and chest and particularly the look in his eyes, understood that Billy was trying hard here, attempting to reach him. And quiet, he listened not only to Billy's words and the deep resonance of his voice in the cave, but to the wind and the forest too, to the rain and the crackle of the small burning wood.

"Doc told me Thomas wrote notes."

"Yeh, there's been notes. But you know and I know he didn't write them. Because he couldn't write them."

"There is one way, Henry, that Thomas could write the notes." For the first time since he had lit the fire Billy looked directly into Henry's eyes. He saw them quicken and blink rapidly. Henry was struck by the depth and darkness of Billy's stare; unexpected, Billy's facial and physical appearance was so boyish and playful it was a shock to be suddenly plunged into an altogether new and different depth. He saw what Billy was doing and supposed that this interrogation was necessary.

"Billy. I didn't teach him. I never taught Thomas how to read or write."

Billy nodded, satisfied. Doc looked from one man to the other and he was intrigued by the talk although he did not understand it, Billy asking questions but not as questions, and Henry unravelling Billy's statement to find first the question, then the answer to it. To Doc it seemed that even the pauses and the waiting were meaningful to the two men, as if silences were as significant as the words between them. Doc wanted to ask Henry something but he felt he would be interrupting to speak now.

"So somebody wrote the notes."

"Yeh. I don't know who," Henry said.

Billy nodded. "We wondered. We wondered if somebody did not want to get Thomas."

Henry weighed Billy's words a long time, trying to catch the gist of his idea. It was hard to follow Billy's meaning, Henry knowing that Billy lived with a different concept of time and a different understanding of life itself, so that the words were not simply travelling in the space between them, not simply travelling from one mind to another, but they traversed a chasm, arcing between separate and alienated time zones, and only because Henry was accustomed to living in different zones himself was he able to deal with Billy at all. He figured it out. A question invoked a myriad of possibilities and none of them might be on the right track. The secret was to stay on the same track and not to waver from it. "Somebody did not want to get Thomas. Somebody wanted to get Morgan."

"Yes," Billy said.

Henry scratched his head. "Somebody wanted to draw Morgan into the forest and isolate him there."

"Yes," Billy said.

"Because of the mine."

"Maybe."

Henry was puzzled. He wrestled with Billy's thought. "Or maybe because of Gail?"

"Yes."

"Nope. It's not me, Billy. I didn't write the notes. I didn't commit the sabotage and I didn't put any blame on Thomas either. Look, Morgan's no friend—but I didn't do it."

Billy nodded, quietly and pensively. "I wanted to know that."

Rubbing his hands over the dying fire, Doc was having a hard time keeping up with the conversation, stuck now on a question out of what was already and eradicably the past. But he believed he could not pursue it out loud.

"Then you are here," Billy said, and he was looking at Henry again. He said the words quickly, surprising both Doc and Henry and commanding their attention.

Henry blinked, searched through himself for an answer. *Yes I'm here and so are you but why are you here anyway? I see. That's what you want to know of me. Okay then. What is it you're afraid of? What's the accusation exactly? I already told you I—So that's it.* "I didn't commit the sabotage, Billy, and I didn't set up this situation either. But now that it has been committed and established, I'm not here to take advantage of it either. I mean, I'm not here to get Morgan."

"Thomas," Billy said.

Thomas. What about—? "Nope. I'm not here to sacrifice Thomas. There's no way."

Billy was nodding again and smiling for the first time. "I wanted to know that."

Sitting still. The three men. Doc presumed that the issue between the other two had been resolved, but when he glanced across at Henry his friend's expression was intent. Doc noticed that Henry studied Billy's features closely, and he detected that the conversation had not been concluded after all, only the positions in it had changed. Now Henry was about to enter Billy and Billy was waiting for him.

Henry was puzzled again. He wanted to know Billy's stake in all of this, why he was here. But he could not accuse Billy of the sabotage, even though he had suspected him in the past: the young chief had reason to resent the opening of the mine, for it would drastically affect the Kloo Ravens and their isolated life. Henry could not accuse Billy of it because Billy had initially accused him, which announced his own ignorance of it and therefore innocence too. What bothered Henry was how to broach the subject. He had to learn Billy's manner of talking. He took his time and slowly developed the clues. The key was always to make a statement that did not question the other man, but which stipulated the limits of his own knowledge, which allowed the responding person to add to it. Henry followed his thoughts hurriedly then, trying to reach the edge of his knowledge. But when he got there he found he already had the answer to his own question, and he said it, "Thomas is like a fuse." Billy looked up and Henry continued. "Yeh, like an electric fuse. The first link to blow out. Because he's closer to the mine and because one lone hermit's more vulnerable than a tribe of Indians. Yeh. You don't want Thomas blown out because as long as he's safe in his reclusion then you and your band at Kloo are safe in yours. But once he goes, then you're next. That's why you're here. To see if the lights are still on or not. To see if the wires are burning yet or not. To see if your house is in flames yet or not."

Again Billy nodded, looked at Henry. Henry did not have it precisely correct but he was close, and Billy told it to him precisely. "Once Thomas goes, then the forest does. Thomas—he is like a weak and old tree in the forest, the first tree to fall in the big storms." Billy shrugged. "When the forest is gone, we are gone."

So you're here to protect the future and I'm here to protect the past—or at least to reconcile it once and for all with what is true and just—and together we have to see that the present is not slandered and does not abdicate its impoverished and tarnished throne—but throne nonetheless. Because Morgan could slander it and decimate both past and future, and

Thomas could abdicate again just as he abdicated seventeen years ago.

Billy added wood to the fire and stirred the ashes. He looked at Doc quickly and Doctor Marifield returned the glance; Doc guessed that something new was coming and this time it involved him. He still had a question for Henry. Billy said, "Thomas's cave is hidden good."

Henry looked at him but he did not speak.

Doc said, "So you know where he lives."

Watching Henry, Billy said, "I do not. So it must be hidden good."

Henry was looking into the fire. When he looked up he scratched his head first, then said, "It's hidden very well. It's impossible to find."

"How do you know that?" Doc spoke sharply. "And what's this business about teaching Thomas or not teaching him how to write?" He had finally poked his question out. "Does Billy mean you could have? You been keeping it back from me, Henry, you've seen him and I don't mean seventeen years ago."

"Don't get upset," Henry said.

"Oh I like that. I like it! All summer long we've been trying to figure out the sabotage, and you tell me don't get upset! You knew all the time Thomas can't write. Right? Isn't that right, Henry?"

"Yeh. That's right."

"So you tell me don't get upset. Bloody hell! You never told me about Thomas. You take off into the woods without me. You don't tell me where you're going. You leave me to put out the fire in your house. Your house, Scowcroft. So I'll tell you I'm upset, all right? I'm upset."

Henry rubbed his forehead and looked into the fire. Billy said, "It's the ashes."

"What ashes?" Doc said. "Don't talk to me about the bloody ashes. I can't read your bloody ashes." Henry put his boots on. "Where're you going now?"

"Doc. Listen."

"What?"

Henry hesitated. Tried to find the right phrase, exasperated by what he saw as a delicate situation.

"Why don't you say what's on your mind, Scowcroft? Spit it out."

Pulling the laces tight and tying them, he said, "It's a trust."

"What's a trust? Speak plain English, Scowcroft. I don't feel like following you through your maze right now."

Henry looked at Billy. Billy nodded slightly. Henry shifted his position so that he could rest his hands on his knees, his knees propped at eye-level. Casually, he picked up his cane and played with it in his hands.

"Well?" Doc said.

Henry looked at him. Saw the anger and bitterness flashing in his eyes and could not determine why it was so strong. Henry sensed he was to blame for the hurt in Doc's eyes, but he did not think he had done anything so drastic to have caused this much pain and anguish. "Why'd you come out here?" Henry asked, but his words were less a question than they were a lament.

"What trust?" Doc said.

Henry stared at him. "I'm sorry, Doc, but—" Suddenly Henry rolled toward the entrance and in an instant he was on the ledge and out of sight. Doc hollered and sprang to a low crouch but he managed only a step when he was slammed into the rock wall and it was Billy on top of him, pinning him. Doc cried out, "Henry! Henry!" and he squirmed and tried to push Billy away and he hollered, "Scowcroft! Come back here!" and he escaped Billy's hold and jumped to the entrance, but Billy pounced on him again and forced his head near the fire.

"Leave him, Doc. He can go alone," Billy said.

And Doc said, "Damn you, Peel! Damn you!" Flat on the floor he felt the same sensation welling within him that he had experienced while reading his logbook two long days ago and he had felt the need to cry, and he had felt it again when Evlin had bridled him for his loss of toughness and enterprise, and this time the tears came to his eyes and he was ashamed, and he fought Billy more rigorously but he failed again, Billy pinning him to the floor and Doc stared into the small flames, and this time his tears did run down his face and moisten the grey-white ashes.

17

TRAMPING THROUGH THE WOODS, Henry was baffled by the difference a few months had made, for at the outset of the summer Doc was still bright and enthusiastic. Together they helped calm the panic and warn against the avarice and sort out the dilemmas; together they refereed the arguments and pacified the flare-ups and outbursts of temper, but somewhere along the line Doc had sagged and become increasingly withdrawn, and Henry had thought it had to do with their failure.

He thought of the eyes of the men staring out from the Rogg House benches, staring out over Cumshewa Sound and over their individual and collective memories, staring out over the sunlit and sparkling water so that they had to shield their eyes to see and interpret the commotion: surveyors, mining people, making the talk true and real then, the Japanese actually were going to develop the copper-sulphate deposit at Lake TaColl, just as the rumour said they would. The eyes stared out but the expressions remained blank, not yielding yet to the forces of either terror or greed, of either panic or lust; they waited, waited for the movements of other men and circumstances to decide it for them. Their livelihoods and their conditions were always subject to the exterior forces of rain-and-sunshine-ratios and the enterprises of others, which only included them after they were provoked into being included, so that they waited not only for the surveyors, and after them the miners, but for men like Henry Scowcroft and Doctor Marifield too, to define and illustrate the significance of the events and moreover the choices. For Skincuttle Islanders abided in a single and coherent awareness of their immunity, so that choices and meanings were not important; they were made safe by their isolation and smallness and moreover by the protection of the elements, the rain rain and constant rain, rain and high water so that all days seemed much the same as the next, and the only points of conversion or trauma were the chants of the gathering storm and the quick bright aftermath of squall or shower or torrent. The changes came, but came disguised, washed in by the sea like useless and colourless and faceless driftwood, so that the changes were propagated, but slowly and diffidently and unobserved by the staring islanders, the landscape changing and rolling and relinquishing itself to the rain and the sea, but the rain disguising and concealing it. The staring missed it. The invasions which had occurred elsewhere and had already been accomplished and perhaps even terminated included Skincuttle Island too, but the movement was subtle and arbitrary, so that it was up to the historian Henry Scowcroft or the doctor Doctor Marifield or sometimes even the Indian prophet Billy Peel to identify and clarify what had rolled in with the tide: to announce the presence of a few industrious, talkative and, in this case, dim-witted surveyors as being the advance force of nothing less than a renewed assault of civilization itself.

And Doc had become withdrawn, and Henry had thought it had to do with their failure to deal with the crises: for they had not expected the action, they had not expected the sabotage, the theft of the surveyors' tools, the burning of their rowboat, and the wrecking of equipment. They had been as surprised as anyone when the harried surveyors returned from weeks in the woods, angry and frustrated beyond reason, telling tales of how their stakes had been planted and replanted and uprooted every time, as if by some invisible and untraceable hand. Finally the surveyors no longer ventured into the forest but hung about Rogg House and smiled and laughed and whenever questioned replied confidently that they were "waiting", that all things would be put right soon—which meant the appearance of Morgan Duff, a seventeen-year exile returning as a specialized road builder, a man who put roads and railways through cheaply and quickly where others claimed it could not be done, a man who had bartered and battled with native populations throughout the world and always got his work done, returning to his native Skincuttle Island and promising to put things straight. But the sabotage only intensified against the newcomer and against the others too, against Doc and Henry, and soon the mysterious notes appeared, a signature only, scrawled in a juvenile handwriting, the name "Thomas"; and Henry was baffled by the change a few months had made, thinking of Doc, Doc who was his friend and who had uplifted him from a destitute and morose condition, whose impulsive and eager nature had stirred Henry from a death-like trance and spurred him to life again. Doc, the mysterious and intelligent and volatile escapee from the mainland, had faltered, had somewhere along the line lost his pulse and rhythm, had given up his pursuit of a fair and palatable fusion of Skincuttle Island life with the opening of the mine, and the changes wrought by such an occurrence. So now, in the forest, in this most demanding and desperate of manoeuvres, he had become a liability, he was not thinking properly or accurately, and in the forest it was dangerous. Henry had had to escape from him and he had known it and Billy had known it too. There was no use in explaining his trust with Thomas Duff, there would be too much to review, and after it was detailed and related Doc would have been left solely with his hurt and his self-pity.

And the change in his good friend hurt him deeply. There had been a shift. Somewhere and during the summer there had been a shift, and Henry longed for the hour, the moment, when Doc would be calm and they could figure it out together. He owed Doc a lot, did not consider it a debt but a trust, a privilege and a gift to be a part of the relationship, a mutual love and need, but now something new had been added: aside from pulse and rhythm and hope there was truth too, the reclaiming of the past, and it was at the point of what was true and evident and real that Doc wavered and sank. Henry walked through the forest sadly. Knew that he had hurt his friend. Hoped the damage could be remedied. But life and death were at stake now, past and future too, and it was obvious that Doc did not really know that yet, that he was still fighting himself and so had to be abandoned, again, for now.

The rainfall was light and gentle and the liberation of his knee made the walking easier for Henry, almost pleasant by comparison to when it was locked. Pains in his leg still, but they were made tolerable by the freedom of the knee, and having left his pack behind in Billy's cave made the going easier too. The lighter rain had improved the range of his ears, he felt safe, confident that he could hear Morgan if he approached near by.

Henry took no chances. Scouted carefully before ascending a steep slope where he would be vulnerable. When he tired he lay on his stomach and overlooked a cliff and scanned the forest. He still had not rested. He was tempted to close his eyes and doze, a quick nap, but a deer family attracted his attention. The animals moved spritely through the woods. Leaping the underbrush and fallen debris, scooting quickly across the surfaces of flat exposed rock. Then Henry sighted Morgan.

Did that grizzly make it?

Look who it is! Scowcroft! Lookin like a full growed man yet.

About that grizzly.

A little bent but standin straight up and down mostly. Still bootleggin, Scowcroft?

Nope. John Rogg does the hard stuff himself now too.

Whiskey's a man's business anyway, Scowcroft. No place for cripples. Yaha!

What I figured is, that grizzly gave you quite a wallop but at least you're here to tell about it so I wonder if that grizzly was so lucky.

Wasn't no grizzly.

No.

I got this in India. It was a Bengal tiger.

And you're still here to tell about it.

That's right. That Bengal tiger didn't make it neither.

What do you mean, neither?

Morgan prowled the woods on the lower tier. His scar began on the crown of his head and two lines ran down his right cheek, joined at his chin, continued down his neck to his collarbone. Deep marks, the flesh parted by the canyons which were white across his tanned skin.

Yaha! You know what I mean, Scowcroft.

Henry had not been the only person fascinated by the scars. The men of Lyell regarded Morgan with high esteem because of them, and drunk one night he had revealed his boils too. The men averted their faces from the boils: living things, they spoke of decay and destruction; the scars, dead things, told tales of full-blooded life and adventure. Henry learned that it was Morgan's way, and remembered that it was true years ago too, to frighten, to instill fear, to first provoke panic in his victim before he struck.

Gail.

Yaha!

Morgan was crossing the level below him and his eyes scrutinized the ground. Henry looked down. Took his eyes off Morgan and looked straight down. And saw his trail. Saw his footprints in the mud and the marks his body made climbing the rock and soft earth. Morgan was only thirty yards from discovering the trail.

The mine.

Never mind the mine. The mine's none of your business.

Sure it's my business. I live here.

So do I! Yaha! Sockeye's my home town, Scowcroft.

No.

Sure it is.

No. Because Skincuttle Islanders maybe become successful here after they failed somewhere else, or maybe they failed here too and somewhere else too, or maybe they were born here and never attempted anything else except surviving, but a Skincuttle Islander doesn't make a success somewhere else and then come back. Once he's gone and made it somewhere else it's like he's excommunicated, you might say, not by any person or thing but by the way things are.

What are you, the pope?

No. Just the historian.

Shut it, Scowcroft.
Did you kill her, Morgan?
Henry crawled in the high grass away from Morgan, acutely aware that his knees and hands left the imprint of his flight clearly and precisely reproduced. Away from the cliff, he scampered to his feet and fled into the forest. Everywhere the soft earth revealed him. There was not enough exposed rock here over which he could move invisibly and silently. So he changed his course, and he did not try to hide his steps, did not want Morgan to suspect he had been spotted while he led him away from Thomas's cave. He moved quickly though and even the impression of his cane followed behind him. Coming to a stream, Henry waded through it upstream. The water was cold and swift. The large brown-and-white-spotted stones were laced with stringy moss. He arrived at a sharp, low waterfall, and he crawled up beside it then ran across the rock outcropping, leaving no trace.

What're you going to do?
Shut it!
I live here.
Out of my way!
Yeh, but then what?

The roots of Henry's fear ran deeper than Morgan's intimidating demeanour or the scars that enunciated what was vile and terrifying. The cause of his fear was not his concern for his own safety or well-being or even life. He feared him, and it was not the fear of the weak man for the strong, but the fear of the backward glance, of his own responsibility, the fear of returning to the time and moment of the event that had caused Morgan to leave Skincuttle Island years ago, and his return meant it could be avoided no longer.

I'm gonna build a railroad smack from Lake TaColl to the sea. That's one thing, Scowcroft.
And then what?
We're gonna build schools and hospitals.
Yeh, but then what?
Those floatin lumber camps are out of date. We're gonna bring a modern operation in here, and there's gonna be banks and stores and businesses and bars.

Yeh, I know, Morgan, but then what?

Then I'm gonna bust every bone in your body. Yaha!

Yeh. Well. You'll have to make it every bone too. I can see where you'd need to do that.

Henry leaped and caught hold of a tree limb. With his cane tucked in his belt he pulled himself along so that his feet were off the ground. At the tree trunk he managed to squirm around it and continue out along another limb. At the end of it he dropped to the forest floor and his first prints were concealed behind bushes. Henry ran through the woods. He was running along the slope of a hill where the trees were less dense and his tracks were plainly marked in the mud. He stopped behind a fir tree, breathed heavily. Looked back: no one. He ran again, his leg hurting him sharply again but he paid it no mind. He reached a formation of stones. He ran behind them and sat down and caught his breath. He peered carefully around the rocks and could see no one. Breathing easier, he smiled and looked up into the lightly falling rain. He opened his mouth, stuck out his tongue, caught the falling drops. Closed his eyes and let the rain gently wash over his face.

Henry did not hear the man. Heard only his own breathing and the rain and the wash sliding down the mountain side. He did not hear the man or even sense his presence. Abruptly he was yanked to one side and a hand was firmly clamped over his mouth, and Henry stared up into the ancient, weathered face.

18

"So we just wait. Henry goes into the woods alone and we just wait."

"He'll be all right, Doc."

"Sure he will. Did you see him? His eye's puffed up. His bad leg must be killing him. His knee might stiffen again—it will stiffen again. And Morgan's out there, you know."

Doc was sullen and bitter. He felt impotent and futile. He spoke to shake off the oppressiveness of his feelings, spoke because he did not want to brood on the one thing he could not get off his mind. Thinking about it upset him, and his thoughts became disoriented. But it popped out: "So Henry knows Thomas. He knows exactly where the hermit lives."

Shrugging his shoulders casually, Billy Peel chewed on a slice of dried venison. "That's right."

"He never told me that, you know. I'm supposed to be his friend. Some friend."

Billy looked at him. "He could not tell you, Doc. He could not tell you because it was a trust. It must be he has a vow with Thomas not to tell."

"Well. Anyway."

Billy stared into the rain. The cloudcover was less dense and the day was brightening. "Think about it, Doc. You been here four years.

Henry's vow with Thomas is maybe ten, is maybe fifteen years old." Billy paused and nodded his head. "We knew Thomas had contact with somebody. Because sometimes we seen him with new clothes."

Doc fidgeted and scratched his growth of whiskers. Admitted to himself that it was true what Billy said. He was still a relative newcomer to Skincuttle Island, so it was not strange that agreements and pacts had preceded his arrival. Sometimes he felt that all things began and ended with himself, but he knew that it was not so. He stood in a crouched position. "I'm going out," he said.

Billy said, "Why?"

"Are you my guard or what?"

"Where you going, Doc?"

"To take a crap, do you mind?"

Billy touched Doc's wrist, squeezed it lightly as if taking his pulse; "Look first."

Doc was properly cautious as he left the cave, looking in all directions including up before he ventured onto the ledge. He walked slowly because his legs were weak and sore and he did not trust his balance. When he returned to the forest he sought a well-secluded spot, lowered his pants, and squatted. Looked up through the branches and leaves and needles. The rain was gentle on his face. Through a gap he saw a pair of crows fly past, and when they were out of sight they cawed back at him. He listened to the rain in the trees and to the streams. He felt drained, and his weariness reached a point of comfort where even malevolent energies were sapped and empty. And having emerged from the dimness of the cave the forest seemed brighter and more distinctive to him now, as though he were viewing it through new eyes. Weary, he detected a freshness and vitality to the woods that had escaped him before. The forest was soothing to him now, quiet, peaceful, and bright. It did not converge upon him and take advantage of his tiredness and lassitude as he would have expected, but offered sympathy and consolation. Doc adjusted to his own state of mind now so that he no longer stood guard against the forest and its power.

When he was finished, Doc stood and searched through the forest.

He did not feel like returning to the cave immediately. Its dimness and dankness repelled him. Instead he climbed the rock above the cave and looked out over the valley and Lake TaColl in the distance. Billy stepped out from the cave below and Doc said, "Take it easy. I'm not going anywhere."

"Maybe you should sleep before Henry comes back."

"In a minute, Billy, in a minute." Billy Peel slipped back into the cave. Doc lay on his back and gazed up into the clouds and rain. As the notion first occurred to him he received it with anger, because it reversed his present peaceful temperment. But the idea stirred and the feeling was difficult to resist for it was a feeling soon, no longer an idea, moving through him, and he recognized it from long association, from years ago during his university days when he used it to become rich as a successful entrepreneur through his working days as a medical researcher, when he used it to fly off on bizarre tangents that frequently led to extraordinary and enlightening discoveries, and in both instances he was commended for his genius. But the feeling, which was actually a force that overcame him and manipulated him, which was actually his own impulsive nature, needed to be controlled and tempered on Skincuttle Island, needed to be guarded as Billy guarded it now, because now it was personal and human affairs with which he dealt. He had not learned, responding to impulse time and time again, and while sometimes he was right, frequently he neglected the worth of valuable lessons and stumbled where a fall proved critical. The past summer had been fraught with tensions and emotions and many times Henry had had to rectify and smooth over his mistakes; yet he had followed his impulses, regardless of how much Henry or Evlin attacked him for it, because the sensation was too sweet, too tempting, the impulse burned through him like a flash fire and before he knew it himself he would be off again. And he was off again now, jogging into the woods, seeking out the rock and the soft grasses where his steps were quiet and undetected; off again and leaving Billy behind; off again to seek Thomas once more, and Henry too, for himself, already visualizing himself rescuing them from Morgan's grip, but feeling guilty too for spoiling the woods' message of tranquillity. Deep into the woods he slowed to a brisk walk and he was elated to find tracks, Henry's tracks, and he followed them up.

Each step hurt him. As if the pain entered the soles of his feet and shot up through his legs. As if the pain dwelt in the land, in the soil, in the forest, and it was passed from man to man as every man walked; but it was a pain and a sadness dwelling here and abiding here but not centred here, for it was a pain of the heart, and Billy knew it. Each step hurt him because of Doc, this foe-in-spirit he must now call friend to keep him alive, this opponent who had been good for him because he had kept him honed and tempered but who opposed nothing now: it was painful for him to see his enemy falter, for there had been a special and particular glory in the battle itself. Their differences had contained the highest of ideals and the most abundant and overflowing of spirits, but as the one side faltered, so did the battle and glory which had held them fast dissipate and collapse. Their conflict from the past centred on the isolation of Kloo, the refusal of the Ravens there to sustain any contact with the outside world; but Doc was the man isolated here, Billy thought, isolated not by any decision or idea, but by his confusion and errors. Billy stayed well to one side of Doc's path through the woods and a good distance behind him. He would let him walk himself out, walk the sadness away until not even that remained to move him. Then he would lead him back to the cave and they would wait together for Henry and Thomas.

The forest suited his desire to brood. The grasses and ferns bent and sagging, the branches sloped low under the weight of the rainfall, the water trickling through the intricate patterns of bark. The forest held the correct tones of gloom and melancholy, mingling with a sufficient dosage of light and harmony. He did not find the woods hostile or threatening, they were not about to engulf him and smother his breath and submerge his body in the bracken to be fossilized and revealed to some distant era; in the quiet of the rain the trees and plants were meditative themselves, each tree withdrawing within itself, each shrub and fern respectfully still and silent, like faithful parishioners attending mass. Doc felt a surge of power and energy. The forest could be manipuated to suit his own mood and need. The forest did not overpower him but was under his control, he could use it to fulfil his own desires. He smiled. Now that he was off on his own again, his hostility toward Henry and Billy too was renewed, and he gathered strength from it.

He recalled his arrival on Skincuttle Island—the town went into an uproar then. First his appearance on the wharf, sick and exhausted from his voyage from Vancouver: he could not move or think, and he slept the night right on the wharf, stretching out on his chesterfield that bordered the bulging pile of his belongings. Pandemonium. People thought he was protecting his property, that he did not trust them, a thought that had not occurred to him but it would have been a wise idea if it had, and the people knew it. But they resented him reaching such a conclusion so quickly. Next he goaded a timorous and sullen cripple by the name of Henry Scowcroft into organizing the entire male population of the town together to transport the doctor's residence and clinic across from Lyell to Kinstuk Island, an impulsive act to be sure, and it offered the town more excitement than it had known in a year. Unfortunately he gave a reason for the move, which was not the true reason, because he had no true reason, just the impulse. He told someone that he wanted the house on Kinstuk Island so that people would have to put a little effort into visiting him, so that they would not visit him needlessly, which naturally had the effect of insulting the entire town of Lyell and stiffening many backs against him. Those backs stiffened more solidly when it was discovered that he burned religious candles and read from an enormous copy of the Bible—it sat huge and impressive in his front room, the largest book of any kind on Skincuttle Island, the pages stained yellow with time—yet he did not attend church services, and in his second month on the island he had had Jonas Gatenby deliver an entire stock of wine to fill a large, deep cellar dug behind his house. What was offensive was not the wine-bibbing or the religious candles and Bible reading, but the two things together, one or the other would be fine but together they were of the devil (some of the women talking now), or at least the acts of a lunatic (said the men). Henry Scowcroft, his new friend, got him off the hook.

"Tell somebody you're a Catholic."

"But I'm not."

"That's of no importance."

And Henry's technique worked, Doc was rescued from contempt and stigma, and his new label could be used as a cover-all for many activities. He was held as peculiar and eccentric but not with disdain, everything explained away by the fact of his Catholicism, which he could not help, being born that way.

All of which had bewildered Doc and scared him too at times. He had felt that he could not step without the vibrations of the movement coursing through the town and having deep-seated repercussions. Even his thoughts seemed to possess a certain volatility that was new to him, and what struck him and scared him was the threat of losing his individual vacuum in which to move and breathe and ponder. The irony of it did not escape him either but lingered to vex him: that he had chosen eccentric and worrisome behaviour in Vancouver as his means of breaking through the regimentation of protocol and custom, as his means of being heard, but here each thought, step, or breath was immediately connected to the life of the town, was noticed and commented upon by all, and this instant communication frightened him more than the absence of it in Vancouver.

Doc learned to adapt and live with it but the past summer had been more difficult. As his mind drifted to the memory of it, Doc lost his smile. He climbed an embankment and lost sight of the tracks for awhile, rummaging about idly to locate them, more attentive to his line of thought than to the trail. When he found the way again, the footprints continued at a right angle to the original route, and Doc followed.

The sabotage during the summer had been unsettling, and he knew why it had bothered him more than it did Henry. Henry found it intriguing, as if he was delighted that someone thought enough of Skincuttle Island to go to all that trouble. But Doc feared it because he liked to know exactly what was happening and who was involved;

sometimes he thought that Henry preferred the mystery to the discovery. The sabotage demonstrated that he did not have control of things, that he and Henry and Evlin and Gerald and Walter were not the only people at the centre of things. Someone else revolved invisibly within their own circle, and he did not like it. He feared it, and more and more he discovered himself relying on Henry to provide some sort of answer or conclusion or at least hypothesis, but none was forthcoming. Two things disturbed him: one was his awareness of how deeply involved he had become with Skincuttle Island life. This had been his intention at the outset, but he had never been so critically involved with people before and he felt surrounded, felt as if he, the helper, had been trapped and nailed into that position. And he was upset by his continued and deepening reliance on Henry, he feared the loss of his individuality. He had helped Henry back on his feet, emotionally and physically too, and now he followed him everywhere like a faithful dog, could not move unless he heard the scratch and jab of Henry's cane preceding him. His spirits sank. Actions came from habit rather than impulse. He lost his ability to see into things, seeing only himself and his self-made prison. Morgan Duff had returned from his exile and exploited his weaknesses. Bearing his scar like a weapon, a warning. His work was to enter where nature struggled to repel him, and Doc realized quickly that he did the same with a man. "If a man knows the peacefulness and valleys and rises of his mind," Doc had written in his log book, staying up at night to think things through, smoking his pipe faithfully and sipping glasses of the finest wines, "then Morgan knows how to enter and disturb, trample and crush." Doctor Marifield expertly avoided any confrontation with the man. The wrenching part was that the townspeople looked to him for his opinion and leadership, but he was caught off-guard by Morgan's ruthlessness and power, and all he could do was to appeal to Henry for his support. When he himself became subject to sabotage, when someone filled his powerplant with water in exact proportions to the gasoline they had removed, that did it, it was the last straw. He felt insulted and abused, but felt also that it was right, he had had it coming, he had let everybody down and so he had had it coming.

Doc ducked behind a pine tree to urinate. Even deep within the forest feeling the need to protect his privacy and solitary nature. "It's time for a change," he said aloud. Finished, he leaned his back against a tree, steam from his urine drifting about his ankles. "I mean I'm already out here. The Duffs chased me from Lyell and Evlin from Cumshewa Town, and I didn't think when I left with Billy, but now that I'm already out here I should turn it all around. A reversal of form. Henry shouldn't have to go it alone. Or Evlin at Cumshewa Town, for that matter. Get on the ball! I can help so I should help. Do something right for a change."

He walked on. He came to a stream that cut through a bed of rock and beyond it the tracks did not continue. He figured that Henry had travelled upward, disguising his trail. Doc climbed too. He was feeling sorry for what he had done to Henry. Knew that when he had been following him and depending on him he had resented Henry for it, that he had persuaded his bitterness and self-reproach to be turned against his friend, and he regretted it now. Doc moved more quickly along the edge of the stream.

The black bird rises *Cumshewa People* the raven flies high *Men of the Raven* above the trees and the rolling hills *Soul-land of our Fathers* higher than the mountain peaks where the eagles nest *The sacred hoop is broken* and sees the circular horizon of ocean *The salmon spawn* and below *The old world dies* the land is beaten by the storm. Below the high-flying and wind-tossed bird the old world has crumbled, as Yestiglee knew it would, as he had prophesied, as he revealed in his visions of invasions and disease. Yestiglee, who told of the whiteman's coming long before it occurred, who told of his people's suffering during their time of greatest abundance. Below are the trails that mark the steps of Connehawah and Leegay, who sought their visions on the great mountain peaks above the pure, wise, emerald lake—Connehawah who signalled the trials of his people, and Leegay who promised the return to glory, and Klakow, the great warrior Klakow, hunted here, the forest still full with his breathing, still silent with his hushed steps, still discreet with his waiting. The old world has crumbled and the new world has not yet begun; and the raven flies high between the two, between the old below and the new that will come from the skies like dew, that will radiate and glisten the earth once again.

Cumshewa People
Men of the Raven
Soul-land of our Fathers
The sacred hoop is broken
The salmon spawn
The old world dies
The new light shines
On the feathers of a bird

Billy chanted in his own language silently to himself, and the names ran through his head—*Yestiglee Connehawah Leegay Klakow Billy Peel*—and he wondered if this was right, if he ought to be hiding in the woods now while Doctor Marifield marched past, his eyes vacantly watching the ground; he wondered if he ought to be involved in this whiteman's business, even though the forest was involved too; and he experienced a moment of trepidation, sensing extreme danger, and he chanted again silently for courage. No one denied it, Billy Peel had rescued his clan from alcohol and syphilis and degeneration too. He had waited patiently for his time then executed a plan with daring and precision: first he raided the bedrooms of Prince Rupert hotels to take back the wives and daughters and mothers of Raven men, which broke a kind of psychic barrier, as Billy knew it would—the men taking back their women—and suddenly pride was rekindled and with it respect; then he had established again the ancient and barren village of Kloo, where the people lived in almost total isolation from the outside world. No one could deny the rescue, but many questioned his methods, questioned their validity in the long run. Through many fitful nights Billy had questioned himself too and wondered if the rescue was truly salvation or not, truly merciful or not. The struggle was a trying and discouraging one, as when Doctor Marifield had been involved, when the children took sick and finally they had had to call for him and the fever claimed three lives, the story of old again, disease again, as if the Indian people were no longer fit to live on the planet, as if the planet had been infected beyond their capacity to survive on it. Doctor Marifield believed the isolation was wrong, that the tribe would be made vulnerable again and one day could easily be victimized again, and he had been a vital, energetic man then. But Billy had made his decision and he stayed with it, lived with it, the only man to deal with the whiteman would be himself, for the protection of the tribe. But he did not ever believe that he lived beyond the need for protection himself, considered himself to be the most vulnerable point in his plan. He called on the chiefs and the prophets of old to stay with him and to guide him through their sacred forest.

Billy lurked in the undergrowth as Doc passed. The doctor had surprised him by suddenly altering his course and walking in a line that would intercept his own path. He waited for him to go by before he stood again and followed. When he came out on Doc's path he noticed the footprints immediately. Henry's were revealed by the telltale stab of his cane, but Billy examined closely and there were two additional pairs. So that someone else was walking the same trail as Doc and Henry. Billy hurried. Where a stream crossed, the trail vanished. Billy hurried up the side of the stream. Climbing a ledge, he scanned the side of the mountain. He could see Doc. He was climbing on his hands and knees and concentrating on the rock formation. Ahead of Doc, Billy sighted the blond man with the rifle.

19

THE MAN SQUATTED with his hands on the ground like a toad, demanded, "Who's comin?"

Henry peered over the rock, back into the forest the way he had come, said, "I think I lost him."

"Who's it?" The man hopped and glanced quickly for himself, hopping like a toad.

"He could pick up my trail again, Thomas. We better get going."

"S'y, it be the man wit the gun?"

"That's right exactly."

They hurried through the forest quickly and Thomas led the way, running ahead, bobbing and weaving like a man running a gauntlet, leading Henry through streams and over rock outcroppings and through rain-swollen pools and grassland, and their steps were concealed behind them.

Thomas stopped once and spun quickly. "Is he huntin you, Scowcroft? Is he goin kill you, b'y?"

Henry panted and waited to catch his breath. "Well. If he finds us together, that's right, he might kill me too." Thomas's one open eye had a glint to it, he was excited and curious. Henry sensed he felt glad and relieved about something. They ran on, Henry stabbing his cane into the rock and pushing with the full strength of his arm and shoulder to keep the pace. But Thomas stopped again and Henry asked, "Now what?"

"What? What?"

"That's right. You first and then me." Thomas looked at him. Henry noticed the closed eyelid straining to open itself. Finally Thomas pushed it up with a finger and stared at him with both eyes steadily. "We better get going," Henry said. "We better hide in the cave."

They had to climb. Thomas reaching back several times to hoist Henry up, Henry securing the crook of his cane on a root and pulling himself up, and when they made it they ran through the big woods. Henry jumped around a birch tree and ran full-face into Thomas, who had stopped and assumed an immobile stance. Henry bounced off him and rubbed his nose.

"Thomas," he said.

He was panting heavily but the hermit was breathing calmly. The man reached down and clutched Henry's wrist. He unbuttoned the top of his shirt and placed Henry's hand against his skin, over his heart, pressing it there.

"I'm dyin," Thomas said.

"You're not dying," Henry said. A strange sensation, the rapid beating of the man's heart while he stood there, quiet and motionless and scarcely breathing.

"S'y. I'm an old man and I'm dyin. Me heart's flappin like a wee bird. Jus like a wee bluebird."

"Thomas. You're not dying."

"All I ever did was pull up them red ribbons."

"What? What's that?"

"And some green ribbons." Thomas ran on, bending low, bobbing and weaving, moving so quickly that Henry lost sight of him. But he knew the way from here. At the entrance to the cave he looked around carefully before he entered. Thomas was lighting lanterns.

"You pulled out the stakes," Henry said.

"It's no reason for nobody to kill me!" Thomas said, his voice suddenly frantic.

"That's right." Henry sat down in a heavy wooden chair and he was careful, for the wood was coarse and abundant with potential splinters. "But we're not talking about nobody."

"You don have no pack," Thomas said. "You didn brought me nothin." He sat in a chair too. "I need lots a things. How come you didn brought me nothin?"

"I left in a hurry this time, Thomas. On account of somebody's out here to kill you."

Thomas shook his head and pulled his grey beard with both hands. "I sure need lots a things." His voice had a dry and scratchy quality, as if the sound came out through the dense growth of beard and was distorted along the way.

"Hear me now, Thomas. A man's out there who wants to kill you."

The hermit opened his mouth and showed Henry his teeth. He scratched his teeth together. "Comin loose," he said. "I'm loosin me teeth." Thomas stood quickly and rapped the table. "Salamander!" he shouted. "Salamander! Where's that creature be now? Hee! There 'tis." He went to the counter and the squirrel wanted to be picked up. Thomas Duff pressed the squirrel against his chest. "Feel it? Feel me wee heart flappin like a bluebird? Somebody's come to kill me Henry says. Henry says so. Somebody's come to kill me but I don know nobody, nobody at all." Turning to face Henry, the sallow lantern light reflecting on the walls behind him and highlighting the patches of water stains, the cave looking like a dungeon, he shouted in a loud, frightened voice. "I don know nobody!" Henry was up and he touched the hermit's shoulders, but the old man pushed him away. "You should brought me some things! You didn brought me nothin you can go way."

"Look. Thomas."

"Henry Scowcroft can go way," he said, and he was speaking quietly now to the squirrel. "He can go way, Salamander." Thomas put the squirrel down.

"You know some people," Henry said.

"Nobody, nobody," the hermit muttered.

"You know your family," Henry said, and he moved behind the table. Thomas was turning. In the dim light he looked like a ghoul rising from the worst of nightmares. He was making guttural sounds that were not words.

"You know your family, Thomas," Henry said again. He moved behind the chair too. Thomas was still turning and he twisted his body so that he went right past Henry, then he uncoiled back again and stared at him with his one open eye. He jumped forward like a toad and slammed the palm of his hand hard against the tabletop. He crouched low and stared at Henry. "You do," Henry said.

"Nobody! No—bod—y!"

Henry was shaking. He felt his own heart jumping in his chest. He stepped to his left and a nerve in his bad leg twitched, hurt him. The pain caused him to blink. "Thomas," he said, and he stepped to his left again.

"Where you comin? Don you come."

"Wait. Wait, Thomas." Henry took three steps to come from behind the table and be next to Thomas. But the hermit circled too, and they were opposite each other again.

"Nobody. Nobody," the man murmured. "Don know nobody, b'y."

"You know me, Thomas." Henry kept his eyes on Thomas's one open eye, anticipating his movements.

"I know you. That's all. Where you comin, b'y?"

"I want to feel your heart again, Thomas." Henry's steps were minute, small quarter-steps to conceal his motion. Thomas still crouched with his hands gripping the table. The hands of a weathered fisherman, purple bulbs and black knots, life in the forest had not restored them. Fingers like the gnarled roots of a tree.

"I know I'm dyin."

"Yeh. So let me feel your heart again."

Thomas stood up straight. "It's flappin!" he cried.

Henry came to his side. He placed his hand inside the man's shirt on his tough, cold skin. Cold like ice, like the skin of a fish. "I can feel it," Henry said quietly.

"It's flappin!" Thomas repeated, and his grin showed his delight. "I'm dyin!"

"Let me listen." Henry undid the lower buttons and opened the shirt. He placed his ear over Thomas's heart. "I can hear it!" he said. "I can hear it."

"Yas you can!"

Standing back from him, Henry placed his hand on the old man's shoulder. "Why's it flapping, Thomas?"

The hermit sucked in air between his exposed teeth, and exclaimed, "I'm dyin!"

Henry shook his head and looked into the man's one open eye. "No. You're not dying. That's not why your heart is flapping."

"Yas! Tis! I'm dying, b'y."

"Let me listen again." Placing his ear on the man's chest he listened to the rhythm of the heart, listened, and he could hear a voice there murmuring, hear a voice there whispering from the cavern of that heart and chest, hear the pump of a voice long besieged and bound by rumour and hearsay, he could hear a quiet tongue now working. "You've been waiting," Henry said. "And now your wait is over. That's why your heart is flapping. You've been waiting, Thomas. Now it's time."

Thomas whirled. "No!" he screamed. "Nobody!"

Henry grabbed him, first by the arms and then by the beard. "It's Morgan! Morgan's back! Morgan's the man with the gun! He's here to kill you!"

Thomas fought Henry off and he fell on the floor and he squatted there and panted heavily, his breathing filling the cave like some great yawn and stretch of the earth, a tree uprooting itself. "Stay way from me!"

Henry put a hand up. "I'm not going to touch you."

"You better go way," Thomas said. "I know nobody."

"Morgan is out there, Thomas. He's out there."

"He won find me. Nobody can find me here."

"Morgan's not like me. He could find anybody. He could come with big machines and tear this mountain down just looking for you. Come. Stand up. Thomas. Stand up." Slowly, the man stood, straightening his knees cautiously. Henry sat at the table and he laid his cane across the table. "I want to tell you a story."

"Morgan won find me. Why's he want to kill me?"

"I'm going to tell you a story and then you'll tell me a story."

"I don need Morgan here. I don trouble Morgan. I don know him no more."

"Sit down so I can tell you my story." The hermit sat but he continued muttering to himself. "Listen to me now. You know those red and green ribbons? They belong to Morgan."

"No! It was the men wit the spyglass!"

"They work for Morgan. Some people are opening a mine up here and Morgan's helping them. Morgan's going to build roads and a railway. There's going to be roads, a railway, and a mine up here, Thomas." The hermit did not speak but he propped his eyelid open with a finger and he stared at Henry. Henry noted his confusion and alarm and he tapped the knob of his cane on the table. "But I got an idea. You said I didn't bring you anything, but I brought you an idea."

Thomas used both hands to scratch his beard. "Me heart's flappin. I'm dyin anyway soon."

"No, you're not dying. You've been waiting for your father or maybe even Gail to come back for seventeen years, and now it's not either of them but Morgan, but it's the same thing, Thomas, it's the same thing. You want to know why?"

"What?" the hermit said.

"Because Morgan's coming here to kill you, just like you figured your father would one day return to kill you."

"I'm dyin!" Thomas yelled. "It don matter." He suddenly felt happy. "Hee! Morgan's comin here to kill me but I'm already dyin. He's goin find me when I'm already dead!"

Henry slammed his cane hard on the table. The sound echoed in the cave and Thomas came to attention. "Let me tell you my story, Thomas."

Thomas bobbed his head from side to side, said. "Hookay."

"First there's the men with the spyglass and the ribbons," Henry said.

"It's right! Then there's the airplanes."

"Right. But after the airplanes there'll be more men and they'll build houses up here, and they'll bring big machines like you've never seen before, machines bigger than a whaling boat, bigger than one of C. Oliver's old trawlers, giant machines that roar in the night and blow smoke all day. There'll be roads, a railroad, trucks and trains, and they'll tear down the mountain and make a big hole. And Morgan and everybody else'll find you because they'll tear down the mountain and open the cave and make it a big hole and everybody'll find you, Thomas, everybody. And they won't find you dead because your heart's flapping because you're waiting, Thomas, that's right, not because you're dying. Listen to me. I have an idea."

"What's it?"

Henry leaned back in his chair. He had to do it right. Had to penetrate through Thomas's mad, lost mind and make sense to him where sense and reason and understanding too had long been neglected. But he knew the place to go. Knew he had to get to the very point and decision that had caused Thomas to flee to the mountains and huddle here in panic and fear for seventeen years. "Morgan wants to kill you first. He's a big man now, a big-shot, like C. Oliver used to be, that kind of man. So he doesn't want anybody telling anybody why he left Skincuttle Island seventeen years ago. Rupert and Jake and Jackson Two and Whitney aren't talking because they're scared, and they keep silent anyway, see? And Sam and Alf and Bud in Sockeye, they've got their families and all that and they don't want any trouble either. But you. You, Thomas. You've been pulling out the stakes and some people think you've been doing more than just that, and you got nothing to lose, nothing, so Morgan's afraid of you. Afraid to death of you, Thomas! So you got to tell what happened. You got to tell me that story and tell it to my friends too. Tell it to Lyell!"

"No!"

"Thomas! Morgan needs you dead!"

Thomas slammed the side of his fist on the table. He opened his mouth and distorted his face so that his lips were pulled back to reveal his bloody gums. "I don care, b'y! I don! Morgan can go head kill me if he wants! He can go head!"

"You got to tell the story."

"No I don."

Henry stood up, leaned over the table. "You do! You do! If you come back to Lyell with me, Morgan will have to leave Skincuttle Island. Maybe it'll take a long time before they open the mine then. Do you want those machines tearing up your mountain?"

"No I don."

"Well then?"

"I'm not tellin no story, Scowcroft. No story."

Henry sat back in his chair. He spoke quietly. "You got to. And you know why?"

"What?"

Henry hesitated. Thomas was looking away from him, as if by diverting his head he could more easily allow his words to pass right through him. Henry hesitated and he felt it close to him, what he too had been waiting for for seventeen years, what he too had been dragging behind him with all its pain and anguish, the pain itself, the history, revealed. He got up and came around the table and kneeled before Thomas and looked up into his face. Thomas was surprised and he fidgeted.

"What?" Thomas said.

"There's two things. But even those two things are one thing. The one thing is this: you can't let Morgan do it again."

"What you talkin, Henry?"

Thomas was sitting with his hands on his knees, and Henry placed his own hands over them and rubbed the coarse skin. "You can't let Morgan do it again. You can't let Morgan kill Gail again, and you can't let him kill this island either." Henry saw the older man yield, saw something in his one eye and in the shape and tenseness of his skin go slack. "Her memory, Thomas. It's all of her left alive now. I hold it and you hold it. But you're the only one who felt bad enough about her death to come into these woods and give up your life. You're the only one who knew how wrong it was. But Morgan's coming in here to kill you and it's not even you he wants, Thomas. He wants Gail again. He killed her in her body and now he's going to kill her in memory too. That's why he wants you dead, Thomas. Thomas? Don't let him kill her again." Thomas was looking at the top of

Henry's head, then he looked at the floor. He spoke quietly and Henry did not hear. "What?"

"Morgan didn kill her."

Henry nodded. Now it was coming. "What happened exactly?"

"Morgan didn kill her none. Nobody did, cept maybe me. She come to where we's fishin and Morgan calls her to his boat. And she's all dressed up, Henry, that's the crazy thing, she's all dressed up in yellow and red and green and blue. Morgan funned wit her. All we come round and we funned wit her too and she's cryin. Morgan wouldn let her go back in her boat. She's all dressed up because there's goin to be a dance in Sockeye in the night and Ma sent her out to the fishin grounds wit more whiskey so's we could be ready for the dance too. Sometimes Ma sent us whiskey when Pa's not round. So we's drinkin and funnin and Morgan took out his knife and Mitchell and Michael they held her and Morgan cut her clothes off. And all we still jus drinkin and funnin and laughin and Gail she's just cryin and callin out. Morgan, Morgan he got on top of her and he pulled his pants down, and we weren laughin, all we jus watchin and listenin to her screamin. I remember listenin to the seagulls screamin too. They knowed. They knowed. She's the cause of all we troubles, the way Pa treated us since Gail's borned. Then Morgan come up wit his knife flashin and he dared us do it too, but nobody wanted. He dared us and he spit on her and he spit on us and he told us again about all the trouble she's. But nobody wanted. But Morgan's flashin his knife and he made Rupert do it too. Said he's the one always takin her round the town and treatin her like a queen. And Rupert's too stupid. He didn know. He got on top of her and Mitchell and Michael and Morgan helped him do it to her. She's screamin. I remember lookin round and seein the seagulls screamin too. After that Morgan yelled at us and he knelt down and he's goin cut her body like a fish. He's goin cut her body down the middle from her throat like a . . . like a fish."

Thomas's voice faltered. Henry was looking at the floor and listening and holding Thomas's hands, and Thomas was looking up now and the tears came from both his eyes, from the open eye and the closed one too.

"She's screamin so much, Henry. Screamin so much. She s the cause of all we troubles but she's jus a little girl and I said, 'No. Don do it now, Morgan!' He flashes the knife in me face. Morgan said, 'You see what we done? You see what all we done? She better be dead now!' And everybody's scared and everybody sided wit Morgan because nobody wanted Pa knowin. Pa would a killed us sure. But I figured Pa would rather she's still alive than dead, and I didn care if he killed me then or not. She's screamin and she's jus a little girl. I told everybody not have her blood on we hands. I told everybody break her motor and pour water in her motor and throw way the oars and dress her and put out to sea and let the sea kill her. And everybody agreed and that made Morgan agree too. I knowed the currents, Henry. I knowed the sea! I knowed it! I's goin go round by meself and I knowed where the current would brought her out and I'd rescue her and I'd take her back to Pa meself and then I'd run and hide. But I never found her, Henry. I looked for her back and forth on that sea and I never found her, Henry. I looked for her back and forth on that sea—but I found the boat, Henry! All smashed and broken up. And she's gone. I didn tell nobody. I let everybody keep searchin even though I'd already seen the boat all smashed up. I didn tell nobody, and then Pa and Ma and the little ones, all they disappeared too."

Thomas stopped, and Henry held his hands, held his hands and it was as if he could see through Thomas's sight, seeing the pictures looming within the hermit's mind—the young girl, friend Gail, terrorized and murdered on the sea. Now he knew what he had already guessed, and the positive knowing returned his grief for a moment. And he could see her battling the currents, paddling with her hands, not knowing that she thereby eluded her one and only rescuer. Henry said, "You tried to save her, Thomas. You tried to save her."

"No!" Thomas cried. He bounced out of his chair and knocked Henry onto his back. "I didn try! I could a saved her!" Thomas banged around the perimeter of the cave, ranting and striking things. Wooden objects clattered on the floor, and Henry could not see what was falling or being smashed. "I never tried. I could a saved her! I could a took that knife right out his hands—I could a beat up his face.

I could a stopped him before he ever climbed up on her and made her scream. She's jus a little girl, jus a little girl, jus—little . . ." Thomas began to whimper in the darkest corner of the cave. Henry called his name softly. The hermit came rocketing out at him in a fury. "Don tell me I tried savin her, Scowcroft. I didn! I didn!"

"Then save her now!" Henry shouted. Thomas picked up Henry's cane and swung it violently. Henry ducked blows aimed for his skull and shouted, "Don't let Morgan get away with it again! Save Gail this time, Thomas!"

"I could a! I could a!"

"That's right! So save her now! Thomas, Thomas. Save Gail this time. Save—Gail—this—time!" he chanted.

Thomas Duff slammed the cane on the table and dropped it. Henry retrieved it quickly. He squinted in the dim light and his heart was racing. The two men listened to one another's breathing. "Yas!" Thomas cried. "Yas, b'y!"

20

THE TIGER HUNKERED in a pool of its own blood and issued its challenge, crouched low and snarled and its teeth shone like polished red jewels in the sunrise. When it leaped he fell back and his knife came up under the beast's body and plunged deep into its hide and the claw gashed his head and face and the teeth ripped his upper arm and his knife broke in the tiger's jaw and the butt of the blade caught the beast's eye and he jabbed again and again and again and the tiger died and the natives came out of the bush, and they were cheering the tiger-killer.

Morgan waited; hid behind a boulder and waited. He had heard a voice, one voice only and one set of steps. Perhaps one man was a woodsman and concealed his steps. He could not make out the words: perhaps the man was muttering to himself. Morgan unfastened his pack and searched through it with his free hand while he kept his eyes on the trail. Pulled out a canister of cigars and lit one, and he relaxed behind the rock. With a shirt he wiped water from his rifle. He heard the man climbing beside the waterfall and Morgan grinned. Only one man. Who was not talking now but scraping and attacking the rock then muttering again, "Climb, climb—climb! What's the matter? Up now, up!" And Morgan stood behind the boulder and chewed on his cigar and let the barrel of the rifle rest easy over his forearm while his fingers clicked the safety off and tightened on the trigger. The man appeared at the top and brushed his trousers, and Morgan laughed out loud.

"Hey, city-man!" he called. "This ain't no place to clean your pants!"

Doctor Marifield looked sharply into the grin, into the barrel of the rifle, into Morgan's still eyes. "Do you mind pointing that thing somewhere else?"

"What's carried you up to these mountains, Marifield? Looking to stake a claim? Yaha!"

"A little to the left or right, please, or better yet, into the ground."

"Or maybe you're the one pulling up the survey stakes. Eh? Is that you?" Morgan puffed on his cigar and the smoke crossed his face like locomotive steam; the train, Doc thought, the first engine of the first train. Doc took two steps to the side and Morgan jerked his gun. "You're moving," Morgan said.

"That's right," Doc said. "I'm just getting out of the line of that gun. Will you move it, please?"

Morgan grinned and shook his head, and the smoke waved like a signal. "Lawd, Lawd, you don't understand. You ain't moving, Marifield. You ain't moving another step."

Doc looked at the scar, his attention caught by the rain funnelled from Morgan's scalp down the scar to his chin. "What are you talking about?"

Morgan grinned, plucked the cigar from his mouth, and knocked off the ashes. "This ain't the city. This ain't even Lyell. This is mountain country, Marifield, the bush."

Doc shuffled his feet, biding his time, not stepping but not standing still either, not challenging him but not yielding to him either, although his palms felt dry in the rain, and his skin felt as if it had been pulled and stretched. Remembering Morgan from the moment he had landed at Lyell and Henry had nudged him and whispered, "Watch it!"; remembering him too from that first night in Lyell: he had had the brain-wave to mix this newly arrived exile with the Lyell Duff brothers, and Rupert and Whitney and Jake and Jackson Two turned squeamish when confronted by Morgan, bowing their heads while he ridiculed them. And Henry had nudged him again, said, "See?"

"So?" Doc said. "What's that got to do with the gun?"

Morgan laughed, lifting his face into the rain and letting his laughter loose like a mad dog. But with equal suddenness he winced, shut his eyes momentarily to a pain, and levelled the gun at the doctor coldly. "What are you doing here?"

"Nothing," Doc said, and his manner was flippant. Even as he uttered the word he knew it was a mistake, felt the mistake suddenly seize inside him and scream to be repealed, knew that it was wrong to incite him, arouse his anger. Morgan's reply was quick, emphatic: he squeezed the trigger, the rifle exploding and the bullet careening off the rock and striking into the forest, and Doc jumped back.

Morgan puffed on his cigar. "It's got a lot to do with me and you. It means I could bury you here and who's to know?"

"I'm a doctor!" Doc protested. "I'm a government official!" His heart pounded so rapidly now that it was hard to catch a proper breath. And he perspired profusely.

Morgan laughed again, and for the first time lowered his rifle. "Relax, Marifield. I ain't gonna kill you. I ain't gonna kill nobody."

Doc looked into the grin again and feared it this time, and believed he had already suffered a defeat. Beaten, he still did not know how, or what had been lost. He hunted frantically within his mind for Henry's support, for anything he might have said that would help him now. The thought nagged him that Henry had slipped a clue, but he could not find it.

Morgan came out from behind his rock. Came next to Doctor Marifield and put his arm around his shoulders. His breath was rank, like an old man with a stomach disease, and heavy with alcohol. "Only kidding you, Marifield, only kidding you. You want some meat?"

"No thanks." Doc felt Morgan's arm around him as a threat greater than the rifle. Morgan was coaxing him along and he had no choice but to follow. He knew that he was shaking and perspiring and he could not stop it, knew that Morgan saw it too.

"How about a drink?"

"Sure."

Morgan stopped to remove the cap from the canteen, and Doc took a swallow of the whiskey. It felt good, warmed his insides. Morgan drank too and he grinned and flexed a shoulder. He asked, "What're you doing up here?" His manner was casual. "This is comp'ny land now."

"I didn't know that." Doc sought desperately for an excuse, some reason for being here that would pacify Morgan. "I came to see exactly what was company land and what was not. I used to come here a lot. I like the lake. I wanted to see how much territory belonged to the mine."

Morgan turned away from him and stopped. Doc thought he detected the man's body shaking. Remembered the boils—Morgan had displayed them once in the beer parlour to a group of awed farmers. When he turned back he was grinning, but his face was whiter than before.

"This side of the lake is ours. All of it. Now why did you really come up here? And if you don't tell me straight I'm gonna blow your head off." Morgan tucked the muzzle of the rifle under Doc's chin and forced his head up.

"I'm looking for Thomas!" Doc said quickly, and Morgan burst out laughing again, then slapped his back.

"I'm only kidding. I ain't gonna kill you. I ain't gonna kill nobody."

Morgan passed Doc the canteen again and he drank quickly. His knees quaked. Looking around he made a quick study of the land, considered escaping. But found it hard to concentrate, his mind drifting to trivial consequences of his death, his unknown and never to be discovered death, like the young Duff sister—Gail was her name—and recalling her name and disappearance, he had to quell an inner rising panic, for she might have experienced this man's viciousness too. The forest no longer seemed dense to him, no place was suitable for hiding, there was no quick escape by leaping into the foliage or darting suddenly to one side. His only hope was in outwitting Morgan and he believed that that was no hope at all. He told himself that Morgan would not harm him, but he was caught now by his own diminished ability of discernment and knew it, and by the long string of misjudgements that had dogged him through the summer. He was afraid to trust his own perceptions. He regretted squandering his talents on self-pity, for now that his life was on the line he was reduced to fear and frail defences. He passed the canteen back. "What are you doing here, Morgan? Surveying for the mine?" He was hoping Morgan could be induced into idle chatter, but was ignored. Morgan scouted the rim of the rock for tracks; Doc saw the tracks, but they began farther in the woods and Morgan missed them.

Morgan said, "I heard about you before I came. I heard you were a trouble-maker. You're one of the people on my list."

"What list?"

Morgan rotated his shoulder again. "My trouble-maker's list. The surveyors thought you might've done the sabotage."

Doc thought he saw something move in the forest, asked, "What do you think?" and fell behind a quarter-step to peer over Morgan's shoulder.

"I told them no. I told them it wasn't you." Morgan was carefully scrutinizing the forest floor for tracks while he circled the perimeter of the rock. "You know why? Cause I'm a good judge of people. I look somebody in the eye and I know who he is," he snapped his fingers, "just like that!"

"So you say it's not me. It could be me." Doc spotted him. Billy. Billy held up two hands for a second then disappeared into the forest again.

"Nope. You're a city man. You're the kind of man who gets lawyers and injunctions and slows everything down by going to court but loses in the end anyway. Yaha! A loser, that's who you are. What you call a real loser."

"Thanks."

"Nope. I told him it's the other one. Scowcroft. And I still think he's in on it. Doesn't fool me with that cripple business. He's the one who got Thomas in on it. Am I right?"

"I don't know."

"You know."

"Then how come Henry's shack was burned to the ground? Do you think he'd destroy his own house?"

Morgan shrugged, rotated his shoulder like he was working out a stiff muscle, said, "That's got nothing to do with it. Maybe he left a smoke burning."

"Maybe. But Henry doesn't smoke."

Suddenly Morgan wheeled and he gripped Doc's coat. His rifle fell between them and banged on the rock. He gripped him, and Doc was taken back in surprise before seeing the man's face, his eyes, the eyes rolling upward, the flesh turning white, and the teeth clenched hard and biting on the pain; gripped him and as his eyes returned to normal; threw him to the ground, retrieving the rifle and standing over him, the rifle aimed at Doc's head.

"I'm a doctor!" he cried, raising his hand as if that would fend off the bullet, as if the upraised hand would entreat the fingers, if not the mind and the being, not to fire. "I can help you with the boils!"

A tree limb cracked loudly and a rock banged down an escarpment. Morgan spun and fired the bullet meant for Doc into the vacant woods. Doc rolled. Morgan turned and Doc feigned a sighting and hollered, "Go Thomas! Run!" Morgan looked back into the woods and Doc scurried for cover behind him, and he heard and Morgan heard a man fleeing through the forest, the thud of steps, the swish of wet branches and bushes, and while Morgan listened Doc ran too. Hesitating, undecided, Morgan twisted back and forth on the rock drunkenly before he finally gathered his belongings and plunged into the forest in the direction of the main disturbance, and Doc saw him go and crouched low, running for his life.

21

CUTTING UPHILL, Billy kicked stones that struck loudly on the rocks. And by no angle or sense or explanation did it feel right to him. Hurrying across a plateau, he remained heavy on his feet to reveal his flight. He was understanding something and it surprised him that it had taken so long. He hid behind a neat row of ferns on the lower incline of a hill and studied his escape route. Waited. Doctor Marifield did not have control of himself. Billy had believed him to be without experience or proper understanding, but he realized now that it was more than that, that Doctor Marifield was no different than a young cub, exploring, getting into mischief, rolling in a sunny meadow only to sprint after a reflection or movement senselessly, propelled by child-like energy and little more. He was a man, true, and capable in his own way, but he did not contain himself, he was subject to the whirlwinds and storms and calms around him, both visible and unworldly too. It was the only explanation for his falling into Morgan's hands. In a forest whose real size and depth could never be measured, he had walked right into his enemy's grip, and it did not feel right to Billy or fair that now he had to save him, that now he had to draw Morgan away from Doc when it was Doc who had created the situation in the first place, it did not feel right to Billy or fair that he was so involved in the whiteman's world that he lived now as a decoy, using his Indian sense and knowledge, and moreover his self sense and knowledge, to save one white adversary from another. Because it seemed to him that it was not really Doc's fault, he could not be held to blame, and so often he had been confronted with just such a dilemma in the whiteman's world, which itself seemed to move without fault or blame, but senselessly nevertheless. And it was so easy to become entangled in its chaotic mesh.

Billy listened to Morgan pursue him up the hill, then stall, and Billy cracked a branch in his hands and Morgan bounded his way. Billy ran, leaped and caught hold of a tree limb, and swung back and forth several times, gathering height, gathering momentum, swinging and feeling the kick of a new spirit dance through his body. He felt like a boy again, felt that same sense of joy and adventure that caught him years ago when he roamed these woods alone, and he released himself from the branch and flew down the same embankment he had already climbed. He hurried through the woods again. He enjoyed the return of this old, familiar sensation, the inner feeling of boyhood, and he ran with it, retaining it, luxuriating in it as in the company of an intimate companion. Looking up: Morgan. He tossed a rock behind him and Morgan slid and scurried down the hill.

Billy ran again, winding between trees and over fallen logs and through the rain-saturated grassland around a cedar grove. Knocking a stone over a ledge created a minor landslide. Throughout his boyhood he had known sharp doses of hardship and confusion and pain, interspersed with forays into the woods where he turned himself over to a spiralling happiness. It was that sense of fulfilment that he experienced now. That sense of running away, of being alone, of having the entire forest only to himself and to the animals. He had begun to learn about the forest then, and it had become his real home.

He could not see Morgan and he walked with long strides, breathing deeply, believing Morgan was far behind but that the trail of noises and footprints would continue to draw him away from Doc and Henry and Thomas. But it was as if the others were not present or involved, not near by; it was as if he walked alone through this forest and he was not the chief of the Raven clan, not the leader of a people who depended upon his guidance, not the chief and not even a man heavy with experience and therefore dread; it was as if he were truly a boy again, wandering aimlessly, escaping the pain of the larger world, safe here and excited, alone and free.

Morgan ran with solid, powerful strides, flat-footed so that he was not actually running but burrowing through the undergrowth. Saplings and branches and shrubs lay crushed and broken behind him. He panted heavily but never slackened, his legs driving as if they had life and energy of their own. He never paused to review the trail of footprints, relying only on occasional, quick glances at the floor. He read the turn of a bush, the break of a branch, the twist of bracken, and pursued.

Stopping, Billy heard Morgan come crashing close behind. Quickly he scooted up the sharp incline of an escarpment, then ran through the woods. His feet sprang from the spongy duff as if the floor hid a layer of cushions. He had been hunted in the woods before, as a boy, when search parties had been sent out to find him and bring him back. He remembered the time he had run into the woods with Evlin Oliver and they hid in the caves for three days and nights. Her father had landed on Lake TaColl in a seaplane, and it had not seemed right to Billy or fair that he could employ such tactics, but Billy had eluded him anyway, and they returned to Sockeye only when Evlin became worried and scared. It was great fun, escaping from those who would return him to the civilized world, and Billy delighted in it still.

In an instant Morgan had noticed the absence of prints, and he climbed the rock face. With his rifle slung over his shoulders, he scaled the slope on all fours and picked up the trail again at the top.

Billy tried to outrun him with pure speed, sprinting through a relatively open section, dodging branches. Leaping logs, leaping streams, scurrying up a rock face again. But he realized that he was heavier than he used to be and probably less agile too; he was not as accustomed to running as when he was a boy, and when he paused to catch his breath he heard Morgan charging through the undergrowth, still close behind.

Morgan breathed in great gasps that sounded like a steam locomotive gathering power and speed, but his shortness of breath was independent of his legs and will, his legs churning like pistons and each step accelerated his rage, and it was his rage that drove him forward. On rocky ground he lost the trail, and he had to search the perimeter of the plateau to find it again.

Billy Peel slid down from a tree, feeling like a mischievous child again, outwitting his elders. While Morgan hunted at one end of the plateau, he left the way he had come, backing off the rock, stepping in his own footprints to conceal his escape. Darting through the woods, he headed down again. He ran low and hard for three minutes, then lay in the shelter of immense and thick bracken and caught his breath. He breathed heavily and lay on his stomach. Felt the ache of his lungs for air. What had bothered him and hurt him, after he and Evlin had returned to Sockeye from their adventure, was that Evlin was immediately banished to the mainland for the rest of the summer, and then, of course, for the school year. So it was ten months before he saw her again, and by then they had both changed. It seemed cruel punishment to Billy, cruel for Evlin and for him too; he had to live with the blame for her chastisement on his mind. It was his first real skirmish with the whiteman's world, and its cunning and meanness baffled and subdued him.

Billy lay under the ferns and let the water drip on his face. He felt a kind of sadness surround him like a docile but malicious ghost, but in a moment he heard Morgan again, stampeding down the slope after him, and Billy was up quickly and running.

And he wondered about this man, felt by his tenacity and will his need to see Thomas Duff destroyed, the forest destroyed, felt the power of his urge to triumph here, as if all his success elsewhere meant nothing to him unless he succeeded here too, unless he overcame the people who had caused him to turn and flee, unless he could obliterate all sign or portent or trace of vulnerability. Billy chose to test Morgan over a more difficult course, gritting his teeth now, and his forehead was lined with seriousness and tension.

He headed for an area of treacherous mountain country. Ran along the side of a steep incline, slipping on the soft mud occasionally, supporting himself by grabbing branches and shrubbery. The mud stuck to his boots and he plodded along like a weary, bored cow. Whites had not been his only hunters. Indians too. He had grown up amidst political turmoil, and some would have had him follow Arthur Rand, whose title of Raven Chief he would inherit, who was powerful and dynamic, but also a criminal; and others wished him to follow his father, Simeon Peel, who was a weak and unimaginative leader, but a simple and good man. Billy would flee from this turmoil into his beloved forest, until the Indians would chase after him and bring him back. It had been at such a time that the idea had first stirred to one day separate and establish a new and isolated village. An idea that had severed his relationship with Evlin, who married the Eagle chief instead, Arthur Rand's son Gerald. He ran downhill suddenly and scraped the mud off, then he jogged through the woods again.

And Morgan followed, although travelling on the hillside slowed him down. Once his backpack caught in a treelimb. He slung his rifle over his shoulders again to allow him the use of his hands. He carried a small stick to scrape the mud from his boots as it built up, then he found a long and sturdy branch he used as a staff to prevent himself from sliding.

Billy recognized the area and knew where to go. He could already hear the waterfall. He increased his pace and followed the curve of the mountain. He had come here one time in the winter, keeping himself warm with alcohol and fires, and was assaulted by evil spirits and wicked visions. After a quarter of a mile the forest became extremely dense, he could never see more than a few feet ahead, the way blocked by the high ferns and by the rotting, moss-covered firs that lay toppled at various angles without space to fall and die in comfort. When Billy had left the forest that time, he had continued on through Lyell and left Skincuttle Island too, mainland bound. The island seemed too terrible and heart-breaking a place to live.

Here the forest floor was covered by inches of water and gave way underfoot like sponge. He came to a broad and overflowing pool, and the wall of the mountain rose steeply, almost straight up, hundreds of feet, cut and revealed by a thunderous waterfall that boiled in the pool below. Billy dove into the pool and the water was ice-cold, and he swam to the opposite bank and the spray from the waterfall stung his neck and face. He entered the forest, shivering, and started to climb.

The trees grew tenaciously to the side of the mountain, and he used the trees that curved out and then up to give him a foothold or a handhold, and to conceal him from the forest below. He mounted steadily. Sometimes he climbed perpendicular rock. His breathing was sharp and heavy, for he had to extend himself to gain even short distances. He heard nothing behind him, all sound obliterated by the drone of the water.

Once the most accessible route took him immediately next to the falls. The large, flat stones made convenient steps, but they were extremely slippery and precarious; looking down, the trees of the lower forest were watching him like enchanted and tense spectators, and the pool below waited like a net, like the fireman's net he had once seen in the city. Commotion had emptied the beer parlour and Billy had joined the flow onto the sidewalk. Firetrucks wailed and jerked to a stop, and as the flames licked the building across the street, the crowd watched transfixed as a solitary man climbed onto an upper window ledge and stared down. "Fly, fly!" Billy had called, and he had been serious, although his companions laughed. And soon the man did fly, leap out from the building and curl his body with his arms and legs spread out. And Billy had thought, "No, not like that," as the man plummeted to the pavement, because he had not seen the net. Later he had returned to his drinking inside.

Billy climbed, and he worked his way up through the wooded area where he could not be seen. He rested momentarily in the crook of a trunk, his legs dangling under him over a drop of a hundred feet, then dug his fingers into the rock and continued up. Straining his muscles, perspiring freely; whenever he paused the rain felt cool and gentle on his head and neck. There was a moment when he felt he had become a part of the rock itself, stolid and patient, receiving the rain, relinquishing itself to the water and wind and ages. He no longer felt young but sensed the loss of his boyhood, even youth, and facing the cracked and split and yielding rock was vaguely like seeing his reflection suddenly in water and viewing an altered but recognizable image of himself.

Making it to the top, an open meadow awaited him, and at the next thrust of the mountain the river continued into the mountain and forest and down the length of a deep gorge. Billy marched upstream, fighting the current, then cut across to the forest and ran through to the next stair. Here the rim of the upper rock hovered over him, sloping outward from its base, an impossible climb without equipment. But Billy already knew the way up. He had come this way when he had returned to Skincuttle Island from his self-imposed exile, returning from the bars of Vancouver and from the Indian reserves of interior British Columbia and Alberta too, returning with a heaviness of heart but with a newly-found commitment to his land and his people; and he had climbed to the tip of TaColl Mountain, the highest point on the island, seeking the cooperation and blessings of his forefathers and a renewal of spirit. He learned that sadness would always be a near companion, and that there could be no freedom without struggle but something else too, that there could be no struggle without freedom. He had come down from the mountain believing that only the free man can fight, and when the time was right he founded the village of Kloo.

He scaled a fir tree, ascending straight up where there were no branches, gripping the trunk with his arms and knees, entering into the branches and winding his way through the maze until he came to a strong and long-reaching limb. Hand over hand he worked his way out over the upper rock then dropped onto it. He paused briefly for breath and to feel the rain wash over his face and chest, soothing him, before he jogged into the forest and found adequate cover under a cedar tree and he rested there.

For Billy, the time and the action itself had to be just right. It was as if his people were on a revolving wheel and at only one point could they disembark. The timing had to be precise and the move well-executed. He did not act until he was ready, after Arthur Rand's death and he had become chief. Then he roused other young men, and they sallied against Prince Rupert hotels and retrieved their women from the beds of whitemen, and the wheel, if not broken, slowed momentarily. Suddenly men and women were respecting one another and things could get done, a new village could be built. People had spirit to fight, and fighting back against those things that had shackled them, that had caused them to shackle themselves to an endless, circling rhythm, gave them spirit. And as others saw his success they had courage to jump from the wheel too and joined the band at Kloo. Billy had the village he wanted for his people, but as isolated as it was he never felt safe or secure or even protected there. He anticipated and feared the decay and collapse of the rest of the island and the planet too, and he doubted that Kloo had immunity.

Billy's rest lasted about fifteen minutes when he heard it again, near by, the beast crashing through the forest again, after him again, crushing all in its path, oblivious to obstacles and deterrents, raging and brutal; and Billy fled, feeling the beat of a drum, feeling the chants of the Kloo Ravens in his bones and his blood, feeling the life of his Indian nation on the run, and feeling, too, the breath and hands of his pursuer, no longer believing him to be a man or even an animal having human characteristics, but a beast, one from the outer rim of darkness, transmogrified and substantiated here by some quirk of the forces of destruction and death. Death, not decay: ultimate and absolute end, the doors sealed, the other world of spirits and ancestors guarded and concealed by the deepest and greatest of nights. He ran and he crossed the ravine, stepping lightly across a fir tree that he had helped place here himself years ago, running quickly, paying no heed to balance or to the slippery bark or to the depth of the fall, and when he crossed he dove into the bushes and waited there.

Waited and breathed heavily. His heart beating as he gasped for air. He wanted to fly to the highest of the guardian peaks surrounding Lake TaColl, to beg sanctuary of the rock and of the approaching night too. But he believed he would be shot down out of the sky.

The forest was quiet. Not a sign of Morgan. Water churned through the ravine below Billy. Billy scanned the forest and listened deep inside himself, but nothing was revealed. And Billy understood. Morgan was on the opposite side waiting for him, fearing that if he ventured onto the log, his prey might have some means of dumping it into the gorge below. Billy had an idea. He crouched very low and slowly made his way along the edge of the ravine, hidden by the trees and vegetation, setting his trap. He waited. He cracked a branch underfoot and kicked a loose stone over the side, letting Morgan know that he was well past the log. Morgan emerged at the crossing, rising up out of the forest as if being squeezed from a tube that was centred in the belly of the earth, and he straddled the log. He crossed, pulling himself along, his massive shoulders working laboriously, like the heavy muscles of a plough-horse.

Billy cut a wide circle. A traceable path. Ran easily and quietly, his mind elaborating on a picture of Morgan's movements. Timing was important. Proper execution essential. Carefully, Billy worked his way back toward the crossing. Crept through a small, bubbling stream that ran down the centre of a hollow, and the three-foot dip in the land concealed his crouched back and bobbing head. Billy paused, breathed, listened. Visualized Morgan at the opposite side of the circle by now. He made it back to the crossing. The tree was gone. Morgan had already sent it reeling into the ravine. Billy's plan to recross then roll the tree had been thwarted, and now he was in danger. Morgan was close.

Billy crawled and flew and scratched and tumbled and leaped his way down the side of the ravine. Cut and bruised by wayward branches and stones. Rocks continued to fall behind him. Reaching the edge of the mountain stair, he leaped, catching hold of a limb. Worked his way down the tree to the lower level. Recrossed the river, the water cold and turbulent. From here he could see in two directions: Lake TaColl in the distance, and he longed for its reverent peace and security, and to his right the stately peak of this mountain, overseeing all, contemplating all, impassive and inert, but intelligent too. Once he had looked across at this peak from a high mountain closer to Kloo, envied its eternal perseverance. The children of Kloo had been sick then and three had died. And Billy saw himself now through the mountain's eyes, saw his flight and the generations of flight: a plaintive, cawing bird, ascending and descending the forest and mountains, searching for a scrap of food and a home.

Billy ran for the caves. Reminded again of boyhood, of hiding out in the caves and avoiding the various searchers. But the memories were not accompanied this time by the feelings of those days or by the experience of them. Arose only as distantly viewed pictures. He located a trail, a deer path, and travelled quickly. Remembered one cave in particular—if he was not too big he could squeeze through it and come out the other side of a jut of the mountain. Morgan behind him. Billy lost time darting in and out of several caves and hurried down a stream to put more distance between himself and Morgan. Finally, he found the cave he sought. A wide opening. In its ceiling was a narrow tunnel that burrowed through about a hundred feet of rock. Water ran freely through it. Hoisting himself up, Billy crawled on his stomach. Twisted and worked his way up, water splashing in his face and running down his shirt. Near the top the tunnel narrowed. He had to suck in his stomach and squeeze his shoulders through. For a moment he feared he was stuck, but strangely the feeling was a familiar one, and he pressed on and worked his way out. Running through the forest again he was confident that he had escaped, but his sense of safety was subdued, there was no gladness or relief in it, he was filled instead by a sense of violation, of himself and of the forest and of his people, and he felt returned to himself, expelled from his boyhood and, moreover, boyhood concerns.

Morgan looked up the narrow tube. Removed his backpack, coat, and shirt. Left behind his knife to keep his waist trim. Sucking in his breath, he climbed up. No trouble at first. Where it narrowed he had to squirm and battle for every inch. He used his rifle in front of himself to chip away at protruding bits of rock. His body plugged the hole so that the water built up in front of him. Afraid of drowning, he fought desperately. The rock pressed his flesh and boils and the pain caused him to cry out once. The water kept his body slick and he squeezed through. All over his stomach and back, skin had been scraped away. Morgan spotted an Indian running across a tiny clearing. For the first time he sighted his prey and saw that it was not Thomas. His rage was renewed, burning now against this impostor. He slipped into the forest, employing a different tactic, moving quietly and only at moderate speed, plotting now to take this man by surprise.

22

HENRY'S STEPS WERE STEADY but sluggish, and he pushed himself forward through a sleepiness that was punctuated frequently by assorted pains. Around him, Thomas jumped and danced like an animated scarecrow released from bondage for a day, animated by an energy born of madness, engendered by the staid eyes waiting transfixed over a lost and diminished horizon, soldered to one point and vision in time, and in memory and hope too, then suddenly released, for a moment. Thomas leaped around him in circles, crouching now, standing tall next, scratching his beard, patting his heart, toppling over a rotten log—a ballet dancer entertaining the trees and the animals of the forest. Entertaining also this one and only human friend of the past many years, this one and only being who arrived at haphazard moments with his gifts of cheese and lanterns, oil and soap, bacon and shirts, who arrived encumbered and exhausted under the weight of the gifts, grinning though, like an escaped fool himself, grinning with the satisfaction of having made it alive and whole, and grinning with surprise too, laying out his gifts and admiring them with him, requiring his reaction for reward and payment or disappointment. Thomas danced, a court jester, in among the trees, before and behind his friend, entertaining him, he hoped, and moreover himself too, preparing himself for this return visit to the company of humans, where he knew he would solidify again and become like petrified wood, scared and condemned and annihilated again by the movements and whispers of men revolving around him like the dance he did now.

Henry stopped and used a twig to scrape mud off his boots. He breathed heavily and shook the rain from his face, like a man becoming annoyed and discouraged by it beyond the limits of his self-control, annoyed and discouraged not by two days of constant rain, but by a lifetime; his mind suddenly apprehended by the notion that there were climates on the planet where the sun was revealed more than it was camouflaged, where the skin could warm in the open air rather than crave a covering, where water flowed only in convenient and obedient streams and pools and did not tumble from the skies amidst rumbles and roars and gathering blackness and doom; annoyed and discouraged and wondering if there was not another place for him to live and stir and breathe. But almost as quickly as it came, Henry relinquished the thought. Without the sweet-and-pungent-smelling mud sucking under his boots he would not be reminded of such necessities as purpose and destination, for he could never keep track of where he was going unless he concentrated on exactly where he was coming from, and the mud told him that.

"We'll never find them," Henry said. He readjusted his backpack over his shoulders. He had retrieved it from the cave where he had left Billy and Doc, and he and Thomas had waited there, puzzled by their disappearance and alarmed by their failure to return. They had heard the shots earlier, and Henry decided to prowl the forest in case there had been a victim. "It's no use. They could be anywhere." He did not want to think that they could be dead.

"I know a place," Thomas said. He squatted on the ground before Henry and hopped like a toad.

"Yeh? What kind of place?"

"For lookin. I can see and I listen to the birds. If me eyes don see somethin, the wee birds tell me bout."

"Let's go there then. But we'll get back to the other cave by nightfall, so they can find us, at least."

"Hookay!"

Henry had to move quickly to keep pace with Thomas. The older man moved through the forest like a wisp, like a being so attuned to the density and shapes and nuances of the material that he was like a fish in a familiar pond, the water not a constriction at all but the very fluid in which it breathed and travelled. Likewise the woods and Thomas: he never seemed delayed or perplexed or even hindered by the trees and bracken and debris, passing through it like the air. Henry heaved and struggled and gasped for an extra breath, and when he pleaded for a rest he dwelt on this curiosity, the transformation of Thomas Duff from a fisherman to a woodsman. He probed him about it.

Thomas laughed. "Always I like the woods. Because I played in the woods, but the sea's always work, work, work. I wanted to trap or fall trees when I's young. Pa wouldn let me, no. He fought me and give me a real lickin! 'We's goin be a fishin family!' he said. Maybe he didn yet knowed he's goin have so many sons. Maybe if he knowed it then I could a gone into the woods early. I liked the sea but I liked the woods the same."

His hands were gnarled, his eyelid slouched like the bulging muscle of a tree limb where it meets the trunk, or like a clump of fungus, his beard and hair as wild and as untamed as the vegetation. He had taken something of the sea into the woods with him, for he was not stiff and slow like the great trees, neither straight nor bent nor solid. Henry surmised that Thomas was not so much the character he appeared to be, not so much the old and frightened and to his own mind dying man, but a being partly invisible, that part concealed and intangible so that it moved through the muck and sluggishness of matter like air, like wind; for that was what he had come to find and retrieve, not the guilt-ridden heart so much as the true story; not the incumbent fear and turmoil stuffed into an aging body but the liberating and illuminating cognition; not the mannequin madness at all but the eye, the sight, the vision; not the man at all but the voice. "Okay, let's climb. But not too fast for me, Thomas."

"You be thinkin," Thomas said.

Henry laughed. "Yeh. That's right."

High above the forest and above the ethereal epicentre of Lake TaColl, Henry and Thomas waited, and crouched behind the rocks

Thomas gave evidence of his talents. He told Henry to keep watch to the south. At least two men were in the south.

"How do you know?"

"It's birds. The wee bluebirds tell me that."

Henry could not hear them but he did not question Thomas either. Accepted it, having previously witnessed his abilities. It was Thomas who had originally located Henry, after Henry had come to the mountains with a supply of soap. The soap was not his idea, any more than the trip had been his idea. He had been intimidated into the excursion and into the offering by Thomas's half-brothers at Lyell. Jake, Whitney, Jackson Two, and Rupert. He was young at the time, seventeen years old, orphaned and earning a living selling bootleg whiskey. He woke up one morning and stepped out of his shack into the bright sunshine. Suddenly the four Duff brothers leaped from the ground and scattered into the woods. That same week he passed them in town, and the moment he was by them their steps ceased. He glanced quickly back and they were staring at him, and not even at him but somehow through him, scaring him. He felt transparent and formless. At night he would catch them peering through his window while he read by candlelight, and finally, while the rain beat violently, while the wind wailed in the woods and howled under the floorboards of his shack like a lost and forlorn dog, the shack rocking precariously on its stilts, the shutters banging and branches thrashing and lamenting like wailers overcome by the grief and misery he himself expounded, while the darkness and night convulsed inward in a great and triumphant pain, there was an additional sound, a banging he could no longer appreciate as being storm-created. His front porch was besieged by a pile of rocks, and another missile already pierced the night air and rain—*crack!*—and nicked his ankle. Henry went after them then. Hobbling like a tormented old man and a madman at that, he chased them all the way to their home. A square, trim house with a pointed roof situated near the sawmill. He marched down the boardwalk, rapping his newly acquired cane on the planks with particular relish, gained the doorway and pounded. When nobody answered he tried the latch, it gave way and he entered. The brothers were seated on both sides of their long, narrow pine table. Henry sat at the head of it and waited. He quickly realized the reason for the activities, it had been their way of summoning him here. He waited. He sat with his hands clasped on the table and the four Duff brothers sat impressively straight, concentrating on a central point between them. He could feel the blood pumping in his temples and brain; his hands perspired and desultory pains awoke in various parts of his body, lingered, and made him fidget. He waited four hours for them to speak, waited and felt harnessed to his chair, waited for the unknown, waited for a voice from the abyss of the house, which was not a home but a memory so intense it had taken physical form and presence and shape. They had built the house themselves, engineered it by their own system of thought, which Henry believed might be no more than a sensory system of feeling and thought, akin to that developed in the plant kingdom perhaps, so that the walls of the house were not simply divisions between rooms for the sake of privacy or order, but were reinforcements of the code, silence, grief; and the roof was not insulation against the elements, but a shelter against the movement and presence of the present itself. He waited four hours, and his knuckles went white from squeezing the armchair and his chest burned as if it had been branded, and he wondered if somehow they were communicating between themselves and perhaps with him, he wondered if this eerie sensation that vibrated in the room and in his body was not a forlorn, unearthly intelligence, rising as a laborious radio signal passing through static, which did not communicate with the mind but with the guts; waited, and after four hours the word and one word only began to come. Jackson Two's lips moved. Henry perspired heavily and squirmed in his seat. The lips puckered. The jaw slackened and even opened once. Jackson Two looked at Henry and he knew it was coming. "S-s-s-s," Jackson Two said. Henry thought that that was it. He was halfway up in his chair when Whitney shot out a hand and clasped it tightly over his, shot out the hand but he did not move or blink otherwise. "Ss-ss-ss," Jackson Two said again. Henry could see that he was stuck on the letter "s", that maybe the four hours had been in commemoration of the letter "s" and its sound.

"Sssss-so," Jackson Two said. In ten minutes he tried again and this time he got it out. "Ssss—so—soap." Henry said, "Soap?" The answer was returned so quickly that it was probably coming anyway: "Soap." Henry brought the Duff brothers soap, although he did not understand why they refused to fetch it themselves, and it took a second and similar meeting for him to learn that they meant it for Thomas, and he was to be their emissary. Henry spent five weeks scrounging around Lake TaColl in search of the hermit, until his mind and sense seemed deranged, out of whack, and he was desperate. He was oppressed by the belief that if he left the soap the Duff brothers would know it, and if he failed his mission he would be subjected to their tyranny. Finally, he sat under a pine tree and spoke in a conversational tone. "Thomas Duff, it's up to you to find me. I give up." And within the hour Thomas tapped him on the shoulder, accepted his gift of a year's supply of homemade soap, and brought him to his cave to rest for the night.

Thomas said, "Look now." Henry looked quickly. In the distance a figure passed over the crest of a mound of bare rock. The forest was sparse there, probably burned out years earlier. The rain obscured his vision, but the black head could only be Billy Peel. He was not moving quickly or with concern, and his direction indicated he might be returning to their cave.

"Okay," Henry said. "Let's go."

"Wait," Thomas said.

Henry looked again. Waited. Felt himself join with the small space he observed, felt beings rise up out of it only to disappear when he blinked. Then a second man appeared. Bare-chested, blond hair. It was obvious that he was tracking Billy. Moving slowly, stepping carefully, discreetly, creeping forward like a man stalking an unwary prey.

"Stay here!" Henry commanded.

"Hookay!"

"Stay here and I'll warn Billy. I'll come get you later."

"Hookay!"

Henry dropped his pack and hurried into the forest. He worked hard to gather momentum and thrust, a nerve pain thwarting him again, knifing upward from his thigh through his hip to his rib cage, but he pushed on and accomplished a movement that was a cross between a run and a hop, a three-legged jog that carried him quickly along one of Thomas's trails. He estimated that Billy's casual walk would be enough to keep his distance from Morgan, who was probably staying back to remain hidden, but Billy could not afford to stop, and Morgan's rifle could bring any distance close. Henry crawled over a ridge and climbed down, then trotted through a hollow and over a roll in the earth's surface. He sighted a figure again, and the moment he took to identify it was too long—he was sighted and identified first—and the shot cracked from the rifle and he heard the bullet sing in the bark of a tree behind him, and he ran. Thinking, *Well that warns Billy, but now who the hell is going to warn me?*

Henry ran hard, ignoring all pains now, leading Morgan away from Thomas and into the thickest depth of the forest. In one area he was able to gain a hundred feet without touching the ground, jumping from side to side over fallen logs and an accumulation of branches, and when he ascended an escarpment he rested and waited. He could not understand why Morgan had not caught him yet. He listened and surmised that Billy had remained Morgan's principal target. Henry returned to where he had left Thomas.

The hermit was not there. Henry's pack remained but Thomas was gone. He traced the footprints and followed them into the forest. He lost the tracks but by continuing straight ahead he picked them up again. About a half-mile through the forest he came upon a clearing and the tracks were joined there by a second set. The two men had held a discussion, for their footprints revolved around each other in narrowing concentric circles. Henry knelt and examined them and stared into the woods where they departed together. Their direction was towards Lyell.

"Okay, Doc," Henry said aloud, "he's all yours."

23

BILLY PEEL REMOVED HIS JACKET AND SHIRT and laid them out behind him. The clothes were soaked through and smeared with mud, but he laid them out on the forest floor in the rain as if they were sacred vestments, folding the sleeves over the chest carefully and pressing the creases. His heart beat rapidly and the ceremony helped him to be calm, to keep courage.

Using his knife, Billy carved a circle in the dirt surrounding him and added the east-west equator. He squatted, facing the east, and prayed. The rain was cool and gentle on his skin. He turned and prayed to the west. For a moment, his prayer took him out of the forest and he floated above the clouds, and he witnessed the march-past of an army of centurions, men who were not Indians nor whites either, but he recognized them as warriors, recognized that each man had known his moment of reckoning, his moment when he had had to place his courage in advance of his fear, and Billy turned his head and saw his death, waiting, and he was in the forest again and a hollowness had carved a huge gap in his stomach.

The grandfathers were gathering in his circle and they gave him strength. They rose from the horizons and travelled to his side, like puffs of mist carried on the wind. They whispered as the breeze whispered among the branches, and they chanted as the rain chanted among the leaves. Their voices reverberated on the taut skin of his hollow stomach like taps on a drum.

Billy applied mud and damp earth to his wet skin, blackening it, and he rubbed his face with the roots of a fern. He placed pine needles across his shoulders and scratched his scalp with bark. He was calling out within himself and he could feel the energy rising. He breathed deeply, filling his lungs, and with each breath his anger rose, flooding him so that his blood and nerves and muscles tensed for the fight, and his mind conjured images of the most fierce and outrageous demons. Thoughts of a warm fire, of a friend, annoyed him, and he attacked these memories with vehemence, as if they were his greatest enemies, and his inner viciousness grew.

He made audible sounds, a low murmur like a snarl, and he could hear Morgan coming. Morgan would pass below him. Billy bowed once to each of the four directions, then kissed the centre of his circle. He did not remove the mud from his lips but wore the earth's kiss as his armour. Carefully, he laid his jacket and shirt in the circle, and it was his life as a man that he was laying down, protected by the grandfathers with their blessing until he returned to it from his animal being, and Billy stood and climbed to the top of the rock.

He crouched and he thought he could smell him, or was it something else, perhaps the ages, perhaps the eons of time surfacing for this struggle, choosing sides, or the grandfathers, gathering and smoking within their circle? Or perhaps it was his own body he smelled, transforming itself into a creature of war. Billy moved back within himself, retreated to a remote station within his mind, couched by membrane and darkness, having only a narrow opening for sight and breath and sound; he could feel his talons grow and his muscles tone and his senses accelerate with instinct and wantonness.

Billy panted and he could hear the steps of his predator, hear his breath like a machine chugging and blasting smoke into the skies, hear the forest sag and yield under his approach. Billy crouched and felt the trees next to him and behind him crouch too, felt the rocks arm themselves and even the overhead clouds steel themselves for the conflict; he crouched and he saw him, the bare chest slick with rain, the head glancing from side to side, expecting him, expecting this, the hands gripping the gun in front of him firmly and with authority, and Billy watched, terrified, as his own body crept an inch forward, as Morgan passed below him, and as he leaped, flew through the air like a silent swooping bird, feeling the rush of air over his wings and torso, and at the last moment he cried out, and it was his own cry, his own voice from deep within himself that pierced the air and forest and rain—"Ai-Yiiiii!"—and Morgan looked up just as this black being slammed onto his shoulders and drove him to the ground.

Suddenly Billy was propelled back into himself as Morgan spun him in rapid circles while he clung to the rifle with one hand; suddenly the animal spirit deserted him and he was on his own, fear and terror seizing him by the throat and guts and it was the loss of this power that scared him, and the thought screamed at him that the grandfathers had fled too. When Morgan slammed him onto the ground he dodged the rifle butt once but the barrel caught his scalp and a white light flashed across his brain and Billy moved by instinct, scrambling around behind Morgan and hugging him, clutching his hands then twisting his wrists into the sores that he had already seen. Morgan cried out, smacked the butt of the rifle against Billy's hands, but the Indian would not let go, ran backwards into the rockface but the Indian stayed on his back, would not let go, and he was fainting from the pain; and Billy worked and kneaded his wrists into the boils and felt Morgan's body convulse and quiver with the pain, grunted and panted and was ashamed of the sounds escaping him for they revealed his fright, but it was Morgan who was the first to plead, yelling, "Let go! Damn it!" and Billy cried, "There! Over there!" Morgan wrestled further, but he cried out and relented and Billy ordered, "Over there!" and Morgan accepted the pact and tossed the rifle to the opposite side of the rock. Billy turned Morgan away from the rifle, then ran for it with Morgan behind him. He fell in front of the rifle and rolled and coming to his feet he flung the weapon as far as he could over the cliff and into the forest, then he spun again to avoid Morgan's lunge.

Billy flashed his knife and wiped a hand across his face. He cried out within himself for his power to be restored, for the spirit of the animal to fight this battle. But Morgan lunged for him and Billy leaped quickly beyond his reach, flashed his knife, and the two men circled one another. Billy concentrated on Morgan's eyes, Morgan on the knife. Morgan issued his challenge like a tiger, taunting, actually snarling from the side of his mouth, but Billy's animal spirit was gone, and he responded with deep, short breaths. They circled. Billy moved slowly when his back was to the edge of the cliff, safe from Morgan's charge, Morgan afraid of being eluded and propelled over the edge himself. Against the wall of the mountain where his manoeuvrability was hindered, Billy moved quickly. They circled, learning the terrain of this battleground, hunting for a weakness in the other's defences. Suddenly Morgan stooped to the ground then attacked with rocks, throwing them hard, and as Billy ducked to avoid one, Morgan's knee came up into his teeth, and a blow to the side of the head sent him reeling. Morgan was on top of him and Billy was desperate for breath, feeling bound and about to suffocate. His knife slid into Morgan's flesh, entered the stomach smoothly and neatly, and Morgan rolled away and looked at the wound in dismay and back at Billy.

Billy propped himself up and stared back at Morgan. He looked at his knife and the blood was dripping into a puddle of rainwater. Billy jumped up and he flung the knife as far as he could into the woods, responding to an instinct he trusted, responding to his need for survival. And Morgan was upon him immediately, pummelling his face and body, and Billy rolled near the edge of the cliff and curled his body to protect his face and groin. Each blow jarred his body so that he wanted to fuse with the rock, to become inanimate and senseless, and the fingers of one hand clawed the rock for support. With each blow Billy fought the temptation to roll on over the edge of the cliff and end the beating, but he held on, to the rock and to himself too, choreographing his own descent into unconsciousness, and the moment that Morgan paused, the instant he stopped and attended to his own wound, Billy caught him under the knees and spilled him over the side.

He could hear him tumbling on the rocks forty feet below. Billy moved away from the edge and lay on his stomach so that the blood would drain from his mouth. The pain was mounting now as the adrenalin subsided. He could not speak, and his thoughts were incoherent, and he beckoned to the grandfathers with a hand, beseeching them to draw near.

24

Dusk had descended when Henry opened his eyes, but not descended, he thought, risen, oozing from the depths of the earth and seeping upward, like smoke, shadowy ghosts dancing and drifting and ultimately coming together, risen, overcoming the undergrowth first and the small animals there, the slugs and moles and worms, then darkening the forest below the branches, distorting and disintegrating shapes and forms, soon to overcome the sky and ascend higher, higher, reuniting at last with the body of night in its still but fertile sleep. Henry opened his eyes and he remained alone. Billy had not yet returned, and there was little time before the darkness would be total.

Sticking his head out from the cave, Billy's cave, birds chirped to the setting sun, crows cawed, a wind swayed the trees and set the clouds in motion, but nowhere could Billy be seen or heard. Henry had confidence in Billy's abilities in the forest, he did not believe that Morgan could catch him, yet—yet Billy had not returned and this was the more cutting reality. One last hope offered itself for companionship, that Billy was still involved in eluding Morgan and so would not return to this cave before nightfall.

Henry waited. Sat up and ate and gazed out over the valley and lake. Suddenly the day turned very quiet, a strange and poignant silence that was like the presence of the air itself, moving wave on wave, inhaling, exhaling, breeding and suffering life, coming to the forefront: the rain had ceased abruptly and all was still, water running but within the bounds of this newly-created quiet, as if to define it and give it dimension. The rain had ceased and the clouds were being chased off the mountains. Henry sat at the edge of the cave for a better view. He shivered, felt his bones knocking together, felt the cold and dampness that enslaved his body as a bag wrapped around him. He sneezed, coughed, shivered, and wiped his nose on his shirt. Memories of warm fires and thick blankets at night tempted him. A horse neighed and he thought he was at home. With horses grazing on the edge of the woods or calling out in the night from the distant farms. Henry's eyes were closed and his mind drifted with his reverie. The bark of dogs. Some drunk complaining while being ousted from Rogg House. Overhead, over his roof and above the trees, bands of roving clouds interspersed with signalling stars. In such a dreamy condition there was no deterioration or decay, only a spontaneous and exquisite celebration of romance and gaiety. The horse neighed again. Henry woke up. It was too real. Not close but real, definite, actual. On his knees he looked out over the sky and water, as if this horse would have wings or was mounted on the prow of a ship, and he saw nothing but he continued to listen, the forest reverberating loudly now, the dripping of water like a cascade he desperately wanted to shut off. And after a moment he heard it again, a high bray that floated across the water and circulated among the trees, sailing on the currents of the coming darkness: a horse neighing to the approach of night.

The whinny of the horse came to him like the signal of an approaching being, a forefather perhaps, as if it came from the opposite side of this life, from the opposite side of twilight perhaps, where worlds meet, where the nether world greets the physical, and the grandfathers talk to their lost children; a bugle call, announcing the hour of sleep to the troops and summoning the ethereal beings to rise. Billy rose, pushed himself up to his hands and knees, felt the night surrounding him move and send shivers up his spine, and he listened for the horse again. The quiet was long and enduring and Billy wondered about the vanished sound, now like a whisper on the mind, taunting, teasing there. A night messenger? Formed by the shadows, instilled with life and a voice by the moon? Or perhaps one of Henry Scowcroft's creatures, carved out of the very muscle and blood of the earth, resilient in its mud and muskeg and weary-boned body, and warm in its coat of moss. Perhaps none of these ancient terrors and friends but something new and therefore more extraordinary, more foreboding, perhaps a being crossing from this world to the next and signalling its good-bye.

Morgan wanted to see it. Pushing himself up he stood on one leg and supported himself against a birch tree. His ankle was broken; when he stepped forward on that foot his whole body collapsed. Morgan crawled and hopped among the rocks and located a firm, solid branch; breaking off the ends of it he fitted it to size, so that his armpit fitted snugly in the crook of the branch, and he used it as a crutch. He adjusted his bandage. He had ripped lengths of material from his pants and wore them as a belt over his wound, and as the blood soaked through he turned the bandage around on his waist to a fresh spot. The belt already had three large splotches of blood. Morgan hobbled slowly through the forest. If there was a horse he wanted to see it. He was cold, bare-chested, and the night would soon make the search for shelter impossible. As he walked he wondered about the horse. He hoped it had a rider but could not guess who it could be. His wound, the boils, the night encroaching like an enemy on personal territory, his broken ankle, the cold: the horse meant his escape, his only way out of here, his freedom and his life.

Billy took stock of himself, examined with blindman's fingers his nose and forehead, eyes and mouth, ran his hands over his bruises and cuts with a feather touch. The bite on his tongue had almost pierced it, two teeth had been knocked out, a third was so loose that he pulled it out himself, and two others were broken. The pain when he moved indicated a few ribs might be cracked. His nose was flattened to one side. He did not think it would take much to put such a small nose back into place, and he could breathe well enough through his mouth for now. But the pain from the break was moving upward between his eyes and into his head, a large, dull ache now, and it was obvious he could not wait here longer, he had to think about surviving. Standing up, walking, his body rebelled, pain shooting across his chest and through his head. Carefully he climbed down from the tier, securing each step and hold before releasing his weight to it, tackling short steps only and taking them slow. He worked his way through the forest by grabbing hold of swinging pine and cedar branches, first one hand then the other like a square-dancer moving through a line of smiling, dancing girls. Billy headed for Lake TaColl in search of his canoe.

The dispersal of the cloudcover brought out the moon, full and luminescent; brought out the stars and declared the last strands of daylight, violet with a deep, surrendering glow. The appearance of the translucent sky above the clouds—finally—carried with it a sense of reward and relief. Henry was concerned about how long it would last. He felt comfortable now, the prolonged movement of the night moving within him too, nurturing a quiet and temperate spirit; yet it frequently collided with his concerns and fears, also ignited by the darkness and by the absence of Billy Peel. Henry called upon his deepest instincts and mulled over what they told him.

Moonlight shimmered on the lake, running water muttered through the forest, Henry sensing a call or refrain, a repetitious whisper that eluded his grasp and understanding. Intent on listening, there was nothing he could garner but his own confusion and dismay.

He thought suddenly of Billy Peel, as if the Indian was beckoning from one side of his mind. Billy had formed his band at Kloo as a break from the established and civilized world, as a partial return to the old ways, as a defiant gesture against the condition of his people and moreover their fate, and he awaited the collapse of the outside world to prove him right; Henry had always believed that that meant him too, his own ideals and hopes, foreseen by Billy as eventually thwarted and extinguished, so that he had always believed that Billy saw him only as ashes on a future world's pyre, and for this reason stood against him, enemies not by spirit or design but by birth. Although it was not as simple as that and Henry confessed this to himself, for there was a conflict of vision involved: Henry the historian looking back, determining the present and the future in terms of their ability to comprehend and reclaim and revalue and fulfill the past, while Billy was the rebel chief, a seer and sorcerer, reviewing the future as a matter of record, already engulfed, inflamed, marching to an end already past. Henry lived the life of a dervish, brooding on the monastic forest life one time, rallying to an individual's needs or turmoil the next, while Billy sullenly prepared his people for survival and failing that, destruction; all of his attention focused on either the future or the distant glories of the past, while Henry hounded the space between. Henry recognized now that their personal territories were not necessarily combative, for Billy had had little choice, to resurrect his clan from their moral and physical destitution required a plan of vision and energy, required the condition of isolation to make it work. Henry had only himself to take care of, as much as he mingled into the histories and minds of other people he left them the responsibility for their own lives, so that he was not as concerned with either direction or accomplishment as he was with perception; he could afford that luxury, Billy could not. He could afford it, Billy could not; Henry now saw that there was no serious cause for alarm between them, no cause critical enough to do battle. His animosity probably stemmed from his picture of himself as an historian, and as an historian he resented the man grabbing his history by the scruff of the neck and disciplining it to a new shape and vision; his animosity and fear and resentment were those of the quiet and meditative man for the man of action. Yet it occurred to him immediately that such a differentiation was not strict, or even valid, for they both crossed and recrossed this line and so diminished its significance and existence.

The water. Running through the forest to the lake.

The moonlight. Shimmering on the lake, the moon pulling the water to a head.

The light reflected on the water and Henry moved to a crouch, his heart quickening, his mind zipping again.

Of course! The water brought it all together. Fused everything into one fluid motion. Annealed all separations and identities. If Billy was hurt and able to move at all, the one and only place he could find him at night, the one and only place where they could find each other at night, would be the lake.

Henry braced his pack over his shoulders and he left the cave quickly, the ledge illuminated by the full moon; but the forest, once entered, was dark and sombre and alive with dancing shadows. After being struck in the face several times by branches, Henry resorted to crawling and sliding along the forest floor, slithering like a snake sometimes, a wise and wary serpent, rising within himself to an old and not-forgotten music, the compelling song of a flute.

Billy became entangled in the undergrowth. The land had dropped suddenly and he fell into a pool of cold water, with long grasses and bulrushes tying up his arms and legs. He fought his way back to his feet and continued through the forest. He could hear the waves lapping on the shore. Even in the moonlight it was hard to distinguish his whereabouts, he thought he might have to wade in the water and study the view from the lake. But crossing a large boulder he recognized it, he had come this way with Doc after ditching the canoe, and he altered his direction, approaching the lake now at an angle with the moon sometimes appearing amid the treetops at his back. He walked slowly, managing the slopes by sitting and carefully working his way down on his seat. After a half-hour or so he came out by the lake, his head popping from under a cedar tree and he gazed out over the water. In the distance a blackness grew. No stars penetrated the western horizon. His understanding failed him, for he did not immediately identify this new and denser movement of cloud, but assumed it was a menace of a different order, looming perhaps on the horizon of his own mind and not outside him at all. He was dizzy and his head jarred with every movement he made. It took him a long time to evaluate his location. Aware that his faculties were labouring, he was careful not to decide anything in haste. He knew he was in trouble now, more than he had diagnosed at first, and he could not take a chance on wasting time, he had to be right the first time.

Billy crawled along the rim of the lake to his left. He made the right choice, for he travelled only about twenty feet when he found his canoe. Well-hidden; safe. He pushed it out over the water. He heaved again. With each shove the craft budged only a few inches. He heaved again. Billy could feel his strength leaving his body, felt barely strong enough to stand and he sank to his knees and shoved again. Inches again.

Then he heard the sound again. He hesitated only a second to confirm it. The crashing and thrashing of the beast in the underbrush, and Billy put his shoulder into the canoe and dug in his toes and pushed with all his weight and might. A couple of feet. Another shove and the nose of the canoe dipped down over the bank and into the water. The beast was very close and Billy jumped down into the water and pulled frantically. Tree branches held the canoe fast. Billy pushed the nose of the canoe up finding the strength now, acting on nerve and fear now only, and the canoe slid out from the land and plopped in the water and Billy fell under it. He heard the bubbles and rush of water. Billy slid the canoe out and hoisted himself into it as it passed him, and pulling himself up he sighted Morgan, a crutch under one arm, a club held high in the other, and Morgan leaped into the water after him, landing on the crutch and his one good foot and bounding after Billy, the club waving and Billy caught him under the chin with a paddle, knocking him back, and with his next movement Billy propelled the canoe into safe and open water. Morgan hurled the club but it landed far from the target, plopping in the water and bobbing harmlessly.

Billy's body retaliated against the exertion. Billy pulled hard once and the canoe skimmed across the water. He slumped over while his body attacked him, while the pains shot up through his chest and bore into his neck and head and back. Behind him Morgan scrambled on the shore and Billy rested, stretching out in the canoe. He wanted help.

He thought it odd that it came to him now, returned to him as a tranquil and favoured experience, although it had never been that at any time—came to him, and perhaps it had to do with the hour of the day, after sunset; perhaps it had to do with his desire now for a warm house and a crackling fire as he crawled through the sopping grass and over the mud—the gentle lullabies of the flute his father would play on Cumshewa Sound, rowing out from shore. The music then would seem to pervade from the night and the darkness and water itself, and something within Henry would quicken, although he'd be embarrassed by it too, conscious of the sneers and insinuations of the townsmen who thought his father strange. There were the times his father played at Sockeye, visiting the church there after nightfall and playing in the empty building, the church that Jim Duff had built following his conversion or re-conversion, which followed and was coordinated with the birth of his daughter, had it built because the old chapel was too small for himself and his huge family. Jim Duff forced his family to attend these nocturnal concerts too, huddle about outside and listen at the door, and Gail Duff was always the first one in line, receiving the notes as if they were sacred.

Henry crawled, slid through the mud; he could hear the waves now, smell the lake, and he thought it could have been Lake TaColl that precipitated the return of his father's music to mind, for Calvin Scowcroft had always had a deep feeling for the lake, as if it were important to his equilibrium, as if it were a place to be renewed and invigorated and inspired again. Henry felt close to his father here.

He came out by the shore. Splashed water on his face to wash the mud off. The moonlight reflected on the silver back of a salmon and Henry's heart leaped. He was sure it was his friend from days ago when he had set out on this journey. If not, it did not matter, the personal relationship was of no consequence, he had joined in the dance of the salmon since early boyhood and the pact was between himself and all the fish. He slithered a few feet to his right along the bank for a closer look. Under an overhanging limb several fish swam. One fish bore a white blotch, the first appearance of its imminent decay, and they were all developing the humps which would precede their deaths. Henry readily sympathized, his own body wracked and destroyed, feeling as if it would peel away from his life and abandon him. But soon the fingerlings would be carried down the rivers to the sea, carried backwards by the currents while they fought their way upstream. Henry felt close to them, a friend. He had been taught that they did not want to go, which is why they attempted to swim in one direction while they were carried in another. But he believed differently. Understood their wisdom because he was like them too. Knew that they pointed their bodies upstream because one day they would return to the place of their birth; knew that they swam with their eyes behind them, with their heads to the rear, because they already knew that one day they would have to return to their past, just as Henry knew it too. Henry let his gaze cross the water, skip on the water like a smooth and flat and well-thrown pebble, dancing in leaps and bounds, as the moonlight did. Then, crossing the shimmering line of light, a canoe. A figure sat hunched in the back. Henry listened to the forest. Then he hollered, "Billy!" The figure jerked, looked around; jerked as if from a sleep and suddenly frightened by this echoing voice.

"Henry!" Billy called.

Henry felt ecstatic. "Billy!" he called back, "It's me!"

One word, quick, like the flash of a knife: "Hide!"

Henry moved, bounding quickly to his right, and immediately he could hear it, the great disturbance behind him, and Henry gathered speed, moved as best he could on the balls of his feet, accepting knocks to his face and throat that he ill-protected with an upraised hand, and he found a tree that was suitable, silhouetted in the moonlight. A low limb overhung the water and Henry crawled out upon it. The thrashing continued a few moments longer and ceased. Periodically, he heard a movement behind him. Billy had come closer and he followed a line parallel to shore. Billy called out to him, his voice clear and gliding on the water.

"Come out when the canoe's close, Henry. Morgan wants the canoe. He is hurt. He has no gun now. No gun. Come out when the canoe's close."

Quiet.

The canoe skimmed over the water easily and slowly and scarcely disturbed the water at all. Billy was a silhouette in the moonlight.

The forest was quiet, waiting, holding its breath.

Henry clung to his branch and waited. Listened to the forest's high whistle, so high it could barely be heard. Somewhere across the lake an owl hooted. A raven crossed the sky.

Billy approached.

Henry dropped from his branch and his legs churned through the water. To his left he saw the form, charging, attacking with a crutch crooked under one arm, and Billy swerved sharply to pick up Henry. Morgan gained rapidly, impossible speed, desperate speed, battling the water with ferocity, reaching out with his crutch and hooking the canoe, Billy swatting now with his paddle, Henry slipping and tumbling into the water, swimming now, Morgan latching onto the canoe and shoving Billy backwards, gripping the canoe now with one hand, Henry ducking below the water and catching Morgan's knee with his cane, pulling him over while Billy jabbed again with his paddle and sent the crutch flying. Henry hoisted himself into the canoe and as Morgan dove for it, one swift flash of Billy's paddle sent the canoe beyond his reach. Another flash and they skimmed into the safety of the open water.

"Billy, Billy! We beat him!" Henry held his arms out like a conqueror bursting with the thrill of victory. "Haha!"

Billy cried out too, strange sounds, like battle cries, "Ee-yi-yiii!" and they came together and hugged in the centre of the canoe.

But Henry caught a glance of Billy's face and he was stricken. "My God! What happened? Billy!" Sucking in his breath, Billy managed a broken and distorted smile. He felt dizzy and fell backwards in the canoe. "Billy!" His side hurt him, and Henry paddled farther into the open water before coming to his aid. Henry held Billy's head up while the canoe rocked drastically. Billy was losing consciousness. Henry splashed water in his face. Billy gripped him by the shirt and held tight, waiting for the pain to ride through him and pass. Billy gasped and sucked in air again.

"It's not bad," Billy said when he was able to breathe easier. "Not injured too bad."

Henry accepted Billy's words as truth, doubted that he would bother with false bravery. "Take it easy now."

"The pain is bad. Sometimes—dizzy. Glad you came, Henry."

"You're glad! I'm the one who's glad!"

"How you doing?"

"I'm okay. Sore too. Doc's got Thomas." Henry worked to make Billy comfortable in the canoe. He made a bed for him out of his pack and jacket and the Indian chief was able to stretch out. Henry paddled, and he became aware of what Billy had noticed earlier, the black horizon to the west. But he did not speak of it.

"Henry?"

"Yeh, Billy?"

"Did you hear that horse?"

"Yeh." Henry paddled and it occurred to him that he did not know where to go.

"It came from the other side of the lake."

"Want to go there?"

"No. There's no time."

Henry thought. Looked at the horizon. "Where then?"

"Nistee River."

"Now? At night! Are you serious?"

"Henry."

"Yeh. I see it. We better go now."

The entire western horizon glowed bright, illuminating the mountain peaks and causing the water to shake and move in a frenzy. The wind picked up suddenly, blowing hard and gusty, and Henry could taste the storm in his mouth and breathe it in his nostrils.

25

THE WESTERN SKY went white for an instant, and they could hear the rain drumming on the water in a frenzy. Doc scrambled among the rocks alongside the Oganjibra River and it seemed the strangest thing to him, for the moon shone clearly above them and lighted their way, but in the west the sky was black again, blackness itself rising as an all-devouring essence, moving upon them, shot through again by sudden and incredibly bright lightning, and it was the strangest thing too because there was no thunder, only the looming mass and the incessant drumming of the rain, itself thunderous as the line of its advance crossed Lake TaColl.

They ran from the storm although that was not supposed to be it, there was no hope in it anyway. They were supposed to be hurrying to Lyell and making what time they could before this awesome storm overcame them, but in truth they ran from it, feeling its tenacious pursuit at their backs, feeling its mad breath signalled in the treetops, the trees whipping to and fro now, assaulted by the confused and circling wind. They ran from the storm for its strength and power and explosiveness evoked the greatest fears that either of them had ever known. Thomas feared the lightning most, the swift reckoning of the shocks; Doc the massive size, the total darkness.

Yet Doc was excited by it too, felt alive and enriched by an energy itself electric and explosive, a complement to the storm. He was scarcely aware of the difficulties and the awkwardness of their descent, following after Thomas easily and keeping his pace, Thomas who seemed to glide over the surface like a ghost fleeing to another realm. Doc was scarcely aware of it, but descending the slope his feet found their way as if by instinct, his eyes revealed the forest and river and rocks despite the dim light, his body moved behind Thomas and felt air-like too, ethereal and attuned but not absorbed by the breath of the forest or by the fretful wind. He was scarcely aware of his body or thoughts, and when he stumbled, he recovered by running forward more quickly, unafraid, feeling giddy and carefree and exultant.

When Thomas stopped, Doc came up beside him.

They listened.

Then simultaneously they searched for a shelter, finding one together under a large cedar tree. They both leaned their backs against the trunk and waited.

The rain approached on the march.

It fell in advance of the cloud line, in advance of the blackness that obliterated all trace of light. As it approached, the loudness became deafening, as at the base of a mammoth waterfall, as if it were not rain at all but multitudes of marching demons pounding on small deerskin drums. And just as it was about to overtake them, lightning illuminated the forest, and only a moment later thunder erupted for the first time, so loudly it seemed to rip open the sky above their heads, so loudly that both Doc and Thomas jumped, and their bodies continued to vibrate afterwards. Their bodies betrayed them, knowing fears of their own. Their bodies and nerves waited tensely for the next thunderclap. The water hit, the tree limbs bending under the force, the rain penetrating through the foliage in only a few seconds.

Still Doc was excited and not afraid. He caught sight of Thomas as the next bolt struck. He could see Thomas's face muscles quiver and his eyes reflect fright and alarm. Doc reached across to him and held his wrist. Thomas was bobbing his head and kicking his feet, as if the storm was sending electric charges through him. Lightning again, streaking across the sky just over the treetops like a frenzied, startled flame.

Thomas gripped Doc's hand and pressed it over his heart. The skin felt cold and stiff under Doc's hand. Doc felt the hurried beating and he waited for the sky to illuminate his face, then shook his head affirmatively. The flashes revealed that Thomas was smiling. Laughing perhaps, the sound of it muffled by the rain and echoing thunder.

Thomas linked elbows with him and Doc could hear him now, a high and musical laughter above the driving rain. Then, just as suddenly, Thomas unfastened himself from Doc's arm, ran in a crouch under the tree limbs and came out by the riverside.

Doc went after him.

Thomas stood with his arms raised and his face to the rain. Doc came to his side and he was startled by the power of the rainfall. He squinted to protect his eyes. Above the sound of the rain and the surging river and the distant muffled thunder—Thomas's high-pitched laughter again.

The hermit commenced dancing around Doc; it seemed like a ritual dance, an Indian dance, and watching him Doc felt uneasy at first. Thomas tried to involve him in the movements, slapping his shoulders lightly, tugging his lapels, and Doc began to laugh also, and he did a little jig he had learned years ago. Thomas was shouting but Doc could not make out a word over the storm. Then Thomas fell to the ground, and Doc was pushed away when he offered him a hand. Lightning revealed a horrified expression on the hermit's face. He was staring into the treetops.

Doc knelt beside him and fought him so he could get a hold on him. He held Thomas's head and the man kicked his feet. After several minutes the hermit relaxed and Doc released him, but Thomas kept his eyes hidden in the crook of his arm. Like a man who had been blinded. Doc led him back to their shelter, Thomas with one arm around Doc's shoulders while the other protected his eyes. They crouched then crawled and worked their way back to their tree.

The two men lay down facing each other.

Lightning overhead. A thunderclap.

Thomas lay with his eyes closed and his hands tucked under his head as a pillow, and Doc regarded him, studied the weathered and gnarled face and hands, astonished by them, as if they were a portent, reflections that surprised him by their familiarity.

And it was not his own image that he was seeing exactly, reflecting through future years and napping beside him in a sleep that was neither restful nor contented; not his own fate, huddled and deformed like a grotesque foetus, not his own potential, and not even the outcome of his own direction. It was not a result, finally, of his own destination, although he could see all of this in the man and he knew why. He was a deserter like Thomas, fleeing family and home and lifelong work for the sake of his own remission, for the sake of his own salvation amid the collapse of his dreams, ideals, and sensibilities. Doc had run, to this island, as distant and as obscure and as isolated a place as his imagination would allow, while Thomas had fled to Skincuttle Island's hinterland, to the deepest depths of escape he could perceive, so that Doc felt a kinship here, and viewed it in the mirror-image of Thomas's face. But it was not his kinship specifically with Thomas that struck him, that alarmed him, but their mutual kinship and bond and servitude to the compromises of the past, their mutual acceptance of a day of reckoning that would find them in default, and lassitude and fear would no longer serve as sources for their defence. They accepted a reckoning that approached steadily, that one day would finally spring and defeat them, and the interlude before it was marked by their solitude and decay. Doc turned onto his back. Studying Thomas was like witnessing his own demise, for he intuited that Thomas had yielded to the force of others when he had known better, and so had precipitated his own impotence and separation.

Doc fidgeted in a useless effort to avoid a stream of water that had flooded his bed. He looked in Thomas's direction, not seeing him now, as the sky was black and the forest was immersed in darkness; not seeing him now and wondering if he was still there, so that he had to reach out and touch him, and as his hand touched the man's scalp and hair and beard, the feel of that skin and beard charged him with an emotional response. He knew that it was more than sympathy now, more than the awareness of their deeply rooted similarity, more than kinship or even friendship that held him to Thomas. He accepted a bond with this man, accepted his pain and sadness as his own too, and moreover concluded that he was responsible also for whatever this man had done or had failed to do—responsible not by complicity in the deed but through his own acquiescence. He had allowed himself to be intimidated as well, had never said "No" to the force behind the deed, allowed it to overrule a deeper and possibly primal renunciation.

They nestled into the ground, and in a way they huddled together, their bodies not touching, but each one adopted the contours of the other. Doc fell asleep as lightning crackled through the leaves.

26

THROUGH THE CLIMAX of the storm, while the skies flashed and scored white and red and green across the entire expanse of its canvas, while the thunder cracked like the seam ripping between heaven and earth, Henry felt on the threshold of a nether world. He did not lose awareness of himself, conscious at all times of his responsibility to Billy and the canoe, alert at all times due to the velocity of the torrent and the fury of the storm, but he was aware too of approaching another world, a different and unknown region which beckoned and enticed him.

The heavy rains flooded the Nistee River as the lightning lit their way. The flood water actually simplified the journey, the surge of water speeding the progress of the canoe, and rocks that might have proven dangerous were submerged now and not harmful. The river overflowed its banks, and during periods of deep darkness they could hear the water slapping the trees and so steered away from the shore.

Manning the bow, Henry was responsible for direction, stabbing the water from time to time with his paddle to avoid rocks or black impressions that might be rocks, stabbing the water and controlling his fear, the speed of the canoe terrifying him, not allowing him time to think but only to react instantaneously as each new challenge emerged.

Billy Peel lay in the stern, his back and head propped into a sitting position but his legs spread out before him, holding his paddle but using it only occasionally to swing his end around, mainly squeezing it like a bit against the pain from his injuries, squeezing it in his hands and hanging on, watching the night fly past, battling the night and the pain in a struggle to remain conscious.

Sometimes the canoe was jolted by collisions, but it held up well, being picked up again by the river and hurried downstream. Henry had no confidence in his own ability to command it, but after a few bad moments he gained confidence in the canoe itself: strong, swift, it seemed to possess a capacity to ride the currents and determine its own path, seemed to avoid hazards as if it were aware all along of their presence. His fear subsiding, Henry experienced moments of intense exhilaration.

Bolts of lightning connected the sky to the earth, split the air and the rain in one quick shot, dividing realms, like a birth; skimming over the water Henry lost the sense of his legs, even of the water, and moreover of the land, felt himself skimming across a different sort of fluid, traversing more than this river but the storm too, the lightning too. The thunder cracked powerfully once more; a second explosion illuminated the entire western sky and the light flashed repeatedly for several moments, taking his breath away. He felt somehow that the thunder had been inside him also, seemed to burst out from his stomach and hammer in his heart—so that looking into the glowing and exploding sky, he felt the loss, not of his body exactly, but of the weight and slowness of it. Suddenly, while paddling, while helping the canoe to swerve and balance, the storm was not outside of him at all: the bolts of lightning were charges up and down his spine, and the thunderclaps words from his mouth. Released from himself, and strong, his exertion was a source of energy and not fatigue, he experienced each stroke and jab of the paddle in a kind of ecstasy, and at the full climax of the storm he was shouting, calling out crazily and working feverishly, a man possessed, a man thrilled and exultant to his marrow, a man cherishing this exquisite contact with his own soul.

The turbulent water drove them through the night. The canoe nearly capsized several times, and it was luck, it seemed, more than anything else that kept them upright—or perhaps not luck but instinct, instinct that both men had acquired unknowingly, acquired and developed through a respect for the rigours and tortures of the wilderness, the same instinct or luck that had kept Billy alive through his fight with Morgan: something that was not so much a part of them, for they seemed without it under ordinary conditions, but something that was always near, hovering, that they could call upon at any moment when survival was at stake. It was something which Henry sometimes identified as a fish, sometimes as a tree, sometimes as a canoe, never able to quite distinguish its qualities and character from its mixture of ether and matter; never able to quite define and understand its mechanism and mobility, but sensing it and breathing it nonetheless, and accepting it as he accepted his own pulse.

With the electric storm well past, the river and the rain bore them through the night. They made it all the way to the ocean before dawn. Waves jostled the canoe like driftwood, and they were able to paddle right into the forest where they moored. Henry pulled the canoe deeper into the woods. Tipping it over, they lay under it with their legs curled and their feet at opposite ends. They lay on their sides with the backs of their heads touching.

"How you doing, Henry?" Billy's voice echoed slightly in the hull of the canoe. The forest floor was covered by a wet moss that was soft and responded to their weight.

"I'm okay. You?"

Billy did not answer. The rain came through the leaves above their spot and tapped intricate patterns on the canoe. Henry listened to the water and tried to hear Billy breathing. "Can make it," Billy said at last.

"I hope the sun's up soon," Henry said. He laid his head on his forearm and closed his eyes. He had no idea of the time, no idea if the dawn would come soon or if the darkness still held a firm grip.

27

MORNING STIRRED OVER LAKE TACOLL, like a hand passing through the mists, hidden veils being lifted. Soon the sun was visible through the racing clouds. The rain let up, then came again, quickly, trotting across the water and plunging into the forest, ceasing again. The wind chased the clouds with abandon, bent back the high trees, disturbed the lake. Whitecaps appeared across the water, and high up, a hawk battered against the force. The wind blew the horse's mane and the sandy-blonde hair of its rider.

Morgan observed the slow step of the horse as it circled the perimeter of Lake TaColl, coming towards him. He squatted in a puddle and peered through the branches and leaves that concealed him. He leaned his head back against the coarse bark and scowled as a wave leapt up and soaked his legs and chest. But he did not move, stayed watching the horse and rider.

The horse was tan-coloured with large white splotches on its underside. It was small but muscular and jaunty, and responded easily to a prod from the stirrups, running in a slow gallop. The water splashed lightly about the hooves, the sound of it like rain on a roof. The woman pulled on the reins and slowly the horse resumed its slow, searching walk again.

The horse was still far off, and Morgan waited impatiently. He moved his bandage but there were no blank spaces remaining, the entire cloth soaked through with blood. He had not resigned himself to dying here, the sound of the horse's neighing from the previous dusk his one firm link with consciousness; the horse was his only means of escape.

The saturated forest was pungent with the smell of mud and wet grass. Water still fell from the branches. The forest seemed impenetrable to her and vacant, and she scolded herself, she was crazy trying to find anybody here. And the years had never seemed so dark and barren in their reluctant acceptance of the passing days, of the passing age, they had never before seemed so solemn and pious and distant, moving at the pace of a funeral walk, years like hunkering icons hidden behind dust and formality, lost years, never to be regained or even rekindled. Soulless, she would claim, if she had not learned differently, if she had not long ago accepted that simple pain, simple injustice, simple absurdity, were intricately interwoven with those life forces she praised and craved. She could remember days spent beside this lake when the sunlight gleamed on the emerald water, the mountains rose as true and loyal cadets sharply to attention, the forest radiated a spirit that caught at her heart. Fine weather—but in those days only fine weather would have brought her here. She restrained her pangs of memory, for something else was involved then too and accountable—her childhood, which was why the years seemed so poignant and lost now. That was the time, and moment, and age when childhood, and a part of life too, came to a sudden and unrectifiable halt: a life vanquished, raped perhaps, murdered perhaps, the sea swallowing the child but not her ghost, not her impression traced on the wind.

Watching the hawk batter a strong gust, fall toward the lake in a confusion of wings and feathers and body, strain for height again; the wind was its match, and the bird turned in a sharp curve and swooped toward the forest. Looking down the shoreline—she saw a man waving a branch.

He could resist no longer, she had moved so slowly, so that finally he had jumped into the open and waved. But as the horse and rider approached at a gallop, Morgan recoiled, he threw away the branch and stumbled against the bank. He was seized, violently, by terror and panic.

"Morgan Duff," she said flatly. His chest was bare and spotted with ugly sores. Erect in the saddle she approached and the man jumped back from her.

"No!" he cried. Morgan stood on his good leg, dug in his crutch behind him and jumped back again. Gaping at her and he could not believe it but at the same time he did believe it and panicked. He broke for the woods.

"Morgan!" she called. He disappeared in the underbrush. Leading the horse back and forth, she searched desperately for an opening that would admit them. She drew her rifle from its sheath and finally forced the animal into the woods. Branches slapped her face and bit into her shoulders and neck. She forced the horse on and the woodland yielded to their entry. She listened for a moment, then followed the sound of the scrambling man. Soon the horse took over, pursuing the man or at least the sound of him or the smell of him, at least engaging in the game, so that she was hurt by a multitude of blows on the shoulders and arms and legs, but in a minute she caught up to him, and he lay on his back and he had lost his crutch.

"No!" he cried. "No!" He could not control his breathing. His chest heaved in great gasps and still he felt a lack of air, as if he were being choked, as if there was no escape from this nightmare and delirium. The woman aimed the rifle at him but it was not his death he feared, but this return. "You're dead! You're—dead!"

And she understood it then. And it seemed appropriate to her now, and right, as if she had returned from the dead just as he had returned from that nightmare of seventeen years ago and reimposed himself on the island, dominating, challenging, releasing his power like a slow poison, appropriate and right then that she had found him here, injured and virtually helpless, his life in her hands. And she was tempted for one quick second to squeeze the trigger and finish it, end it, accept the culmination of time and lost years; and what frightened her was that it was within her domain to do so, within the bounds of her own sensibilities and choices, she could do it, press the trigger, annul the life, bury the carcass, and it was almost as if she could feel her father's hand tighten on the gun, feel his heart quicken with a sense of power. This and the ease and simplicity of it more than anything else changed her mind.

Swinging her leg over the horse, she jumped down. She still cradled the rifle and he still stared up at her, horrified and numb.

"Relax," she said. "I'm Evlin, I'm not Gail."

All through the night she had railed against the storm, endured its madness. And she had had to struggle with the mare to keep the animal safe from its own striding terror, its fear as rampant as the storm that had ignited it, its body made iridescent by the coloured flashes of lightning, its own power and strength left frail and trembling under the assault from the thunder. Claps of thunder had made her jump and cry out. She'd been soaked through to the skin and chilled to the bone. Whenever the lightning ceased for a time the pitch blackness had been startling. But through it all she had been aware of a link, as if she had fought this fight before, as if it were merely a continuation of some previous black swirl she had been cast into, like a recurring dream.

He had covered his face with his hands. When he looked up again his breathing had returned to normal, although his flesh was still white and death-like. "You're C. Oliver's kid."

C. Oliver. The signs along the wharf at Sockeye and over the cannery and the general store boldly wore the name. So that it was no longer a name but a designation. "That's right," Evlin said. "Only my last name's Rand now—I'm married."

Morgan struggled to his feet, standing on one foot finally and balancing against a tree. The low branches brushed their heads. "You look like her," Morgan said, and Evlin thought to say that she felt like her too, like the reincarnation of her lost friend, or at least like her deputy, granted the responsibility to continue and fulfil her life while she was gone. It was a question of justice, she thought, but it was desire too. There was her own need involved in it.

Seeing her looking at the blood-stained cloth, Morgan said, "I had a fall, lady. I bust my ankle too." Morgan twisted around and displayed the ripped pantleg and his injury, but Evlin did not bother to look. She stared him in the eyes steadily and trained the rifle on his chest.

Early on she had cried. It was the feeling of being a child again, coupled with the remembrances of Gail Duff again that were renewed by this expedition. Feeling small again, frail again, feeling tiny and exposed, as on the days when she returned to her mainland school and the children of Sockeye waved to her from the harbour, growing smaller, infinitesimal specks finally beyond a narrowing and rising horizon, Gail Duff waving too. The picture of her town and home and friends growing smaller stayed with her always, returned to haunt her often, the image of the jaws of the inlet clamping shut and spitting her out, alone upon the sea, became inflated, and she grew to feel it about herself: one tiny being, sailing off onto the abyss of ocean and world.

She fought against it. Sometimes erratically, sometimes without conviction, but in one form or another she had fought against it through most of her life, battling her father's tyranny eventually too, and she was with him when he died, C. Oliver, still fighting him as he struggled to remain strong and potent and forceful despite his disease-destroyed and age-destroyed body, despite the impending collapse of his feudal kingdom and the outrage of the rebellion he was losing—of his daughter against his force and domain. It was a war she had waged without reward, for it would recur, that sense of herself overpowered and brutalized by forces that cared only for their own infatuated and bloated fantasies of strength and rule; so that she cried under the onslaught of the storm, feeling small again, and broken and alone again, before catching hold of her strength and warring spirit, before rising up against the storm and its fury and denying it sovereignty.

"What's the gun for?" Morgan asked, and he grinned and examined her. Evlin did not flinch under his scrutiny. Her anger was building and it came from meeting this man again. As a youth he had intimidated her and the other children of Sockeye, and she hated him for it, hated him for Gail's death too, hated him, but at the same time she was wary of him. "Nice horse," he said.

"Why were you running?" Evlin asked. Her expression was cold, remote. She was studying his eyes. An additional layer over the cornea gave him a glazed and distant look, like a man whose mind connects very slowly with his surroundings. He did not answer. "Why were you running, if you thought I was Gail?"

"Yaha! I thought I'd seen a ghost!"

"You believe in ghosts?"

"Yaha! I'm an old fisherman, don't forget. Sure, I seen ghosts before." Morgan adjusted his weight against the tree trunk and broke a thin branch in front of his face. Evlin stepped to one side to keep a clear view of him. The horse nuzzled her back.

"But I didn't look like her ghost. I didn't look like the ghost of a twelve-year-old girl, now did I, Morgan?"

"Look, lady—"

"You look. You look and tell me why the appearance of your sister, who's been missing for so many years, makes you run away. You hid. You hid, you—" The anger was surfacing now, Morgan was surprised by it, for everybody on Skincuttle Island had held it in, not daring to provoke or disturb him. And the woman was holding the gun as if she intended to use it, he recognized the stance and the pressure of her hands on the rifle. Every time he looked at her she still reminded him of Gail, a grown Gail, the anger making her appear like his sister all the more, grown in age and size and moulded in a spirit of vengeance in which he was the intended and rightful victim. Suddenly the woman let the rifle drop to her side. "I know why, Morgan. It's obvious. And when we get Thomas out of here, everybody else will know why too."

For Evlin the night was one of the worst she had ever known, and it was not merely the physical force of the elements that had made it so, for to flail against the storm she once again had to reach down into her own body and summon her full strength and courage and cunning. Consequently the memories and the furies of the past came up also, as if each battle fought resurrected the old battles again, as if all her struggles and failures, victories and defeats, were all part of the same continuing war—which she understood, the storm hammering away at the guises of time, the interludes of time and change that distorted the ongoing and never-ending battle itself, and she was furious with herself once again for periods of tardiness and lament, for her periods of indulgence and sleep, for she had to atone for them now. In summoning her strengths, her weaknesses were assaulted, and when she cried again it was because she fought alone once more, and she pitied herself for that.

"I don't know what you're talking about, lady."

In one swift motion, Evlin mounted the horse. "Suit yourself," she said.

"Hey!" He came out from the tree, gripping the branches for support. "You can't leave me here."

Evlin slipped her gun back into the sheath, patted the horse's neck. "Yes I can."

"Lady—I got a broken ankle. I need the horse."

"That's not all the matter with you."

"What d'you mean?"

She jerked her chin, pointing to the makeshift bandage. "Who'd you fight?"

"Nobody, lady. I fell."

Turning the horse's head, Evlin retreated through the woods. Morgan called after her and she could hear him stumbling along the path. When she came out on the lake she waited for him, passed the time by rolling a cigarette and lighting it. The wind blew out two matches before it caught.

She had stood up finally, while the horse still neighed and kicked in its corral, still pulled against the ropes. And standing, she endured it, the rain beating hard, her hair flattened against her scalp and neck and back, her face covered by water, the lightning reflecting in her eyes and sparkling on the beads of running water; she endured it, allowed the rain and lightning and thunder its full attack; she endured it and saw the faces of the children of Cumshewa Town where she lived, saw the faces of the old men, saw the faces of the women, saw the faces of the drunken men and their beaten wives, saw the lightning flash between the heavens and the dark, awesome forest and knew that she could only do what was within her to do, carry on.

When morning had come, she washed, brushed her hair, changed her clothes. And she was aware of a link that had helped carry her through the night. She had come, she thought, in search of Doc, although her thoughts were soon embroiled in the whole spectre of events—the hermit, the return of Morgan Duff, Henry's disappearance, Doc's state of mind—but climbing into the mountains it was the memory of Gail Duff that returned again and again. She had tried unravelling the peculiar connection to her that had outlasted the years, so that in the morning she finally resolved it, accepted that Gail's memory lingered latent in her mind, charging out at her from time to time, just as the wild, frightened horse did, and struggling with the horse brought out her strengths and moreover her need to triumph. Evlin had groomed the horse thoroughly in the morning, attending to it as to a child, keenly sensing with some remote part of her being that the animal had spoken to her, had imbued itself in her mind.

Evlin felt an energy excite her nerves, swell through her body. She wanted Morgan to ride with her on the horse, and more, she wanted him to discover it was the memory of Gail he was riding.

Morgan appeared. He had found his crutch, but he stumbled on the bank and collapsed into the water. He got to his feet swearing and spat water from his mouth, and Evlin had to pull hard on the reins to keep the horse from bolting.

"Some Indian!" Morgan shouted. "He jumped me from behind and stuck his knife in me. He even shoved me over a cliff! That's how I bust my ankle."

"Who?"

"I don't know him."

"It's a long way back to Lyell on one leg, Mister Duff."

The horse turned in small circles, snorting and breathing hard, shaking off the water.

"What do you want from me? What the hell do you want from me?"

"You're losing blood. No clothes. No food. I don't envy you at all." Evlin turned the horse, and the animal walked away from Morgan and parallel to the shore.

"Wait! Wait, damn it! I seen him!"

Evlin stopped. "Who?"

"Who do you want? I seen 'em all. I seen Scowcroft and I seen that doctor from town."

"Where?"

"Where. Where. In the woods, where. But way in. Yesterday—they're gone now." Morgan hobbled along the shore desperately as the horse resumed its slow gait. He pursued, but pleading with Evlin he lost the concentration he needed and stumbled several times. "They're probably half the way to Lyell by now. No—wait. Scowcroft went with that Indian who jumped me. They took a canoe across the lake, towards the river over there. Wait! Will you slow down! What's the matter with you? Listen—that doctor's probably on his way to Lyell by now. What's he doing up here anyway?"

Evlin stopped the horse and turned it, while Morgan stumbled forward to catch up. He stopped and looked up at her and he was breathing heavily and his eyes were red. It was his eyes she studied. Hate there, vengeance already looming, but controlled, meaning that he would wait for the right time. "You better convince me of something fast, Morgan, anything, or I'm leaving."

He pleaded and waved his hands in the air. "What can I say—what can I say? Look, Scowcroft called that Indian 'Billy'."

Evlin stared at him between the horse's ears. She had assumed that Doc had gone down to Kloo to see Billy. The canoe story seemed plausible, only Billy or other Indians from Kloo would have canoes up here. "And Billy's still alive?"

"Sure he's alive! I'm the one who's hurt!"

"And Henry and Doc are alive?"

"I seen 'em. If they're dead the bears got them, not me. I swear it on my mother's grave."

Evlin clucked her tongue and the horse approached Morgan. Morgan ran a hand across the horse's neck. "Throw that stick away," Evlin said.

"I need it."

"Throw it away."

Morgan dropped the crutch into the water.

"There's only one way out of here on a horse, Morgan. I know it and you don't. Understand?"

"Sure." Morgan leaned against the horse and tried to pull himself up. But Evlin backed the horse away.

"What's the matter with you?" he said.

She watched his eyes flare, fascinated momentarily by the hatred, the violence there.

"Nothing," she said.

28

SKULLS. Bones. Long skeleton fingers with tufts of skin at the wrist. Henry jerked awake suddenly. They were drifting into shore again. This time Billy too had fallen asleep so their idea had not worked.

Billy lay in the front of the canoe, facing Henry. Henry pulled on his paddle again and forged away from the wave-assaulted rocks that lined the shore. Their thought had been to face one another and to keep watch over one another, but it hadn't worked.

Henry let Billy sleep. He did not follow the shoreline here but headed across the bay to save distance, cutting across to Big Boot, a peninsula jutting miles into the sea. Billy had warned him not to leave the shoreline, but he was asleep now. Henry splashed water on his face and continued paddling, the cedar canoe mounting the grey swells of the incoming tide and slipping down again into the hollows. An off-shore mist that had concealed the ocean was lifting now, but it was being buffeted inland and soon touched the tops of the higher fir trees and Sitka spruce. A wave rocked the canoe and Billy stirred. The swelling had gone down around his mouth and cheeks, but increased above his nose. Both his eyes were bloodshot and surrounded by black bruises, so that his face looked like a painted, distorted mask. "What are we doing out here?"

"Shortcut," Henry said.

"I told you, stay by the shore," Billy said.

Henry thought that Billy did not trust him as a canoeist. "I'm doing okay," he said.

"Okay. Do what you want. But it's a good idea to stay near shore. We might meet somebody."

Henry had not thought of that. "From Kloo?"

"That's right."

The prospect of a rescue made the morning seem brighter to Henry, took his mind off the long paddle ahead of him. When he reached the shore again and travelled parallel to the peninsula, he scanned the forest constantly, sighting men again and again, only to have a branch or rock take shape on closer inspection.

Time passed; then finally, "There."

Henry looked. "Where?"

"Straight in," Billy said, and he sat up in the canoe and waved. And Henry thought it was no accident that these men were here.

They lay on their backs and waited side by side while the four men finished making stretchers. Henry was not familiar with this part of the forest. From the sea it had seemed much more dense than it looked to be now, and he gazed at it upside down, pulling his head in so he could see behind himself. The new and strange territory delighted him, but he was apprehensive about the stretchers.

"I think I can walk it," Henry said again.

"We go on the stretchers. You can sleep."

Stretchers reminded him of his accident, and of his family. His father had held one end of his stretcher when he was carried out of the woods following the landslide, and through his pain and shock he had viewed also his father's grief, and by reflection his own, for Calvin Scowcroft still had to attend to his son and cast out the thought of his wife's death, so that his grief etched marks of pain along his cheeks and forehead. Restrained and controlled and put out of his mind, his grief attacked and reshaped his body.

A band of crows flew overhead. "They're going to Kloo to pick our garbage." Traces of pride in Billy's voice. For Kloo was a place where the crows would congregate, a known place, a place that existed and lived again. Sometimes he wondered if his village had really taken root; reassurances came from the crows and the bears and the deer and the wolves when he saw that they had accepted it.

Suddenly his body was lifted up, and Henry felt a moment's panic, as if abruptly he was back at the time of his injury, the impressions of those hours flooding his senses. He was placed on the stretcher and carried up, and swaying over the ground, watching the high leaves fly past, he became sleepy in time and closed his eyes, dozing off. Felt himself drifting away. And at that time, drifting away through the layers and fluctuations of his pain, coming to his senses from time to time to harp on the future, suddenly diminished it seemed now that his body was distorted and his mother gone, already lingering on the past, a reprieve from agonies real and imagined, and so it suited him still. When he opened his eyes again the trees towered overhead, and against the blue sky they looked about ready to topple. Billy and Henry were carried single file through the woods and they crossed a stream over a log, Henry seizing the sides of the stretcher in fright. On the opposite side the men rested and Henry squatted beside Billy.

"This is good country," Henry said. "It's a good stand of timber."

Billy laughed. "Do you want to cut it down?"

Henry reacted angrily to Billy's joke, said, "That's not what I mean."

"We were joking."

"Just because I'm white doesn't mean I want to cut everything down and dig everything up," Henry declared angrily. "And just because you're Indian doesn't make you the only protector and keeper of all this."

"So," Billy said.

"So."

"This is the land of our fathers and our grandfathers." Billy looked directly into Henry's eyes. Henry did not move. He felt an emotional rush envelop him. He suddenly felt exhausted and depleted and sick and alone. He felt as though the ends of his limbs were being unravelled and becoming undone. He had to fight back tears, and when he failed he wiped them away with his hand. He stared up at the sky through the highest trees. He saw his parents for an instant, floating past on a puff of white cloud. Exhaustion swept through him, like embalming fluid displacing his blood. He was not sad for what was wrong or broken or missing, but for all that he knew to be true and perfect, and because he was alone and weak now. Billy turned his head and looked through the grasses and shrubbery. "And our children too."

Henry looked at him, blinking rapidly. Billy's "our" omitted him and he felt hurt. A constriction burned his throat, a pain there brought on by his emotion and by his need to speak. As if his body resisted with all its power the release of the words. As if his body, sick and crippled and weary, still fought against his being and will. "Billy," Henry said, and he looked at him again, needing to speak to this one and only man who had the capacity to listen and moreover to understand, "the forest, the forest is, is my mother. It's my mother, Billy."

Billy Peel was wondering about the world, the many cities he had never seen and never would see, the continents and countries, the oceans and plains, the different peoples. One thing that had set him apart from other young men in his clan had been his wanderlust, his desire at an early age to explore, to visit the centres of the whiteman's world—Toronto, New York, London—to travel through Asia and Africa and Europe, to break and smell new ground, to see and taste new life; his yearnings led him away from Skincuttle Island for a while. Although he never got farther than a poor reservation in Alberta, where he lived for a year, he stayed away three years altogether, and in that time he never lost his desire to roam but felt compelled to return too, sensing something new that was greater than his own imaginings or desires, the gravitational pull of his own land and seascape and people. Sometimes he still fancied himself to be a gull, trailing tramp steamers, roving from one port to another, except that he knew himself better now, he was a bird of a different order, a different colour, a scavenger perhaps, living on the fringe of the civilized world, but one who stayed close to home, searching through its domain of forest, sea, and cycles of time. His penchant for travel and his need to be rooted and at home sometimes pulled him in separate directions, sometimes caused him to envy men who were free of responsibilities. Men like Henry Scowcroft. For it had seemed to Billy that there was nothing keeping Henry on Skincuttle Island, except fear and laziness, and Henry had always read books and discussed the outside world with the same enthusiasm and interest that Billy knew, yet he had never left. Vancouver and Prince Rupert were the farthest limits of his travel. Billy had never understood why until now. He had never understood that Henry's bond to this island held him as tightly as did his own.

It's my mother, Billy.

At the same instant Billy felt both elated and disturbed.

Henry's statement voided the isolation of his village because it voided the exclusiveness of his vision, yet it signalled too the existence of something deeper, something real and tangible that undercut the disassemblage of their lives, that connected them to one another just as surely as they were each individually connected and sewn to Skincuttle Island.

"So," Billy said, and caught Henry's eye. "That's what it is."

The historian met the rebel chief and neither one looks to be in too good shape. Henry addressed his thoughts to the forest as he swayed from side to side on his cot. He could hear the rush of a stream near by and the first drops of a shower patter in the treetops. And through it, the tramping steps of the four quiet men who carried out their work with the solemnity and reserve of pallbearers. The forest went alternately light and dark as clouds of varying densities crossed the sun. *Who's in whose hands? I can no more warp my history to suit his needs than he can mend his future to satisfy my past. Sometimes I'm afraid. Should I tell him that? I'm so tired. He must know it for himself anyway. Sometimes he's afraid too. All we can do is meet and hope that that moment will suffice for us both, to fulfil and rectify the past, to announce and purify the days to come. God, sometimes it seems like such seedy business, like a plot against mankind, when all we're doing or all we ever wanted to do is to go on learning.*

The two men were carried through the forest, and the motion made Henry feel dizzy and sick, he lost his concentration and bearings, while Billy winced from his bruises. The four men who carried them seemed tireless, resting when Billy commanded them to, or after a steep climb. Henry asked them to stop beside a stream. Several humpbacks huddled in the water—rotting salmon with distorted bodies. Henry knelt beside the stream and Billy came up behind him.

"Is this the price, Billy?"

"What?"

"Is it?" Suddenly Henry slapped the water repeatedly with his cane, laughing wildly and calling out, "Is it? Is it?" He jumped up and ran through the forest. The forest seemed to fall back from his charge. He broke onto a clearing and before he could check his stride he crashed into a platform and landed on the ground. A pile of bones tumbled on top of him. Billy hurried to his rescue; Henry was screaming.

In his dream he was fighting to wake himself up: in his dream he remembered Billy escorting him through the mortuary ground and through the forest and across Kloo River, and there they were, overlooking the village, with the children and dogs now staring at them both, and one girl came running and brought them to this teepee; Henry could feel the perspiration pouring through his skin, knew that his head was lurching from side to side in desperation, and quietly, easily, like the gentle opening of a flower, he woke up. Billy was being attended to across from him. Henry propped himself up on an elbow. "Hey, Billy," he said.

Billy got to a sitting position. Next to him an old man prepared a plaster for his nose. The nose was swollen and had been jerked back into place. "We thought you'd sleep all day."

"How late is it?"

"It's still early. You been asleep only an hour."

"Billy. I got to get back to Lyell."

Billy shrugged. "Eat first."

"All right." In a few minutes they ate together. Billy signalled with his hand and they were left alone. The food made Henry drowsy again, he felt dreamy again. "It's good."

"Yes." The flap of the teepee was blown back and flies buzzed about their bowls. Outside, there was still considerable consternation. Their arrival together, and especially Billy's appearance, had upset the usual calm.

"What's the idea?" Henry asked.

"What do you mean?"

"Teepees. Cumshewa Indians never had teepees."

"It is something we learned when I left Skincuttle years ago. The first night sleeping in a teepee we had a vision. We respect the power of the teepee." Billy shrugged. "It's something new for the people. It gives us a feeling of our purpose."

"Which is?"

Billy chewed on a tough piece of meat. He was looking out through the opening. "You know," he said. He shrugged again.

The fire was flickering. Twin flames licked the last small log.

"You are going fast to Lyell," Billy said.

"As fast as possible. I guess I'll take Doc's boat back."

"Want to go faster?"

"How?"

Billy nodded. "Go by war canoe. With twenty men to paddle, you go fast. Go halfway up the coast then cut across to Lyell. We'll give you a guide."

"I doubt if I can walk very well."

"An easy trail. It goes downhill. We will give you two guides," Billy said, laughing. "They will carry you if you can't walk."

Henry joined in the laughter and thanked him. The fire was dying. Henry studied it and soon Billy was staring into the ashes too. When the last flame went out they were quiet together. Then they looked at one another. "What do the ashes say, Billy?"

Billy used a stick to poke the cinders and burnt logs. He poked for a few minutes, then he was quiet again. The last puffs of smoke curled slowly upward. Billy made a fist, and when he spoke he shook it slightly. "We're tied to the forest, not like a man to a woman, but like a bird to a tree."

"Yes."

"But you, you are a son to your mother."

"Yes."

"In time, a son leaves his mother."

"Billy, no," Henry said quickly, "that's impossible." Henry felt a kind of agony rise up from his diaphragm, rebellion battling his sensibilities.

Billy smiled. He looked at Henry and his glance spoke words, words that both men knew were best to remain unuttered, for they were unutterable; words that decreed that tomorrow is not the same as today, just as yesterday is not the same as today; words that hinted of what was still unknown and mysterious and unmentionable, still the property of the future and of the deepest past.

"I better go now," Henry said. When they stood they hugged one another tightly and quickly. Billy went out and Henry changed into clothes that had been brought for him. His old clothes stuck to his skin, it was like peeling away a layer of tissue to undress.

Henry walked through the village slowly. It was all new and exciting to him. The scents, the children, the teepees, the dark longhouses, the beaten path—like being returned to another time. But he was aware too of his steps in the soft earth, felt them falling out behind him like ephemeral and untraceable beings. A young girl ran to his side and thrust a bearskin over his arm. "Please take this to Doctor," she said, speaking so fast that the request came out as one word. She ran away again. At the waterfront the canoe was waiting. For Henry, stepping into it was like physically stepping into the past, into the beauty and magic and lore of his history, but when he turned, grinning, eyes dancing and seeking Billy, Billy had already turned and was walking towards the village And Billy did not look back as the men cried out and stroked the paddles through the deep water.

29

Ezekiel. Jeremiah.

Thomas moved off to one side of Doc who skirted the riverbank, moved deeper into the woods so that Doc saw him only sporadically and at times as an indistinguishable form of colour and movement that danced among the trees. Once he broke ahead of him, running quickly, Doc unable to see the man's legs and viewing only a floating, headless torso winding through the woods. The hermit's movement was so fluid and easy that Doc thought he might emerge riding a bicycle—he anticipated some kind of trick. Thomas came out ahead of him though and balanced on a rock, circling, faster and faster, like a child wanting to make himself dizzy—but it was Doctor Marifield who felt dizzied by it—leaping down next and cavorting in the river, the water splashing up to his knees while he danced.

Isaiah. Malachi.

Doc laughed. The sunlight, the brightness and sweetness of the forest, Thomas's antics, the spiralling wind gusts, and the surging Oganjibra River—a conspiracy, he figured, to make him feel good, to make him feel purified and regenerated.

Thomas returned to the forest again, following a trail parallel to the water and Doc's route, and Doc fell into a sunny but deep mood. His meditations were directed on himself, and he was eager to explore various ideas. Recalling his period of regression in Vancouver, Hebrew prophets sprang to mind. He turned the names over in his mind as if chewing on them, tasting them, luxuriating in the juices. The men had inspired his eccentricity, but he wondered now if he had been beguiled by his picture of them, by their form, while paying no heed to the significance of their words and intensity. He had loved them, but it occurred to him now that it was the names he had loved and not necessarily the men. He had never bothered to know the men, admiring their passion, their fusion with life and sky, sun, universe, man, but his fascination had not plunged him to the source or strength of their inspiration. Instead he had used their vitality and zealous spirit to fashion an image of himself, not as a prophet exactly, but as a man of fortitude and vision, emancipating vision—an image he saw as silly now. On Skincuttle Island he could not play the fool. For his audience comprised the very people with whom he lived and breathed, doctored to, with whom he ate and drank. The loss of his self-respect in the city could be camouflaged by harebrained behaviour, but the trick did not work here. So much was stripped bare here, positions, power, even bloodlines and passions and pain, so that his exuberant tangents were not simply dismissed by one and all as extreme and nonsensical, or as dangerous and insane, but were followed backwards to their core by a few curious individuals, friends, such as Evlin and Henry, and the root of the activity observed. He couldn't take it. Could a man not be a fool without his foolishness revealed? That was the difference. And it was crucial. In the city, men and women sighed and said that they could not understand him; on Skincuttle Island men and women sighed and said they did. *Ezekiel. Jeremiah. Isaiah. Malachi.* A defender of righteousness, but a fool; an idealist, but without conviction: he was not an honest man. He saw that he had been victimized again, not by the exhortations of the prophets that had sent him off raving like a lunatic; not only by his intelligence and capabilities, to which he had succumbed and submitted his inner wishes and feelings and beliefs to the point where madness became his only release; and not even by his impetuous nature that had allowed him, conveniently, to escape any struggle at hand, but by his refusal to stop cold, and stare, and catch a glimpse of himself as he flittered past.

Doc watched Thomas prance and romp for a while, walking on, feeling immeasurably more sure of himself, finding pieces of his being and sensing the discovery of himself as old skins and coats were removed. Thomas's energy and youthfulness made him feel alive too, and he delighted in it.

Suddenly bears emerged from the forest as Doc rounded a bend. He froze in his tracks and his body seized, lost weight and its ability to function too, and the mother and her two cubs looked up the river at this odd apparition, sniffing the wind for his scent. Doc was struck by the realization that he emitted a smell strong enough to drift upon the breeze, and he was startled, as if his awareness had suddenly magnified, believing for a moment that he was that scent, floating, drifting, a refined essence.

Thomas broke out of the woods and charged after the bears, and immediately Doc felt liberated too, charging too, hooting and hollering at the top of his lungs. And the amazed animals retreated to the woods again, while Doc and Thomas collapsed against boulders, laughing and gasping for breath.

And farther downstream they dove into the river after salmon, rampaging through a quiet pool, and the fish skirted this way and that and avoided them easily.

Doc looked around him. Felt the presence of the forest and blue sky. He became aware that he was no longer afraid of being fused, nor even of being overwhelmed by the elements, understanding then that he had always felt vulnerable to fusion with the earth, sky, sea, because deep inside himself it was his desire to be so united. And he recognized that this was still a potentiality, but because he simply was not ready for it, all was well, he had nothing to fear, the earth, sky, and sea would not rise up against his will to snare him, although one day he might discover them as friends, waiting to welcome him home.

Doc continued on toward Lyell feeling a little more sober and subdued. By afternoon the sunlight shone brilliantly on the white water—sharp, piercing reflections—and reflected from the high leaves too: a kind of crystalline awareness that he felt in his own being, the warmth and clarity spreading through him like a final process of purification. He enjoyed his companion, this animated and zestful troll who had also been inebriated by the sunlight and made dizzy by the descent, and he joined him in a quick and chilling swim. Rising out of the water, Doc experienced a sadness, a wave passing through him that hovered and lingered on. Suddenly the forest seemed like home, and the intercourse of light and foliage, of shadow and air, was impressed upon his mind and senses. He felt like a devout man departing from an altar to return to a less miraculous, less decent realm.

Immersed in his moods, he had maintained no concept of time or distance or altitude, and soon Lyell spread before his vision like a mirage, a trick oasis, somehow unreal and extraordinary under the glare of sunlight. Beside him, Thomas went rigid. As they walked he could feel the man's stiffness and fear. Gone was the dancer's gait, the bouncy step, and the lithe movement of the torso. His facial expression was like stone, like the granite of his home. He looked like an old man who had aged many years, suddenly and without prior warning.

30

THROUGH HER FATIGUE, through the numbness that seemed to invade from the body of the horse and rise up through her legs, Evlin was conscious of Morgan's body at her back. She felt brittle, her waist held between his hands, as if he could snap her life in two. His every twinge and movement triggered a response through her, electrical charges that startled her to wakefulness and fear again. His breath was sour and stale and reeked of liquor and decay.

Frequently Morgan dozed off, leaning to one side or forward against her, but the movement of the horse would grate against him, causing him to gasp as pain from his injury or wound or boils pierced his leg or chest. He was pale and weak from the loss of blood.

Shaking herself awake suddenly, Evlin discovered that the horse had stopped to graze. Neither she nor Morgan had noticed. The light through the trees and the birdsong and the drill of a woodpecker made the moment a languid and pleasant one. She shook herself again, decided to rest here and eat.

Evlin made bannock over a small fire, using a tin can as her stove. She used the upturned bottom of the tin as a grill, and a section of one side had been cut away for ventilation. Morgan leaned against a fir tree. The paleness of his skin had shocked her, he seemed drained of all strength and energy. Eating the bread, he finished his portion in quick, large bites while Evlin nibbled and chewed slowly. The food invigorated him a little; soon he was leering at her.

"Stop it," Evlin said.

"What's wrong, lady? Yaha!"

"I can still leave you here."

"Don't threaten me, lady. If you know what's good for you."

Evlin smiled and nodded her head, said, "You haven't changed."

Morgan moved and lay beside the dying fire. He selected a twig that still burned at one end. He drew the hot ember across the biceps of his left arm. The skin burned. Morgan looked straight at Evlin.

She jumped to her feet, kicked the can aside and tramped the fire under her boot, pressing the ashes into the wet ground. "You think I'm afraid of you?"

"Yaha!"

"I'm not. I'm not afraid of you. I'm not a kid anymore, when I used to run away from you like a scared rabbit. That part of me died, Morgan. Died the same damn split-second that Gail did. Think about it. You thought you were seeing a ghost. Maybe you were. Think about that."

Morgan glared at her and she mounted the horse quickly. Anxiety showed in his face and Evlin backed the horse away. She was mad enough now to leave him here, but looking at him she saw that he was dying. "Well?" she said. "Come on!"

Morgan stumbled forward as best he could. Putting weight on his good leg shot pain through his stomach. He hopped forward but as he reached for the reins the horse was startled and jerked its head away, and Morgan collapsed on the ground. He looked up at her from the forest floor and crawled ahead. The hatred was intense in his eyes, controlling his pain and exhaustion, waiting for its moment, its reward of vengeance. Leaning on the stirrups, he pulled himself up beside the horse.

"Do you think it was like this for Gail?" Evlin asked.

Morgan stopped and looked at her again. He didn't speak.

"Well? Do you?"

"How the hell would I know, lady?"

"Exactly."

* * *

The trail was a secret one, she had learned it years ago from Joe Crigger, who had loaned her the horse, and it followed connecting deer paths and bear routes, winding its way to the western end of Lyell by the sawmill. Mosquitoes and flies assaulted them, and the warm, humid air increased their drowsiness. The horse's ear flickered constantly as it tried to shake the mosquitoes. The rolling, plodding gait of the animal reminded Evlin of the motion of a small boat. "How do you think she died?"

"Shut up about it, why don't you? What do I know?"

"That's right—what do you know, Morgan?"

Morgan cursed her under his breath.

"You know when I saw her last? Your mother was sending her out to you and your brothers, with what? More whiskey. Did you get that whiskey, Morgan?"

"I don't know what you're talking about, lady."

"You know. I saw the empties. She made it to the fleet. What happened after that, Morgan?"

"The sea got her. The sea smashed her boat."

Evlin slapped her forehead, then a shoulder. The mosquitoes burst on her shoulder and blood was smeared on her jacket. The jacket was hot, but she would not remove it, needing the additional layer of protection between her and Morgan's sweating skin. Glancing over her shoulder, she noticed that the mosquitoes bit into him but he paid them no mind. "That's why you left Skincuttle Island? Because the sea got her?"

"Time for a change."

"That's why Thomas disappeared into the mountains? Because the sea got her? Sure."

"It's none of your business, lady."

"It's my business. Like it or not. It's my business."

They were quiet for a while, and sometimes sunlight broke through the foliage and they had to squint. Time seemed expanded here, marshalled and measured by the heavy, prodigious walk of the horse, mud ploughed and turned over by the hooves; time seemed elongated, stretched out, the forest's life suspended, no shadows, no recesses in which things were evaluated and redone or destroyed, as if the two of them and the horse were trudging across a planet where all movement had abruptly ceased and awaited inspection. "She was my closest friend," Evlin said, and she was surprised to hear herself speaking out loud. But she continued. "She was always so bright and energetic. Not innocent, I don't mean that, and not pure, but something like that. Refined. In a carefree way. Do you think she was refined, Morgan?"

His reply was indistinct.

"No. Not even refined," Evlin said. "She was just a little girl and sweet, despite a tough life. She loved it when the sun came out. Then she didn't have to live under that tarpaulin. She couldn't even see under it, she was led around like a blind person. Maybe that was it. She knew what it was like to live in a cage, so she really appreciated being released and she conveyed it, other people caught her zest and happiness too. You must have been very sad when she died. Were you sad, Morgan?"

The man slumped forward against her. Evlin twisted herself around and pushed his head back by the hair. He was unconscious. "Yes. I bet you were," she said.

The sleep was in her legs, they felt numb and distant, and it encroached upon the rest of her body. Morgan's weight against her wore her down further. Crossing over a rise she saw the sunlight sparkling on Cumshewa Sound, the water lightly rippled and moving. A sudden gust of wind rushed through the foliage. She continued on through a darker patch of forest and dozed in the saddle several times, her head snapping back each time, and she exhorted the horse to press on. Near Cumshewa Sound she thought she saw a horse and a face, and her own horse whinnied as if in surprise—she thought she saw an Indian in full regalia watching her, and the horse he rode had a brilliant green stone between its ears. Looking around wildly, she saw nothing. But she felt alert afterwards, and for some time her hands and stomach continued to tingle.

The final fifteen yards of the trail were overgrown and concealed.

The horse had to squeeze through tight spaces and the slapping branches stirred Morgan again. When the horse leaped a fallen log Morgan woke with a start, clutching his side and gasping in pain.

"We're here. You better hope Doc is here too."

"Shut up, lady. I've heard too much from you already."

They trotted onto the clearing, the sawmill to their left, and further left, Cumshewa Sound. The saws were whirring, and smoke from the inverted-cone furnace drifted lazily skyward. The land sloped upward, then down again into the hamlet of Lyell. Morgan's hands tightened around Evlin's waist. "Watch it," she said.

"You watch it. I've had enough from you."

"Leave me alone." Evlin tried to kick her heels into the horse to get the mare moving, but Morgan blocked her. She squeezed her knees and the horse broke into a gallop, but reaching around her Morgan yanked the reins hard, pulling the animal's head back. Morgan had a hand on the rifle as she struggled to free it from the sheath, and the horse was panicking now and spinning in circles, rising slightly on its hind legs, whinnying, its cry echoing off the surrounding forest like a high-pitched siren. Evlin held her position in the saddle, digging her feet into the stirrups as Morgan tried to throw her off. She punched with her elbows and heard him gasp, but he fought on, and what she felt overpowering her was not his strength or size or muscle, but his flesh, sickening her as it pressed against her, encompassing her, she felt herself sinking into it, and she heard herself screaming with terror. Yet when Morgan pushed her off the horse she moved instinctively to bring him down with her, suddenly convinced that he could not be allowed the horse, that that would be more than a concession, but a defeat. And they fell heavily on the ground and Morgan was over her, squeezing his flesh into her, and she screamed, screamed, no longer aware of herself, but only of this massive body submerging her, suffocating her, and while he laughed and pinned her arms and spat in her face, she writhed and cried out and cried.

Then suddenly they were surrounded, she was aware of the feet and legs, and in an instant Morgan was off her and she was released from her trance. She jumped up quickly and ran. She stumbled, and when she looked back Morgan was down on all fours and snarling, snarling like a beast, like a wild and ferocious cat, a cougar or a tiger, and his four brothers, Rupert and Jake and Whitney and Jackson Two, were slapping at him with lengths of two-by-four.

Evlin ran, her heart pounding wildly. The horse bounded ahead of her and darted from side to side in confusion, and she called after it, "Horse! Horse!" as if it were a lost and terrified child.

31

THE SHADOWS WERE LENGTHENING in the late afternoon, the hills and trees casting brooding, dark blots over Cumshewa Sound, although far out from shore where a fish jumped, light shone on the expanding ripples, and Doctor Marifield turned his gaze away from the water and retreated deeper into his home, lighting a lantern in the far corner of the room above his desk. His log book and his enormous Bible lay side by side. He alternately flipped through the pages of one, then the other, smiling to himself as if arriving at a satisfactory compromise or decision, revelling in the names again too, the clear, tough names of the prophets. He left the log book open to the first blank page, the whiteness of it shining in his mind's eye, and he slumped onto the chesterfield, propping his feet on the coffeetable.

Thomas was asleep in the bedroom. When he first came in he had pressed the mattress tentatively and tested it with his weight, and lying on the bed finally he had rocked from side to side. Doc had laughed as Thomas bounced up and down, grinning again, laughing soon, and he had left him to it. Only the occasional snore or cough was emitted from the room now, like persistent reminders of his presence there and purpose.

The house held a unique and endearing quality for Doctor Marifield, a life of its own which seemed to manifest itself when the day was quiet like this. A perceptible breathing, the regular inhale and exhale of the old timbers, and the sloped floors and slanted ceilings, the cracked walls and doorways out of whack, were not the natural consequences of old age, he believed, but the result of this internal breathing, this restructuring, which was not decay but development, a laborious renewal that one day would be brought to birth and perfection. The familiar smells, the usual universe of dust motes moving in mid-air, the shadows and streaks of light, the furniture like patient, loving friends—Doc was struck for an instant by the patterns, saw his own life intricately interwoven through this house, and he was seized by a tremor of anticipation that the house seemed to know also.

The rooms had been tidied in his absence. Doc suspected that Evlin must have been down to Lyell from Cumshewa Town, perhaps looking for him, and he wondered if she might still be in town. He wished he could go to look for her, but he did not want to leave Thomas alone.

One of the springs in the big-cushioned chesterfield was breaking through the fabric; when he moved it called out—*sprong!* The sound made him laugh, and he got up again and banged out a couple of dance tunes on the piano that he remembered from university, then pounded a few great and impressive chords, the sound filling the room, causing it to vibrate and resound with new hope.

He returned to the screen door. Birds chirped outside, the breeze rustled the leaves. The sound of children's voices on the wind. And from far off, the screaming saws from the planing mill, like the unattended, piercing cries of the day descending into dusk. Something was awake inside him, he was not certain—excitement, spirit, premonition—and despite the bone weariness of his body, he did not want to sleep.

A canoe bumped the wharf and Doc opened the door, bending low to peer under the leaves. He recognized Evlin by the sunlight reflecting off her light-coloured hair, and he hurried down to greet her, calling out her name.

As she saw him coming Evlin was stung by an overriding sense of relief, for seeing him safe and sound made it easier for her to accept the same thing about herself; much of her worry and strain was lifted, so that she smiled brightly, laughing, reflecting his smile and happiness, so that when they came together they hugged and hopped on the wharf like ecstatic children. Evlin said, "Boy, am I glad to see you!"

"It's good to be back."

"You can say that again! You look worn out, David."

"I bet I do. Hellish rain. I went up to the mountains, Evlin."

"I know."

They walked arm and arm to the house, idly, looking at each other often, as if to affirm the other's presence, as if to reacquaint themselves with each other.

"How did you make out?"

"Ev, I brought Thomas Duff back. He's sleeping in the house right now."

Evlin's eyes went wide and she stepped away from him, gaped, "You didn't!"

"Yeh. I did," Doc said, and he grinned slightly.

Evlin wrapped her arms around his neck and hugged. "David! That's terrific!"

On their way up the stairs, Doc said, "That's an odd blouse you're wearing—for you. It looks—"

"—like an old woman's blouse?" Evlin laughed and linked her elbow with his. "That's because it is. I borrowed it from Thelma. I went to her place to wash and eat and settle myself down. I needed a place to scrub the dirt off. When I came out of the tub she handed me this thing—I couldn't say no."

The screen door banged shut behind them. Evlin remained on the interior landing while Doc continued into the living room. "What dirt?" he asked, but another question was nagging at the back of his mind and he couldn't get to it.

"Forest dirt. I was filthy."

She was looking at him steadily, as if aiming her regard and perceptions, so that Doctor Marifield returned her gaze in puzzlement. "You were in the woods?"

"Yes." She made a motion with her hands as if trying to use them to speak, as if she wanted to blurt out something but had to wrestle first with blocks and apprehensions; she said, "I was riding. I borrowed Joe Crigger's horse."

Doc had seen this expression before, and the motions of her hands. "What is it you want to tell me, Ev?"

She smiled. "So you're not as dim-witted as I've heard."

"What is it?" Then another question finally became clear to him, and Doc stepped closer to her. "How did you know I was up to the mountains anyway? You seemed awfully sure about it."

"Ah. Well. I went riding—um—also, to Lake TaColl."

Staring at her; and something came together within him, and in coming together snapped: the summer, his retreat from clearly drawn battlelines, his retreat from his own ideals and responsibilities, none of it lived or repudiated without consequences. Seeing that now, the consequences coming together now and snapping inside him, and snapping, he was swiftly furious at himself for having faltered in his duty, which if anything was to keep himself toned and prepared for conflict, let alone reconnoitring the conflict, let alone engaging in the conflict itself. He had forced Evlin to enter the woods to back him up, just as Henry had entered the woods without him; forced Evlin to enter the woods alone, just as Henry had entered the woods alone—and Billy too, except that Billy had grudgingly carried him along. Only Henry's tangent he could suffer and accept, and Billy's he could ignore, but Evlin's was too incriminating and beyond his means to readily acknowledge, for it implicated his own flaw and fault severely, conclusively, so that he was equally furious with Evlin, for exposing his blame among themselves, and for daring to care this much about him.

"What the hell do you mean? What the bloody hell—"

"David—"

"Are you crazy? You went alone?"

"Yes."

"Alone! Evlin, for God's sake!"

"Well, when you left I knew you'd either gone to Kloo or back to Lyell. I wanted to know which. I mean, I had to know where you were going, what you were going to do. So when I got to Lyell you were gone, nobody had seen you, so I figured—hoped, really—that you'd gone up to the mountains. Henry once told me that if Thomas lived anywhere it'd be around Lake TaColl, and that's where the stakes were pulled out. So I waited here but—well, you were gone and Henry and Morgan were gone too . . . so I borrowed Joe Crigger's horse and went too."

"Evlin—Oliver—Rand! What's the matter with you? Don't you know what could have happened?" Doc slapped the banister of the interior landing. It had always seemed a peculiar article to him, the inside landing and its railing, as if the house had once been built inside out. It suddenly bothered him to be looking up to her, and he pulled her off the landing into the living room and held her by the shoulders, facing her. "Morgan was up there too!"

"Yes, I know."

"He's crazy! He's out of his mind."

"I know, David."

"You know. Yet you still went up there? Alone?"

Evlin placed her hands on his chest and smiled in a girlish manner. "Calm yourself. I have something to tell you."

"No," he said, but he was yielding to her. "I refuse."

Evlin pressed herself against him and laid her head on his shoulder. "I brought somebody back to Lyell too. And it wasn't Thomas, and it wasn't Henry, and it wasn't Billy, and it certainly wasn't you."

Doc tilted her head back with his forefinger, looked into her face. He said quietly, "Oh no."

Later they strolled around the perimeter of Kinstuk Island, and the gentle lapping of the waves among the rocks was pleasant, lending a rhythm to their steps and inner tempo. Smoke lolled skyward from the sawmill in puffs like departing souls, and the shadows were long and cool in the early evening. In the distance, across the water, a dog barked angrily from one of the farms. They shared their stories again and fought off mosquitoes, and something transpired between them that frightened Doc, it welled up inside him and expired in less than a minute. The sensation was not emotional but ritualistic, as if a ceremony had been conducted, but the meaning of it had long been lost. Walking, he felt deprived, and brooding on this feeling he speculated that something had been missed or neglected. He thought it was like missing the funeral of a friend because he had not been informed of the death, although he had sensed it anyway.

"He's injured badly, David. If he can't come himself he'll have to send for you sooner or later. Pride or no pride."

"It's a wonder he hasn't come yet."

"Should we look for him?"

Doc was thoughtful. "No. I'm afraid to." He leaned against a large boulder that extended out into the water, then crawled up to sit on it and Evlin joined him. Doc took her right hand in his, said, "You know, I feel really badly about letting you down. We wanted to make this summer an important one, make strides, no more stupid concessions to the mining people, but I didn't pull my own weight. I didn't do my job."

"David—"

Doc held up a hand to stop her protest. "When I think of you and Henry, going into the woods alone, I feel sick. I shouldn't have left it all up to you two. When I think of you going in there alone—bringing Morgan out—God." In deference to her courage and accomplishment, Doc felt it both necessary and easy to confess. But Evlin was shaking her head.

"Please, David. Don't go on about it. There's another reason why I went into the woods. It wasn't just to check on you, because I thought you'd be safe in Billy's hands anyway. And it wasn't to check on Henry, because since when is that possible?" Evlin looked out over the water, breathed deeply as if drawing in the courage to speak, as if storing the air inside herself to make her voice strong, so it would not quaver. She looked back at Doc, then turned away and said quickly, "It's crazy because I never admitted it to myself. The whole trip up and down I didn't admit it." She squeezed Doc's hand, needing to speak because it wasn't right for Doc to continue apologizing to her. "I mean I was concerned about you, really concerned. You scared me running out the way you did! Into that storm! And I kept feeling Gail Duff. It's like I wanted to do something for her. . . ." Evlin looked back at Doc, who waited. "But I wanted to see Billy too, David. I don't know. Maybe that's really why I went up there. I was hoping to see him again."

They looked out over the water, listened to the waves wash on the shore. Evlin slapped a mosquito on Doc's wrist. She said brightly, "So don't blame yourself for my being there! It was all my own foolishness. Okay?"

Doc smiled and hugged her. "Okay. Okay."

And later they waited inside, darkness embracing the house gently, the blackness overcoming the final rays of dusk. And as the minutes plodded past their anxiety grew, as if Morgan's refusal to come placed not his life in danger but Henry's and Billy's.

"Why hasn't he come?"

They sipped gin and the night enveloped them. Each sound caught their attention and their nerves tensed. The lantern flickered and shadows paraded on the walls. The woods on tiny Kinstuk Island were alive with movement and prescience.

"I'm going to check on Thomas," Doc said.

The hermit was sleeping soundly in his clothes, lying on his back with his legs spread apart and his feet overlapping the end of the bed. Doc brought a candle into the room and removed the man's boots. Whistles and occasional snorts from his mouth: a deep sleep.

When Doc returned to the main room, Evlin's head was nodding. "Wake up! Wake up!" he called, laughing. "Who knows? Fall asleep and we might be visited."

Evlin groaned, yawned, and stretched. "I'll make some coffee then. Have a cup?"

"Stay there, Ev. I'll make it."

"No, no. I don't mind."

"Stay!"

Doc lit the oil stove in the kitchen, turning on the fuel, dropping a flaming paper into the hole. He dunked the coffee pot right into the water barrel and placed it on the cast iron grill, and soon the water dripping from the outside of the pot spat and fizzled. Evlin joined him in the narrow room.

"You've become quite the homemaker," she said.

"What do you mean by that?"

"The house looks great. I'm impressed. When I came here the first time—while you were away—I thought you must have moved out and somebody else lived here now."

Doc put the tin of coffee down and looked at her. In the light from the lamp it was impossible to read her expression. "You didn't clean up?"

"What's to clean up? The place is immaculate."

Still looking at her, Doc put the lid back on the tin and returned it to the cupboard. "Ev. I left this place in a shambles. It was in its usual disastrous condition. Are you kidding me?"

"No. I'm not."

"I presumed it was you who tidied up."

"I didn't. David?"

"Beats me. Who would do such a thing? You're the only person who's done it before."

They fixed their coffees and returned to the main room. Doc was perplexed, sensing the presence of other beings residing and fluctuating around him. He no longer felt secure or safe here, his nerves tensing at the prospect of what Henry might term ghosts and mercenary ghouls. Sitting on the chesterfield, he put his coffee down and left it unattended while Evlin sipped hers. "Who?" he asked.

Evlin shrugged, smiled, and said, "Either a thankful patient or a fed-up one." And Doc joined in her laughter.

But suddenly there was commotion in the bedroom, muffled shouts and the thumping of the bed on the floor, as if it were being dragged along the floor, heaved upward, and dropped every few feet. Doc, followed by Evlin, made it to the door in an instant, and opening it, only the blackness of the room was revealed, and the shouts and the banging continued, and Evlin ran away and returned with the kitchen lamp.

"Where's me feet? Where's me feet be?" Thomas was wrestling with a pillow and a blanket and as his body convulsed, the bed was jolted back and forth.

"Thomas! Easy now. Thomas!" Doc managed to clutch him by the shoulders.

"Where's me feet? Me feet are gone!"

"His boots!" Doc cried. "Get his boots! Under the bed!"

Evlin retrieved them quickly, and the moment they appeared Thomas Duff grabbed hold of them and held them to his chest. "Me feet," he said. Doc released him and the hermit put his boots back on calmly, absent-mindedly it seemed, and Doc was concerned that he might not know where he was or why he had come here.

"Thomas? It's me. Doc. How're you doing?" The older man did not answer, but concentrated all his efforts on tying his boot laces. "How're you doing, Thomas?"

"I'm dyin," he said.

Calm, direct, his voice startled Doctor Marifield. "What's wrong? What's the matter?"

"Me wee heart's flappin. Me heart's flappin like a wee bluebird. "

"Can I listen to it?"

"Hookay! "

Doc hurried out of the room and returned with a stethoscope. He listened to Thomas's rapid heartbeat but he was not alarmed by it. "It's the excitement. That's all it is."

"I'm dyin," Thomas said casually. "That's all 'tis."

Evlin stood with the lamp just inside the doorway and at the foot of the bed. Her movements caused the shadows of the two men to sway on the walls. Doc said, "Do you remember me? Are you awake now, Thomas?"

The hermit pushed both his hands into the mattress, let it spring back. "Hee!" he said.

"I want you to meet someone," Doc said, and he assisted Thomas to his feet.

Remembering Morgan's reaction to her, Evlin introduced herself quickly. "I'm Evlin Oliver. C. Oliver's daughter? Do you remember my father? I was a friend—a friend of Gail's."

Thomas looked at her but he was unable to penetrate the glare from the lamp. Evlin purposely kept the light in front of her so that he would not think he was seeing Gail. They left the room, their feet shuffling on the bare wood, Thomas's boots cracking sharply. Evlin went first, then Doc and Thomas, but suddenly Thomas dropped to the floor and commenced hopping. Hopping past the chesterfield and into the centre of the room. Doc laughed, but he was afraid at the same time. Thomas looked up and seeing Evlin he screamed,

"Gail!"

"No!" Evlin cried out, ran to his side. "I'm not Gail. I'm—not—Gail, Thomas. I'm Evlin. My name is Evlin. I only look like Gail." As she knelt down to him he sprung to his feet again, stared wide-eyed at Doc.

"What is it, Thomas? What's the matter?"

He glanced back and forth and around the room quickly. Evlin held him by an arm. Turning back to Doc, he said, "Morgan."

And Doc was relieved, for the man's voice had become his normal one, and declaring the name indicated that he had found his bearings. Doc said, "He's not here. You don't have to worry about him now." Again Thomas scrutinized the room, then laughed and dropped to the floor again, Evlin releasing him, and he hopped for several feet before stopping. Motionless. As if he were not breathing. As if all his pulses and rhythms had ceased.

"Thomas," Doc said.

"Wait!" Evlin whispered.

"What is it?"

"Someone's coming!"

A step; then one foot being dragged. Repeated in rhythm. "It's Morgan," Evlin said. "His crutch!" The jab of wood on the porch steps. Thomas was stone-still, squatting on the floor, his eyes intent on the door while his fingers touched the floor for support, trembling. Doc and Evlin glanced quickly at one another. The screen door creaked open and they saw no one. A moment later the visitor appeared, and Doc threw up his hands, crying out.

32

THOMAS TOO. Leaping to his feet and throwing his hands into the air. And crying out. And Evlin pressed one hand to her chest and used the other to brace herself against the chesterfield, breathing a sigh of relief while the men celebrated. Henry Scowcroft's grin extended from ear to ear.

"Look who's here!" Doc cried, and he shook his friend's hand and looked into his eyes. But Henry was already looking past him at Thomas.

"We were afraid you were Morgan," Evlin said.

"Hi, Evlin. No, I couldn't be Morgan. Hi, Thomas! It's good to see you. How are you?"

"I'm dyin!" the hermit said gleefully, pushing out his chest. "I'm dyin, Henry!"

"He's complaining about his heart," Doc said seriously. "But it seems all right to me, only fast."

Henry laughed so hard his eyes watered. "Sure he is! He'll outlive us all. You better watch that kind of talk around here, Thomas. You're liable to get operated on."

The hermit looked from Henry to the doctor nervously, as if comprehending fully.

Evlin asked, "Why couldn't you have been Morgan?"

Henry kissed her cheek and tossed a bearskin over the back of the chesterfield. He went to the front of the couch and dropped into it. Thomas Duff squatted down on all fours like a toad and stared at him with his one open eye. "Because he's still up in the mountains. And he's hurt. We'll have to get a search party—"

"No he's not," Doc said.

"He's in town," Evlin added.

Henry looked from Evlin to Doc and back again; ventured, "The horse?"

"That's right," Evlin said.

Henry shook his head from side to side. "I should have known. The surveyors?"

"Not exactly," Doc said, grinning.

Henry looked from him to Evlin. She smiled and mimed a curtsy.

But before the full realization struck home, while Henry still gaped at her, Thomas leaped and crashed into the coffeetable, sending it into Henry's lap, and Henry automatically reached for him and grabbed him by the beard and was pulled along as Thomas spun away. "He's in town!" Thomas hollered. "He's here!" Because it was different here, he was vulnerable and exposed, not invisible as he had become in the mountains. And Henry rode him into the floor, where just as quickly as he had erupted he fell still, motionless, scarcely breathing.

Evlin and Doc came close, but Henry warned them away. "Are you all right now, Thomas? Don't worry about your brother. You probably won't even have to see him. You're just here to tell your story. That's all. You're just here so Morgan knows you're here so he'll go away and leave you alone, that's all. That's all, Thomas."

Doctor Marifield rescued the coffeetable, placing it upright again, while Evlin picked up the pieces of their cups. Thomas lay still with both his eyes shut. "I'm loosin me teeth," he said quietly. Henry helped him up and he sat in a chair.

"Are you all right now?"

"I'm loosin me teeth."

Henry breathed deeply, relaxing his own tensions, patted the hermit's shoulder lightly. "Okay," he said. "Okay."

*   *   *

Henry listened, guzzled beer, gulped down a sandwich. He was absorbed in their stories, but aloof from them too, and not aloof, he realized, although that's what he thought at first; that's what he thought when he could not genuinely share in the experience of their stories or add his own to the pot. Aloof, he thought at first, as if he were untouched by their courage and daring and hardships, endured now but not forgotten, for even amid the laughter the lines of strain showed through; aloof, as if their stories were common to him and not worth much at all, so that he felt ashamed to even be sitting here and listening, belittling their lives, but he realized with a start that he was not aloof but scared, that it was fear separating and silencing him. The fear itself was not easily traced and identified. It grew out of the image of these two friends ascending and descending the mountains, entering and escaping the primeval forest, and therefore all the dangers and horrors the centuries had known and created, as if every tree and rock and formation of rock and tree had been influenced and persuaded by all that it had ever seen and known and heard, by all the defeated and broken and triumphant men too who had ever passed through, so that every known danger or horror or triumph had found its expression and therefore continuance in the forest and mountains, so that what scared him then was not the knowledge that they had survived and even triumphed, which made the forest and all its stories a part of them and a part of their stories too, but that Morgan Duff had escaped and triumphed too, resurfacing from the rain and forest and flood and his wounds as if he had never left, still here, still possessing his own ruthless form of command. So that Henry was absorbed in their stories but not involved in them, and he did not offer to reveal his own experience, because it was all contained by the forest anyway, and by each and every one of them, including Morgan, who waited to finish it.

And it occurred to Henry that Evlin's and Doc's sharing of their tales was not idle, not the simple outburst of relief and thankfulness now that they had escaped not only alive, but with cheer and accomplishment too. The learning and understanding of one another's parts to the story was crucial to the whole of it, because the need for knowledge had sent them on the expedition in the first place, the need to know Thomas's history and pain. And the blocking of that release was Morgan's whole purpose and single-minded, ferocious intent. Knowledge remained the key in their duel with Morgan Duff, in their quest to shape their destinies according to their mutual will; knowledge and the bearing of it, the carrying of it, and Henry's fear rose and fell as he dwelt upon what he did and did not know.

Doc stopped in mid-sentence. "Hey. What's that?" Picking up the bearskin he turned it over in his hands.

And Henry laughed. "Don't worry. Your girlfriend's not two-timing you. She asked me to bring it to you."

"What girlfriend?" Evlin asked.

Doc scoffed at their teasing and donned the bearskin, said, "She's just a kid with a crush on her white doctor."

Henry winked and he and Evlin laughed. They didn't notice Thomas rising out of his chair. All at once he leaned over Evlin and curled his lips back, exposing his teeth and gums. She yelped in surprise. Thomas wiggled a tooth with a finger, said, "Me teeth are loose, loose."

Doc and Henry pulled him away gently, talking to him, soothing him, helping him into his chair again. When Evlin finally found her voice she said, "We have to do something."

Sitting again, Doc said, "I vote we just wait. If Morgan is hurt it's up to him to come to us—to me. Or at least send a message."

"I don't know about that," Henry said.

"We can't just go looking for him. He might be laying in wait for us."

"I don't know about that either."

"I think David's right," Evlin said. "We're safer here. But we should plan something, to be ready."

"I think we should go get him. Wherever he is. Who knows what he's up to? Better get to him now while he's hurt and we're still healthy."

"No," Doc said. "Evlin's right. We're better off waiting for him here. Our territory, our terms. Maybe we should prepare what to say to him?"

Evlin saw something in Henry's displeasure, in the severe lines across his face, saw something indicating more than his stubbornness and more than his conviction that in this instance he was right. She saw him alone and grieving, and for a moment she was terrified. For suddenly she was propelled back to her own sense of anguish and aloneness that had pursued her in the forest, suddenly she was submerged by a wave of hostilities and unrequited passions. What she felt for Henry at that moment was neither anger nor sympathy, nor anything in between, but something out and beyond both planes, almost out and beyond herself too, neither sympathy nor anger but a form of bereavement. It was as if he had passed through her or she through him, and in the interchange she had learned to love him and despair of him simultaneously, to honour him while at the same moment and instant she was repelled. And she thought that this mental excursion of hers was not so much owing to Henry or to anything about him, save the worry lines marked on his face that had prompted it, but caught her at familiar extremes, worshipping what she condemned, condemning what she loved. As if there were no repose, no sleep, no space between the fibres and tendrils of her life for her to breathe and be at ease, freely. She felt a wave of sadness, not emanating from Henry but including him too, and she fought it off by leaning forward and speaking to him.

"What would be the point? It's safer here. It is."

"The point? The point? What's he doing?" Henry stood up to vent his anger more freely. "For all we know he could be on his way back to Prince Rupert already, and then what? He'll be back again to haunt us! Look, what's the use of hanging around? Let's go find him."

"How can we go with Thomas? And we can't leave him here alone."

Henry nodded, relented, having no argument. He sat down again but he was still disturbed. He drummed his fingertips along the arm of the chair until both Doc and Evlin glared at him. He fetched another beer from the icebox in the kitchen and drank quickly.

"That can't be very cold," Doc said.

"Sure it's cold," Henry said.

"No," Doc said.

Henry and Evlin looked at him. He went to the kitchen and checked for himself. Fresh ice in the box. "Somebody's been here," he said. "Henry. Somebody tidied the place while I was gone. And there's new ice in the icebox."

Henry shrugged. "You have friends."

"Who exactly?"

"Take your pick. I'm not going to worry about that now."

Thomas had fallen asleep in his chair and Evlin and Henry laughed at his snores. Doc paced behind the chesterfield, then said, "I'll be back in a minute."

"Doc! Come back here! Doc!"

He ran through the kitchen and out the back way.

For a brief moment he felt transported, another region of mind and sense, transfixed suddenly by the cool night air and the darkness, the breeze moving through the leaves and needles and across his face, the stars bright and clear between the branches. And what he saw instantly was not himself but a four-legged silhouette resembling himself, not seeing it exactly but visualizing it, as if a remote part of his mind and being that worked independently of him had summoned it and he had placed it out there, among the trees and waves of moonlight, and it fled into the woods and silence. As if he had created something and given it form and purpose, mission, and looking into its space, vacant now, Doc took a certain pleasure in setting it free, returning it to the wilds. And he remained rooted in his steps and heard the commotion behind him, Henry and Evlin running out, but he did not respond to the excitement or questions immediately, continuing in the pleasure of the sensation. He drew his hand along the fur of the bearskin and felt the absence of the animal, lifted and weighed the paw and felt something gone from him too, not knowing what because he had never identified it, but now that it was gone he felt lighter and electric.

And he knew, he just knew.

"Come with me," Doc said.

He took them to the shed behind his house, opened the door and found the flashlight where it hung from a nail. Shining the beam on the red powerplant, he commanded Henry to start it up.

"You fixed it?"

"No. I left it just the way it is—full of water with all the gasoline drained out. Go ahead. Start it up!"

Henry shook his head and bent down beside the powerplant. Switched the starter on, adjusted the choke, gave a sharp tug to the cord. The engine sputtered and the overhead light flickered on briefly.

"Filled with water," Doc said, already making his point, "the damned thing was filled with water! Three-quarters full! Just like it was three-quarters full of gasoline. Now look! Still three-quarters full! But it's not water anymore. It's—"

Henry pulled the cord again and the engine started, the overhead light came on, and a light shone from the house too. Doctor Marifield stepped up to Henry while Evlin waited in the doorway.

"And someone cleaned the house. And put ice in the icebox. And someone fixed the powerplant—"

"Doc—"

"Wait a minute! Hear me out. I told only the two of you it had been sabotaged. So who knew? Who knew except the person or persons who sabotaged it in the first place?"

"Doc—"

"So it wasn't Thomas. He was with me. Ditto Morgan. Ditto Billy Peel. All the prime suspects are properly alibied. So will you tell me what's going on here!" Doc shook his hands in front of himself, pleaded, "Will you tell me what the bloody hell is going on?"

Henry said, "Doc." Placed a hand on his shoulder. "Easy."

Evlin said, "You're right, Henry."

Henry nodded, "Yeh. Let's cross over to town. We're not going to learn anything here."

33

WAVES FROM THEIR BOAT smacked the old and rotting wood pilings under the wharf, and they found a place to moor and climbed up. No one had spoken a word during the brief crossing from Kinstuk Island, and Doctor Marifield had rowed, thinking it best, not wanting to disturb the still night and water by employing the motor. He did not know whose boat he had borrowed, choosing it only because it was convenient when he had crossed to the small island with Thomas hours earlier. The practice of mooring at a common wharf and borrowing whatever boat was handy was a common one that Doc enjoyed; it gave him a tangible sense of community, and he was tickled that he had learned to bring himself to it, borrow freely without permission, adopting the local custom without having to think twice or feel uneasy. Once up from the boat, he caught whiffs of wet grass and pine and beer; a deep breath filled him with energy and anticipation. The nerve-endings of his fingertips tingled. Face to face. Soon. Morgan Duff again. He was anxious for it.

Thomas Duff was the second man out of the boat and he stared one-eyed up the slope of the green at the visible portions of Lyell. Lantern light shone from the homes and shacks, electric light from Rogg House where men drank and shouted. Eerie and frightening to him after his sojourn in the mountains. Evlin stood beside him and Henry climbed up last.

At the edge of the green, Henry Scowcroft knelt and the others stopped around him. Still no one had spoken, and no one spoke now, each person aware that they had no direction or plan, each person waiting as if it ought to become plain to them without their searching for it. And they were quiet. And Henry's eyes scanned the green, its edges and shadows. Lyell was quiet too, the sounds of talk and drink and the persistent bark of an angry dog only touched it, did not penetrate it. When Henry stood up again, shorter than the men and now Evlin too, because she was higher on the slope, he said, "They're watching us."

Furtive glances along the rim of the green, but the others saw nothing. "Who is it?" Doc asked, his voice low.

Standing on his toes, Henry whispered in Doc's ear, "We'd save ourselves a lot of trouble if we turned him over now. Whatever it is they want him for."

"What's that?" Evlin came closer.

"Who?"

"You weren't the only one chased out of town by the Duff brothers," Henry said, still whispering.

"What?" Doc asked, taking a step back but squinting in the dim light.

"Me too. They got me off my ass and sent me into the woods too. To get Thomas out of there. See, they're the ones who sent me into the woods all these years, bringing him things."

"Wait a minute," Doc said, snapping his fingers.

"He'll be safer at their house than anywhere else. Safer than with us."

"Wait a minute," Doc said.

Catching up to the conversation, Evlin said, "They defended me against Morgan. He should be safe with them."

"Wait—one—minute!"

"No," Henry said. "No." And he scouted the rim of darkness, felt the presence of eyes, the rhythm of breathing. "We'll talk about that later."

The grass was soft and thick underfoot and puddles of water still lay in the hollows. They crossed Lyell's green with the moon at their backs, side by side, with Evlin and Henry guarding the outside of their unit while Doc and Thomas were pressed between them. Glancing frequently at the hermit, Henry was amazed by his rigidity, glancing up and reading the severe and stolid face, wondering what fear had cost this man the coordination of his limbs and his natural, fluid motion. Here he was not an invisible being, he did not gyrate upon the waves and currents of darkness or dance with the beings from worlds behind it; here he was victim to his own ageing and deteriorating body, held and bound by it, stiff and slow and fearful. Moonlight shimmered in a puddle and Henry intentionally smacked his boot into it, as if trying to break a spell, to excite activity and life in Thomas where there was only inertia and dread.

"Where are they?" Evlin asked.

"They'll be there ahead of us," Henry said. "You'll see."

At the hilltop they mounted the boardwalk and their boots banged sharply through the still night, echoing off the wall of forest and skipping across the water. Henry found it hard to breathe, his lungs constricted by his trepidation, while his mind was nagged by a problem. Evlin experienced a rush of giddiness, a kind of fulfilling happiness, as if she rode a great wave that had welled far out from shore and surged upon the beach. The answer. She could feel it, run her fingers over it like a smooth stone. Treasure it. She knew the Duff brothers from her childhood at Sockeye—knowing them only from a distance since then—and she had had a special relationship with Rupert Duff. He had been Gail's constant companion, they went together everywhere. And what was striking her now was something she had forgotten, Rupert painstakingly etching the names of his brothers in sand or dirt or mud, Gail coaching him and encouraging him.

Doc could hardly contain himself, and as they neared the Duffs' house he broke past the others, Evlin laughing, and he waited at the walk leading to the door like a guard of honour, adjusting his bearskin. He was excited by an answer too, although he did not understand it, not requiring that it be understood.

At the walk they stopped. Each person studied Thomas. Who stared at the door. He propped open his closed eye and stared. Sallow lantern light illuminated the small windows. Thomas looked at Henry finally.

"The things I've brought you all these years, remember it was your brothers who sent me. Wait with them while we're gone, okay?" Thomas hesitated; Henry touched him to nudge him forward. "Go ahead. They want to see you."

Thomas turned and walked slowly toward the door. His steps were heavy on the boardwalk and measured, as if each one required thought and decision. Just before he reached the door it opened, the lantern light streaking into the night, transforming him into a black silhouette that was quickly enveloped and submerged. The door shut soundlessly behind him.

Evlin and Doc and Henry watched the house, and it seemed to be empty, as if it were not a house at all but a door that once shut seemed unlikely to open again.

"Okay," Doc said, "let's talk."

"Not here," Henry said.

"Wait!" Doc called, but Henry was already continuing down the boardwalk, then he jumped off and was marching through the grass. Evlin and Doc hurried after him.

"It doesn't make sense," Henry said, speaking the moment they caught up to him as if he had been speaking all along. "I mean it's true, Doc, they could have sabotaged your powerplant, and they could have burned down my house too, but what the hell for?"

"Don't you know?" Evlin said. "They wanted—"

"That's not what I mean. I mean, why resort to such drastic measures? You know how they are, Doc, you've dealt with them. Why would they start out by burning and wrecking? They have other methods of communicating with us."

"True enough," Doc said. "But if they did it, it explains the cleanup and the repairs, because they were around to do it."

"And it's just like them to be nice to you once they've got your attention."

"Where are we going?" Evlin asked.

"Looking for Morgan. Since we're already down here, I figured the first place to start is the last place you saw him. I want to check on something, just to make sure."

"Okay, but it's spooky here."

They walked past the sawmill. The smoke from the furnace, grey and delicate in the moonlight, was challenged by a breeze as they trudged past, curling back towards them like a long arm curling back to snatch them off the ground. They averted their heads and had to hold their breath. Evlin ran ahead quickly. Henry coughed and he could taste the ashes in his mouth, and a queer sensation caught at his stomach. He continued walking, but his knees were weak and fluid.

Doc was enchanted by the sawmill, still and captured by the moonlight, the roughly hewn sheds and wall-less buildings appearing as an ancient ruin, the tiers of planed lumber like ceremonial rock formations, the peacefulness lending a tone of reverence to them, of holiness. For a moment he saw himself on one of the high stacks, admonishing sin, exhorting men to be steadfast for the end of time was near. Smiling to himself, he felt joyful, turning himself over to a rising exhilaration.

"Henry?" Evlin said. "I don't think the burning and the powerplant were the first signs. Maybe they did all the sabotage."

But Doc was on her quickly, incredulous. "That's going too far! I can see them coming after Henry and me when it looked like Thomas was in danger, but the whole thing? No. They're idiots, remember."

"I've told you not to call them that," Henry said.

"You too?"

"No," Henry said. "No. They're in the clear about the rest of the sabotage."

"So you think Morgan and his surveyors were sabotaging themselves? It was all a ruse?"

"Could be," Henry shrugged.

Evlin said, "But that doesn't explain—"

"Look!"

Henry found the two-by-fours. Evlin held Doc's arm tightly, the memory of her battle with Morgan alarming her again. Shadows fooled her, she saw prone bodies strewn about. Henry tossed the pieces of wood back into the forest.

"Now what?" Doc asked.

"The beer parlour. Then his room. We'll find him."

They marched back again, past the sawmill, past the Duffs' house, across the top of the green toward Rogg House. "Unless we missed it," Henry said. "Unless they were signalling to us all along and we missed it. That would explain why they became so extreme. Or maybe they just became frantic, realized all of a sudden that Thomas was in danger and that we weren't really doing anything about it. So they acted the way they did. What do you think, Doc? Did you miss any signals?"

"Not that I know of."

Evlin said, "Maybe it's something else you missed."

"What?"

Her answer was thwarted by the commotion greeting their appearance in the beer parlour. Curious men queried them on their recent whereabouts, and Doc and Henry struggled to work their way through to the stairs. Evlin slipped through to the bar and spoke with John Rogg. Rejoining them, she said, "He hasn't been seen. He's not around."

Henry nodded. "He could have sneaked up the back stairs. Because he's injured. Let's check."

The door to Morgan's room was locked. No answer to their knocks. Henry worked on it with his penknife, breaking in. But Morgan was not inside. His belongings lay undisturbed about the room. "He hasn't been here." Henry turned things over, looked under clothing, opened drawers; Evlin and Doc were grinning, and noticing them he blushed and smiled too. "So I'm a snoop," he said.

It was Doc's idea to go down the back way and avoid the beer parlour. Evlin was sent to fetch three beers from John Rogg and meet them outside. The outdoor banister was wobbly and the steps creaked loudly underfoot. Henry felt his fear rising, and it was the fear of the unknown, the knowledge of it escaping him and leaving him destitute. They met Evlin on the front porch and sat there and drank, Henry finishing his in a minute. They were quiet together but it was a restless quiet, each person holding a thought that the others dismissed, each person's view of the events blocked by the others' obstacles.

"Henry," Evlin said, deliberately speaking slowly in order to focus Henry's attention, "exactly why are the Duff brothers in the clear?"

But Doc answered. "Why keep harping on that? What do you think, they're so concerned about the social consequences of the mine that they planned the whole thing?"

"No, but—"

"They could have done it to get Thomas," Henry said, and the tone of his voice was wistful, as if he were talking to himself and dwelling on something that had seared his imagination. "After all, they've been sending him supplies for fifteen years, through me. Maybe those supplies were not so much to keep him alive but were intended to coax him back. And when it didn't work they tried something else. Sabotage—pinning the blame on Thomas so people like you and me would go in there and chase him out."

Doc laughed, but Evlin slapped his arm lightly and shushed him. "Go on," she said.

"See, I know that Thomas was the one who was uprooting the surveyors' stakes. Because he was offended and disturbed by them. That's when people started talking about Thomas again, so maybe the four brothers got the idea from there. Then when the surveyors stopped going into the woods, the brothers committed sabotage in town. That was a problem. Because then Billy's name came up, and my name, and Doc's—Thomas was mentioned only rarely. Until the notes scrawled 'Thomas' were left behind. But when you and me, Doc, even after the notes, and after Morgan arrived, sinister as all hell, when we still didn't go in there and get him, they came after us in their own way, shocked us right out of our comfort and stupidity and into the woods."

"They planned all that!" Doc said. "Ha!" He drank from his beer in disgust.

Evlin and Henry were quiet. "I think that's what happened," Evlin said.

"No," Henry said.

Evlin jumped to her feet. "You keep saying that! But why not! Why not?"

"The notes," Henry said calmly.

"That's right!" Doc said.

Cumshewa Sound was peaceful, and Doc's gaze crossed the water, and he felt himself drifting there, bobbing on the light waves and gliding upon a current. Henry was looking to his side, into the forest, into the darkness and quiet there, thinking about going for a walk to soothe his nerves. Evlin said, "No."

"What?" Doc said.

She looked from Doctor Marifield to Henry Scowcroft, then at the ground. She moved dirt around with the toe of her boot. "That's not right," she said, "because Rupert can write names. I know for a fact he can." Then she breathed deeply, painfully, as if her next words were impossible to speak. "Gail taught him."

Henry and Doc looked at each other for a moment, but Doc broke the peace by shaking his head violently and jumping to his feet. "No!" he said. "No, no, no!"

"Why not?" Evlin asked quietly.

"Because why the hell didn't they just go get him themselves if they wanted to rescue him so badly, if they wanted him back in town so badly? And why do they want him so much anyway, so much that they're willing to risk his life—his life!—to get him here? Tell me that, eh?" Doc shook his head, snapped his fingers. "There goes your theory. Pffft! Like that."

And Evlin felt an enormous heaviness take hold of her, paralyse her, for Doc was right. She had wanted it to be true so desperately, to know that men would struggle and plot to be reunited with a brother; she had wanted it to be true so desperately that it had become a need, the answer to her own struggles at Cumshewa Town, and to those battles within her too. Her answer to her periodic and brutal lapses into aloneness: needing to know that others fought, that others had cares and deep loves too. She thought she would cry soon, and she looked at Henry.

And Henry nodded. He reached across and drank from Doc's beer, then said, "For the same reason they never sent goods to him themselves, but used me." Doc had wandered away several yards, but he came back now, looking at Henry intently. Evlin drew closer too, and she felt her body lifting, as if she was about to fly. Nodding, Henry said, "Gail was raped before she died. She was raped by Morgan, and because of Morgan's intimidation, by Rupert too. And they were all in on it, they all watched it. It upset Thomas the most, I guess. He had feebly tried to save her life and failed. So he bolted for the forest. To hide. The brothers at Sockeye, they wanted life to carry on. They singled out Rupert's crime as being greater than their own and banished him from the family. These four are a group, they stay together, which always suited the rest of the family perfectly. So they were all banished. But they know they can't really handle things on their own. You know, they're working in the sawmill—but they're fishermen! See. So they wanted to be reunited with the one brother who had cared on that day, and who felt badly enough about it that he'd banished himself for life. They wanted to be reunited with the one brother who would care for them. Yeh, I see it now. A lot falls into place. For seventeen years they've been working to bring Thomas home." Doc shook his head but Henry held up his hand. "Let me finish. The reason they didn't go after Thomas themselves is because they don't know if they're forgiven or not, they don't know if he's forgiven himself and could even think of forgiving them. They don't know if Thomas would accept them or not." Henry slapped his thigh, shook his head, pressed his lips together. "Damn! I should have known. It's the notes that beat me."

"Wait a minute," Doc said. "You're still forgetting something."

"What?"

"They're idiots. They're morons! Imbeciles! They don't have the brains—"

"No!" Evlin screamed, horrified, and her emotion caused Doc to jerk.

Henry leapt to his feet and slammed his cane in the earth just before Doc's feet. "Damn, damn!" he hollered, and he clutched Doc by the lapels. "How many times have I told you they're not idiots! How many times?"

"Lay off!" Doc wrestled against Henry's grip and venom, and Evlin, shouting their names, tried to wedge herself between them. "They're retarded! You know that!"

"Like hell! Maybe they're slow, but they're not stupid!"

"They're morons!"

Evlin cried, "Just listen to him, David. Please, please! Listen to him!"

Henry released Doc, who combed his hair with his hands roughly, said, "All right. I'll listen."

Henry said, "They did exactly what they set out to do. All these years they had me supplying Thomas with stuff he needed. And when presents couldn't coax him out of the cave, they plotted something else." Henry counted each point by pulling back the fingers of his left hand.

"Come on," Doc said.

Henry turned on him. "They succeeded, Doc! They made it! They committed the sabotage against the surveyors. They watered your powerplant. They burned my house down! The morons did, the idiots did, the imbeciles! And they planned it so Thomas would be implicated. And when Morgan came they planned it to put Thomas's life in danger. And when we, you and I—us!—who are supposed to be the brains around here, when we still didn't do a thing, they chased the two of us into the woods, to go in there and bring him out. Which we did!"

Doc clucked his tongue, moved away, and sat on the porch again. Head bowed. Noticed that his beer had been finished. "All right," he said, raising his hands in submission, "I'm not saying anymore that I don't believe it. But I sure as hell don't understand it."

Henry sat beside him. Touched his elbow briefly. "Maybe you don't want to. Maybe that's the problem."

"That's right," Evlin said, but she looked at Henry for his explanation.

"What do you mean?" Doc asked.

Henry nodded, as if to a thought that was only just coming, then faced Doctor Marifield. "Maybe you don't want to understand it. Because you don't want to accept it. Yeh, I think that's it."

"I don't get it."

"Well. Think about it."

And strangely Doc and Evlin found themselves looking at one another, as if this was not his problem alone but a mutual one. Doc could see her whole being pleading with him to get it, to understand it, once and for all and finally. And Doc smiled, for what he was aware of most was that he did not want to flee, run pellmell into the night, he did not want to escape, but wanted more than anything to be right here right now and to learn; and he realized that this was the spirit he had set loose, that had vaulted out of him, and he brushed the fur of the bearskin, wearing it not for comfort, but for confidence. He still did not understand, but it seemed to him that Henry was preparing to explain.

Henry said, "Maybe what you don't get is the sense of it, the intelligence of it, because it's the intelligence of it you can't fondle or manipulate. Yeh. You can't even repudiate it or disclaim it. You can't praise it or command it. Because it comes out of what's maybe alien and terrifying to you—to me too, but I respect it at least. Because it's guts, Doc. Guts and heart and blood and—Ah, look. Gail was raped and murdered on the sea. I carry that with me and Evlin carries it too. And the brothers too, even more so. Isn't there any room for that kind of intelligence inside of you, Doc? Isn't there any space at all? Or does absolutely everything have to be categorized and tagged? And you're so chicken you can't live by what you feel at all."

And Evlin had to wipe her eyes, and Henry breathed deeply. And they sat together quietly, sitting in a row on the porch, watching the play of moonlight over the water. Doc nodded, said quietly, "There's room. You're damn right there's room." And he could feel the island swell and heave, feel the sweep of skyway and the wash of rainwater, feel the rock sigh and exhale and the trees stretch and rise through a multitude of pains and turmoils into a still, rueful ecstasy, but ecstasy nonetheless.

"And all those years," Doc said. And sticking to it, he thought, and not only sticking to it but admitting to it, bearing it constantly and refusing to shrug it off, preferring to seek and deserve its eventual dissolution.

"Never mind all those years," Evlin said, and she was looking at Doc with a glance he found hard and cold. But it was not that, and Doc squirmed again, felt energy curl and twist and panic inside him. "Never mind *their* years."

"What do you mean?" Doc said; his voice faltered, he swallowed hard. Henry was looking up. At Evlin and Doc both.

"You know," Evlin said. Sighed. "You know very well." She was looking at the water now. "You don't follow through. You're going to look at the Duff brothers, their years, and marvel. But will you look at your own, David? Or even ours?"

The suggestion alone scared Doc; it did more than knife through his defences, it evoked the awesome, the conglomeration of pain and hope and need spanning eons that was both too human and too personal at the same time to bear. Now he felt like running again.

Evlin pleaded sharply, "Henry?"—requesting him to take over, for she was losing herself in something.

And Henry felt a huge presence snuggle into his lap, surround him with its arms and breath, like a moving sphere of air and mind and sense; snuggle into his lap, and he held it upright between his hands, afraid and not knowing what to do with it. But he ventured, slowly, "Let's say, or pretend, or anyway admit *that it's all one thing, and not only or even one thing but just—one*—let's say, Doc, that *their quest and need is as great in you and me as it is in them, of course it is, because it's the same need and quest exactly, only seen, or admitted to in different degrees;* that maybe what the Duffs have been striving toward is the same thing you fled Vancouver to find, with maybe the difference that they at least recognize it and acknowledge it. But you fear it too much to do either. *I'm talking about a point of pain, Doc, or fire, you know what I mean. I'm talking about—joining.* You fear it too much to look it square in the eye—and not only you. *Me too.* Doc—maybe it's their mental state, their strangeness, I don't know, that has diminished their fear or increased their desperation, but they've been reaching out—daring—in territory where you and I still walk timidly. If at all."

Henry still held the balloon-like, fluid-like presence in his hands and lap. He spoke again, quickly now, the urgency striking him, "And

Doc, they've almost made it! If Thomas forgives them—If Thomas forgives himself, why—" Henry stopped, alarmed by his own discovery. "Why—who knows?" *Indeed, who knows? The Duffs will be released, Thomas included. Maybe, maybe me too. If that whole dread will vanish. And Gail too, her spirit finally unchained from this planet, let her sail through the universe.* Suddenly the balloon-presence was gone, and Henry felt as if he had been abruptly set down into the night. The closeness of his friends, of the woods, birds, and insects, of the nocturnal, restful water, the light-washed sky, all so poignantly impressed on him, all reborn and refreshed. But he lingered in this sanctioned time only briefly, turning to Evlin as she raised her chin and eyes.

Evlin spoke what each of them wondered, "Do you think Thomas will forgive them? He went there, didn't he? Do you think he'll stay?" So that simultaneously they turned their heads toward the square squat house they could not see, their hope and breath and pulse centring there, beating there, humming there, so that they felt hypnotized and subdued.

And as they stared, a figure appeared over the crest of the rise, moving stiffly, robot steps, as if he had no sight and walked blindly in a straight line, his torso like the trunk of a petrified tree, his arms motionless at his sides, willing to turn only if he bumped into something, and then only if it was too big and stubborn for him to smash right through it.

"Oh no," Evlin said.

Doc said, "Damn. Damn."

"Thomas," Henry said.

34

DOCTOR MARIFIELD SPRINTED TOWARD THOMAS, and Evlin was close behind, chasing him, as if to collar him and hold him back so that he would not meet Thomas first and be on his own, as if to catch him and delay him enough that they could meet Thomas simultaneously, so that she could guard against Doc's impulsiveness at the same time that she questioned Thomas, as if she expected and needed to reach down into both of them and pull up the same thing. But Doc did not heed her calls and he maintained and increased his lead. And Henry hobbled as well as he could, swinging his body between his good leg and cane, landing on the lame foot, falling forward to lodge his cane and foot in the ground again. He was soon far behind the others, cursing as he ran, lamenting his slowness now when so much was open to be won or lost. And running, swinging his body forward, he caught sight of a stretch of sky that seemed to bob down with him as his head bobbed, bob down and touch and fire the forest and the distant hills, and he sensed the appearance of a great gap, a huge opening in the forest where all life was formed of space and the space was unmenaced, free of demons and ghouls and rising plutonic ghosts, the corners and recesses illuminated by starlight. He realized exactly what it was and understood it, saw the sky moving in and out of the forest as if flapping on a hinge, as his body rolled backward and forward. And it was space and light moving into his corralled history, the sins redeemed, the demons apprehended and struck dumb by this entry of friends, by the opportunity now to have his history shared and revealed outside of himself; no longer wholly bound and distorted and smouldering within himself, as if by spreading the knowledge and burden of it the spirits of that realm had their power diffused, dislodged. Henry's stomach was tight with fury, his great exhilaration—victory within sight—and alarm, too, close as Thomas trudged towards him.

So that he did not have to run and swing and hobble far. Already Evlin and Doc were returning with Thomas between them, Thomas marching as if out of mind, without thought, his one open eye staring straight ahead as if all his intent and essence had been funnelled into the one activity: flight, again.

"You can't go now!" Doc said, repeated, claiming again and again his right to make the choice for Thomas, repeating the command again and again as if to apply it to himself, to each and every time he had fled and had subsequently regretted it, each and every time he had spurned his own conscience and belief and propelled himself down one chosen chasm or another—and as if in response to his own repeated choice he waved his hands in the air, frustrated. "You can't—can't go now!"

And Evlin tried to enter a calm voice through Doc's frantic protests, her voice choking and made harsh by a rising sense of failure, again, as if failure should have been considered all along as the only possible result, again. For failure was becoming the only recourse, the only path and self-sustaining grace that knew at least a measure of harmony, of consistency. As at Cumshewa Town, where all effort and all discourse and all achievement would fall eventually, again, again, again, to the bottle or disease or rage or somnolence, again, again, inexorable failure. Yet she strove, and Evlin said. "Thomas. Please. They care for you. And they need you. They mean you no harm. Thomas. Please. They—need you."

All of it, Doc's rampage and Evlin's entreaty too, stopped by Henry, who did not stand to one side but set himself straight in line with Thomas, challenged the rigidly marching, cold-bodied form, and when it was about to trample right into and through and over him, called out the name, "Thomas!"

And the old man stopped.

"Thomas," Henry repeated, quietly this time. The hermit stared over his head, the thick, weathered lines of his face accentuated by the moonlight, the moon and the few sporadic lights of the town mirrored in his one open eye, dancing there like reflections of a fire. "What's happened, Thomas? Where are you going?" And the man looked down, looked into Henry's face as if trying to recognize it, as if trying to focus not only his sight but his mind too, his senses too. Thomas raised a hand, and Henry followed the slow movement of it. Expected it to strike him, to cut him down for ever daring to aspire and divine. The hand passed before his face, then lay upon the hermit's own chest. Henry placed his hand over the man's heart, expecting the rapid beating and the flutter again, but he couldn't feel a thing. He worked his hand between the buttons of Thomas's shirt, lay it on the cold, taut skin over his heart. The heartbeat was slow, faint, distant. "Thomas?" Henry said. The hermit lowered his head and nodded slightly. He stepped around Henry, past the others, and continued his regimented walk.

"Henry!" Evlin cried.

"I'll go after him," Henry said. "You two run to the Duff house. See what's up, but for God's sake be careful."

Henry did not hesitate longer but skipped after Thomas, calling out his name quietly, catching up to him finally and holding him by the elbow as they walked. Doc and Evlin watched for a moment, then glanced at one another, then turned and ran toward the small house.

Running hard, heart and lungs and legs; and Doc believed it was right and proper that he go, because Henry had said it to him long ago, and he had refused to believe it then or even to understand it: that the vision and determination of the four brothers overruled their intelligence, or lack of it, or particular form of it; the vision was connected to their culpability. He had refused to believe it then or understand it because he had not wanted to acknowledge such diligence, such self-incrimination—the two things he had shied away from in his own life—so that Doctor Marifield believed it was right and proper that he was going to them now, to praise the diligence he had previously slighted but envied now, and to revere the harsh judgment they had brought upon themselves, because they had recognized him as a man who could have helped, but he did not, and they had seen him as a man who could have understood, but he had not. So he owed them something now. Evlin ran beside him and her breath was short, a sharp pain hurt her abdomen; she ran and was terrorized by her own imagination, a budding premonition that Morgan Duff was involved in this. That would rectify it, absolve it, if it was Morgan who had turned Thomas back to the woods; so her imagination raced with her, generated by acute memories of Morgan, the smell of him, the gestures of his flesh, the hatred ever-watchful in his eyes, the hot ember being drawn across his arm, his snarls as his brothers had surrounded him and driven him off her. She ran, but not as fast as she was able, holding back, for he could be there too, he could be inside that house, and she believed he was.

At the boardwalk to the door they stopped. Listened for any sound beyond the door. "Morgan," Evlin said, catching her breath. "It's possible he's there. Then—" Doc nodded, understood. Wishing too that it was Morgan, that that would explain it. They stepped silently, almost creeping as they moved forward on their toes and the balls of their feet. Reaching the door, Doc rapped hard. Silence. Pounding again, with authority—the slow shuffle of feet.

It was Jackson Two who answered the door. Scarcely looking at them, he held it open and they stepped inside. Relief swept over Evlin so strongly that she was tempted to let herself fall and cry. She was grateful that Morgan was not here, even though the implication was worse, for now the onus was on Thomas. He had rejected them.

Rupert and Whitney and Jake were seated at the table. Doc scrutinized the room for any clue or indication of Morgan's presence, feeling disappointed that he was not here, for having finally readied himself for battle he felt lost, puzzled, now that his opponent had not shown up. Evlin and Jackson Two remained at the door, Evlin leaning against a stand of some kind, and Doc, awkwardly, seated himself at the table. The four brothers regarded him, one collective glance, and Doc was struck by the intensity, which he believed was not that but simply the uniformity of one glance, one thought, one mind, causing him to lose his inner balance, as if his inner diversity and contradictions were helpless before it. He looked at each man, but he only had to look at one to know them all, the individual thoughts and minds pooled together for the common need, for warmth, and for survival.

"I want to thank you," Doc said. He looked at each man individually again and studied him, not evaluating him but learning about him, out of friendship and respect. Rupert's eyes were red. The eyes seemed lost in the mass of deformed head, as if they were surrounded by a deception they could not comprehend, a deception with deep and unknown motives. Rupert had been the brother entrusted with Gail Duff's care. They had been friends and close companions. Gail had been the pride of his life, the jewel in the eye of his seeing that made all things luminescent and understood; he had raped her and lived now with the guilt of it as his companion, the eyes overwhelmed by the bulk of head, without focus anymore, desperately clinging to some dim memory of whiteness and love. His eyes were red. He had been crying, the tears not comprehended either and forced back into the lost and terrified eyes.

Jake's hair shot up from his head as if shocked, his tongue lolled from a corner of his mouth as a sign of defeat, the body pulling its victim apart, distorting and distending him, obliterating speech and nullifying thought, relegating the victim to imbecility but not quite, for Jake clung here, tenaciously, to these brothers he had known from the cradle, whom he no more knew to be separate from him than he knew anything at all, so that his cowering and dislocated being triumphed yet, overriding the forces of disintegration and numbness and death.

By the door, Jackson Two waited, but he was not bound by the normal confines of time or decision, waited with a patience that would outlive the temporal and transitory grief here. In a sense he was their leader, even his name given the luxury of a number, a title, like a king, for the first Jackson Duff had died at an early age, and this replica of that earlier son was not a leader by intelligence or speech or even vision, but because he refused the illusion of time. He repudiated the seeming victory of the hours and minutes, the days, weeks, and years, conformed all time into a single and uniform moment, containing all.

And beside Doc, Whitney returned his gaze. His job, Doc thought, to watch and listen—and over the course of events, months, and years, to plot and plan. It would have been Whitney who had seen opportunity in the coming of the miners and in the sabotage precipitated by Thomas. Whitney read him, Doc thought, probably not in any ordinary sense, but simply and succinctly, detecting and interpreting the sensations in his own guts and trusting them from there.

"I want to thank you for repairing my powerplant. It was good of you to replace the gasoline." And saying it, Doc realized the source of their idea: likely they had seen the motor on Gail Duff's boat wrecked in a similar way. The image had been burned on their minds. And burning Henry's old shack was simply a continuation of work they did at the sawmill, burning scrap.

Doc knew they were attentive to him. "I also wanted to tell you how sorry I am that Thomas is gone again. We're going to try to bring him back again." For there must have been a rising of hope, an expectancy, followed by the realization of the loss, of failure. Yes, Doc thought, they see it in Rupert. The mongoloid's eyes watered, stirred by confounding emotions. Yes, Doc thought, you live closer to us than the rest, which makes it harder on you. Evlin came from the door and placed her hand on Rupert's shoulder. The man bowed his head. "Henry, Henry went after him, to talk to him." Doc felt he detected a perceptible break in their concentration, as if this news forced them into a kind of mental retreat, lasting no more than a second. "You must love him very much," Doc said. "And you must need him. Thomas could free you from the sawmill. Together you could return to the sea again. I guess he would be your captain then."

Doc realized that he trusted them. He did not know if his words meant anything to them immediately, but he had confidence that somehow his meaning would filter into their understanding. So that he was no longer appalled by their stoic reactions but trusted that his words found a home.

"Rupert," Evlin said, and she stroked his shoulder. Then held him, this man who had devoted himself to Gail from her birth, and who had unwittingly given himself up to fear and a form of adoration, wanting to smother her screams and protect her from her terror, mounting above her to hold her tightly, to quell her panic and extreme fright which was his too, while his brothers undressed him and coaxed him, and he pressed himself over the being he adored, his body convulsing in some incredible thrust and release that mesmerized then shattered his senses. But afterwards he had known what he had done, and that it was more terrible for Gail. For she could have expected such torture from Morgan, pinned on the floor of the boat, his body plunging into her like a sword, but she never would have expected it from Rupert, her most beloved companion in all the world. Evlin held Rupert, and something broke within her too as his body shuddered, wracked by a new and terrible orgasm, the tears flowing now for the first time in many years, the tears flowing now and washing over the pain like water over a stone, but the stone did not yield. Whitney came around the table and knelt beside his brother. He did not weep, unable to comprehend it, but he experienced it inside himself in his own way, and he burrowed into his brother's back and shoulder until Rupert grasped his head and held him tight. Then Jackson Two and Jake made their way, slowly, to their brother's side, circling Evlin and Rupert and Whitney, binding them into one tight ball, and Doc felt it hurtling through space. Rupert cried and moaned for them all.

The knock resounded on the door and Doc stood up to answer it. All eyes turned toward the door. Doc opened it and Henry stood before him, his face white in the pale light, his eyelids drooping in a peculiar manner, as if they concealed what lay behind them. Henry stepped into the room and looked with confusion at the pile of bodies. Doc gripped his jacket with his fist. Henry broke free, said, "He's gone. Thomas is gone again. I guess for good this time."

Rupert pushed his way free in the centre of the pile. His voice rose up like a siren, wailing across a faceless, dreamless void, piercing the barrier, the code of silence,

"Thoooooommmmmaaaaaaassssss

35

THEY WALKED SIDE BY SIDE, and it was Henry who was the first to jump from the boardwalk and walk through the grass. Evlin and Doc joined him, and their boots swished through the tall grass.

"It's incredible," Doc said. "Seventeen years." And that alone was enough for him, to marvel at the effort and stamina and endurance, as if the only thing that mattered was that they had tried and put their lives into it. It excited him, propped up a kind of scaffold within himself, and he could look at things from a new height and view.

"But they failed," Evlin said, and she was looking across Doc at Henry as they walked. And it was not enough for her that the Duffs had tried, fought; was not enough that they had pitted themselves against not only a world and its mercilessness, but against themselves too; was not enough that they had engaged in what seemed the only possible and necessary engagement. It mattered more that they had failed, mattered more and affected her more that defeat loomed again like some hysterical, eternal, feudal lord.

"Maybe so. But I think it's incredible just the same. Planning and scheming and waiting for seventeen years. Seventeen!"

And she loved them for their courage, but hated them for their failure, and not them but the approbating council of deeds and opinions and visceral fauna and life that culminated in them and in the failure too. And this same sorrow was rendered against herself once more, as she despised what never managed to complete itself within her, while at the same time she praised it and needed it and secured it tight: compassion, love, broken down, pounded down to their impurities and regrets, herself too. She said sternly, "But they did not have to fail. Maybe there was a way—"

"What can you do?" Doc asked. "Thomas left. I look at it this way—"

"In fact, I don't think they did fail. Not—them."

"And you're looking at me?" Henry asked.

"Us."

"No," Henry retorted, "you're looking at me." And Henry only wanted to move away from here, from them, but the farther he walked to his right made no difference, they stayed with him, without direction of their own, glued. "What was I supposed to do? Drag Thomas by the hair?"

"You have your ways," Evlin said.

"Look!" Henry said, stopping. "He wouldn't come back. He's a zombie now too. How am I supposed to reason with a man like that?"

"Forget it," Doc said. "Let's go for a beer."

"Maybe you should have dragged him by the hair. It would have been worth it. Think of what the brothers have gone through." Evlin wanted to get next to him, to open a slit down the side of his body if she could and slide into him, duel with him there. But she had nothing to cut through to him with, and he was sneaking off, she could see him separating and going off, and she could not reach out, bring him near to slice him. They walked on, approaching the beer parlour. Evlin fumed and brushed hair off her face. The Duffs had come so close, and Doc did not seem fully aware of it; they had come so close, and suddenly Henry was beyond caring. And Henry offered no explanation or courtesy. "You and your damn secrets," Evlin said.

Henry did not reply. Doc glanced at him from time to time, weighing and evaluating his mood, stopping finally and holding his arm gently. He spoke quietly. "What about it, Henry? What happened out there?"

Henry jerked his arm free. "Leave me alone. That's all." He had to separate from them.

"Come on."

"There's nothing to say! Do you hear me? He's gone—gone! There was nothing I could do about it and that's it."

"Look—"

"No! Forget it! Just forget it! I'm going." And he seized the opportunity to break from them, hobbling quickly toward the beer parlour.

"Henry!" Doc called.

"Let him go," Evlin said. "He wants to be alone. That's obvious."

"Morgan!" Doc insisted. "What about—"

Henry stopped, turned. He leaned his weight on his good leg, sticking out a hip to prop his torso up. Evlin and Doc drew closer, and when they were next to him, Henry said quietly, "Don't worry about him. He's gone. He shouldn't be back. You can forget about Morgan now." They couldn't see his face. His body swivelled on his foot and he left them again, the lights from Rogg House illustrating his outline.

Evlin and Doc watched him go, looked at one another, shrugged. There was no point to protest; they would draw details from him another time. Doc was concerned though. "He doesn't have a place to sleep tonight."

Evlin laughed lightly. "Henry will make do. You know he always does. I just wish he'd tell us what's bothering him."

"Yeh."

They borrowed a short, fat boat and rowed across to Kinstuk Island. A breeze rippled the water, but Cumshewa Sound was flat and quiet. Away from the moon the stars sparkled, and only the occasional small cloud drifted overhead. Rowing, pains crept across Doc's back. He was ready now for a good, long sleep. And sitting in the stern, one hand trailing in the water, Evlin nodded from time to time. Her eyelids drooped, and when the boat bumped Doc's wharf her head snapped back. She shook herself awake and was trying to remember what had been on her mind, but her longing to curl up on the couch and sleep forever was too great, she could not concentrate. Inside the house she slumped onto the couch and Doc sat alongside her.

But neither slept. Or closed their eyes. And Doc stood up once and lit a kerosene lamp and the light made shadows gyrate along the walls. And Doc moved about the room, sitting in different chairs, while Evlin turned and twisted periodically on the couch. Until finally they sat together, not speaking, for they were tired and drained and distant now, their thoughts lapsing into areas where they could not be followed, Evlin curling her body under the arm and shoulder of Doctor Marifield, and together they watched the flame flicker and burn, and the shadows dance.

"So he's gone," Evlin said finally.

To Doc, her words seemed to come out of the flame, vibrate among the shadows. "Yeh," he agreed, then he sat straighter and firmer in his seat. Evlin had to readjust herself against him. "That's something anyway."

"Yes. It is, you know. When you think of it. I guess we should count our blessings, right?"

"Mmmm."

"Hey! Maybe we should celebrate!"

They laughed together, although their voices were odd to them, echoing as they did among the timbers, being absorbed among the timbers to resonate long after the sound had ceased. "Champagne and a brass band?"

"Let's dance!"

Laughing, mocking their spent muscles and limbs, feeling the weariness imbued in their bodies secrete a fine, delicate euphoria to every pore and thread, they nestled into the pleasure of their triumph, shaping it out of the murkiness of the dim room and their tired minds, fusing it with their hopes and ideals, measuring it against the backdrop of the night and still sky and humming forest, comparing it to their failures. Their rest was fitful. Only when they finally fell back, caving in, discovering the hollows and edges of one another's bodies, only when they came together in a kind of tacit fusion of their torsos and limbs, only when their heads slumped back over the top of the chesterfield, merging as a vibrating silhouette on the wall behind them, did they sleep at all.

*   *   *

All right then. We've won a reprieve. A victory of sorts, if it's not examined too closely. Morgan's out of the way. That'll slow the machinery down, at least. Aaach, but there's still a secret, dark and forbidden, abandoned by all except me. Ghosts, the night beings, suck on it, on me, there's nothing so tasty to them. They know I can't expose it to the light of day. It's all theirs. So maybe they're the enemies, not the secrets like I always thought, or the burden of them, but the beings and spirits that are nourished by them. They use me as their fool. It's them I should attack and execute. But it doesn't work that way. I'm in the middle again. To protect this I got to protect that. The old story, continued.

Henry drank his beer slowly, brooding. Men who approached him were waved away, and they detoured around him, recognizing his mood. Farmers and fishermen looked at him askance after that and a few scowled, but Henry ignored them, was not even aware of them.

Because what I'm talking about now is the point of pain that survives each and every fire and not even that, not simply surviving but perpetuated, and more than that, revived, so it's not even a matter of coming down to the same thing, or coming around to the same thing, it's simply reborn again and again and again, continued. And I'm in the middle of it. So

Henry did not drink quickly this time, and when he stood up he had not finished his beer. He waved to John Rogg and nodded to the men at a nearby table, who waved back and winked and appreciated his unexpected attention, and he went out through the front door. Outside, he moved quickly into the shadows, stood still, listened. Voices from inside, an angry shout from one of the homes nearby, the quiet symphony of forest and sea, of insect life and birds; Henry crept quietly along the porch and ducked beneath the window, staying close to the wall. Touching ground, he moved through the shadows along the side of Rogg House to the rear. Here he looked around again. He breathed deeply, trying to calm his nerves. He mounted the stairs slowly, pressing his weight on each step in order to reduce the tell-tale creaks and cracking. He opened the door at the top the minimum amount and squeezed into the hallway.

He felt safer inside. There was movement from one of the bedrooms, probably a surveyor and the Indian woman who had befriended him. Henry moved stealthily along the corridor and he entered Morgan's room. He drew the curtains first, then switched on the light.

Henry Scowcroft worked quickly. He went through the drawers and tossed the articles onto the bed. Then he hauled out the suitcases from under the bed and stuffed them full. He filled his pockets with the ammunition he found. When everything did not fit he made a sack by tying the ends of a shirt together, and he filled that too. He scrutinized the room carefully, then left with the two suitcases and the bundle.

He propped the door open with his cane and transferred Morgan's belongings to the outside landing, then crept down the stairs with it all. He scouted ahead of himself, searching for the darkest and most obscure route down to the waterfront. It would be safer to take a boat than to cut across land. His path led him in a semicircle, moving away from the line of vision from Rogg House then curling back in again. A canoe lay on its side on the beach and Henry heaved it out onto the water, tossed the baggage in. He splashed through the water, pushing the canoe, mounted it and paddled. Staying close to shore, he ducked low to keep himself hidden behind the bank. The water was still and each dip of the paddle alarmed him, he felt revealed and convicted. He paddled close to the sawmill undetected and beached the canoe there. Crouching low, he crept toward the furnace, carrying Morgan's bags with him.

At the sawmill he rested. Looked up at the platforms and saws and at the moonlight washing through the network of timber and machines. The shadows were long and still and peaceful now. The mill was peaceful now. Through the shadows and unseen patches of darkness there pervaded a spirit again, daunted, unfulfilled, that brooded on him and suffered his lament just as he brooded on it and listened to its prolonged exacted call. Henry had to catch himself quickly or he would have cried. And he knew that the tears he thwarted were not for himself alone, although once again he was hearing it, knowledge unrequited and unredeemed; nor were they for

Thomas alone, who knew his remorse to be prolonged and renewed here, who knew now that the seed of his first crime had not died but bloomed again, flowered again, a kind of perpetual and tough weed; and his tears were not for the lame Duff brothers alone, although they had reduced themselves in this, their guilt did not merely endure here but was magnified, and not at all for Morgan Duff, his body carved and sliced by the screaming saws. His tears were for the crystallized being, caught and trampled for her primal radiance, instant and lucid and warm, whose spirit still drifted like the whiffs of cloud overhead, homeless above the sky and sea and earth. And not even for her, because ultimately and intimately too he had to accept and had already accepted that she was gone, diminished from sight and sound at least, absent from touch or mercy; so that it was not even for her, but for that part of her that existed anyway, defensive against the butchery and assailed by the slaughter, existed anyway, if not as one whole being then as a part of many, of himself, he knew, and so many others too, perhaps all others, despite the reign of enemies. He was grieving for the men who had come this way, Indians, ancestors, wanderers, who had faltered right here, pausing as he paused now, for they had tested mettle and blood against all that intended to destroy them or the intimate parts of them that made them whole and real and free. Yet they had faltered, weary, distressed, and sick of the cycles of blood and the ongoing craft of deception. They had laid down exhausted in the grass. Quitting the vigil, they let their drive expire, their almost holy work infested by common ailments. They let the rain slide over their skins. Till suddenly they were alarmed again, charged again. They clutched hard to the grass, not to cling to it, but suddenly needing desperately to know it and know their own breath too, their own fibre too, their softness and stringiness and hotness and rhythm, panicking at first, but as they emerged, they apprehended trust in themselves and a spirit within themselves to cull some perseverance and future out of what they had come to see as breeding only despair. Prone on the ground and faint-hearted, they had sprung high again from recognizing the simple gesture of the grass, leaves, clouds, stars, and had straightened up, their heat subsiding, lingering. Henry grieved for those who had glimpsed something distant from themselves, itself in the nature of a promise, if only to themselves, that they held to be stronger and truer than the near and blatant cycle of things, the harrowing circle of things. Men such as Rupert and Whitney and Jake and Jackson Two Duff. Grieved for them because of what they had always to recapitulate.

The Duffs had been drawing a line to thwart it, their defiance nearly total, almost absolute. Their way to stymie the damning chronicle, to interrupt the circling trail of blood. And they didn't do it for themselves—they'd accomplished that already with the walls of their shack some kind of severe division—but they did it for Thomas. And for Gail too and me and the others. So we wouldn't be left in our cave, in our spirit-void. And! They almost created the damn line, unwavering from it! Except finally they compromised again, unleashed the very thing they were trying to eradicate, again perpetuating the legacy they thought they had repudiated.

So close. So almost close. Nearly arresting the constant drone of it. They almost created a prepared place, with all of their pains and sorrows and regrets—with their crimes—redeemed. A sanctuary of sorts, a meeting place where everything could be recognized, nothing pushed down below the surface and held there, no struggle to drown what always bobs to the surface anyway. Maybe they didn't know it, but in their own way they saw it. A home for their brother. Where now he can't stay; Gail neither, nor any of us.

Henry Scowcroft kept his grieving short. As if the true and actual grief of battle was not the counting of the dead or the gathering of the wounded, but the demands made upon the surviving. No victory had yet been won. That was the true grief, but it required no time or token energy of grief, and insisted on none, so Henry held his head in his hands and pressed the tips of his fingers against his eyes, pushing it all back inside. His aching intensified so that he could not stand it any longer, and he stood up. Looked around him. He gathered the bags and ran in a crouch to the teepee-shaped furnace. Peered in through the opening. The fire was dying; there were only small, scattered flames, and the smoke drifted in periodic waves to the chimney. Henry entered the furnace and he felt the close presence of death. He opened the suitcases and spread the clothing gently over the flames, and the fire slowly consumed them. He laid the suitcases on the fire too, and the flames moved over them cautiously, curiously, tasting them first before igniting this material too.

Henry retreated to the doorway. Beings rejoiced in the dancing light. He studied the grey ashes that alternated their tones with the movement of the fire. Perhaps Morgan's ashes had already been scattered by the wind, he thought, or perhaps they lay here still, inert and dry.

But going this way you're not gone, Morgan. Going this way you're still here. Not victorious exactly, but not defeated either. Gail is exiled and you are not. Going this way you do not die but perpetuate yourself upon and through and into all who come behind, who come this way and follow; going this way Gail's tissue of soft inner light and breath is assaulted again, wronged again, and not even by you, but by your enduring

Smoke caught at Henry's nostrils and the fire was heating his face. He stepped out of the furnace and knelt in the shadows again. Suddenly he wanted to be away from here, and he began to run as best as he was able, digging his cane into the soft, sawdust-covered earth and pushing off on it. He rested against a tree by the water and caught his breath. He wished he could go to sleep now. But he discovered Morgan's ammunition in his pockets. He would have to paddle out onto Cumshewa Sound and drop the packages overboard. Do that first, then he could look for a place to rest.